I0736602

THIRD CHILD

C. A. MITCHELL

BOOKS

RAMPART BOOKS

Also by C. A. Mitchell

Beneath the Veils
Beneath the Lies
Beneath the Conflict
Girl in the Middle
Third Child
Sixth Victim
Double Deception
Angel
Tinker Tailor Conman
Children of the Mask
A Woman Called EVE

THIRD
CHILD

1

For over fifteen minutes, Cecelia had waited for a woman who said she had a story that needed telling. Glancing at her watch, her feelings were that this was quickly turning into a hoax. As a female journalist, you were advised never to go out on your own. But what was their suggestion? Take a male colleague, someone to sit and hold your hand. And who do you think the person would prefer to talk to? Of course, the man.

So, where was this woman now? She tapped her foot and looked annoyed looking from left to right. It wasn't pleasant sitting at the table by herself. She felt as if she had been stood up.

Rejection was always Cecelia's problem. It followed her through every step of the day in whatever she did. But this was not how she should think. She was not a victim in life; she was a survivor.

True, she had arrived early, ten minutes in fact. She believed if this woman thought her story was so important, she would have been there already. Before one o'clock, not after.

This morning, she had been so eager to speak to Cecelia, emphasizing how important it was for her to be there. She was the one who asked—no, demanded this covert meeting, not her.

The red purse required for recognition was something Cecelia didn't own, and this was another thing she had to buy for this strange rendezvous. It was plainly on display on the top of the table for the interviewee, but for god's sake, where was she?

Five minutes more, and she was going.

Looking at the menu was tempting. Running her eyes up and down, too expensive for her pocket. Maybe one day. But there again, why would things for her ever change? It never had in the past.

'Cecelia! There you are. You have to forgive me; I was caught in traffic.'

A voice, then a hand on her shoulder, followed by a kiss on each side of Cecelia's face. It was a shock, such affection coming from a stranger.

'And, how are you? It's been such a long time—how long has it been now?' the woman withdrew the chair opposite Cecelia and bundled herself into it. Wiggling her butt, she made herself comfortable.

Rules were, you spoke when you needed to speak and listened when you had to listen. For now, this woman wanted secrecy, so there must be a reason for it.

'I'm fine. How are you?'

'Oh, you know me. Muddling along,' she shrugged, picking up the menu. 'My treat as I kept you waiting.' She read the menu as if she was reading her financial report.

Blonde, and probably natural. Her hair was held back in an elegant bun. Perfect. No hairs frayed out; it was surgical, which said healthy and disinfected. A pretty face, slim nose, neat lips, and hazel-brown eyes fanned with long eyelashes. A little makeup here and there just to highlight those features, which became all the better for it. Overall, this face said kindness, said compassion. It also said she respected others and was discreet. Were there really people like her these days, the kind who put other people's interests first? An impossible way to live when everyone was climbing over the other to make it to the top. Some angel must be looking out for her.

And another thing, she was pretty, too damn pretty, and everything which was feminine; her hand displays were delicate. She looked at the menu as if she was familiar with it. Had eaten and enjoyed the food here many times before? So, happy with this world, it made Cecelia jealous. These sorts of people, it seems, do exist, the ones who have been blessed by good fortune. It was unfair that she sat opposite someone who was so perfect.

Yet, despite how confident she was, Cecelia's sharp eyes noticed this woman's nervous actions. Her hands shook while she softly chewed her lip. A noise made her jump and then she laughed at herself. But when she looked up from the menu, she gave Cecelia a beautiful smile.

'I'm so glad you came. I didn't think you would?' like her eyes, her voice was gentle and musical. It made Cecelia feel like a grouch.

'I think we should talk about the reason you asked to meet me.' Overcoming her envy, the other thing Cecelia didn't like was having her time wasted or pretending to be in some kind of relationship when none existed.

'Do you think we could order first and get that out of the way?' the pretty woman's eyes now darted all over the place as if she had suddenly become aware of the world around her.

Naturally, when asked, Cecelia's eyes went straight to the menu. One never had to ask her twice, especially as she was not given expenses. Why had this woman asked to see her? Glad that Cecelia was a woman because only a woman would understand. Was it to tell her about her boss and how he had made a pass at her? Had she dragged herself away from her desk to discuss her rights as a woman when she wanted a proper scoop? Cecelia wanted a big story which would make her name, not one about how he put his hand on her leg when people were being murdered, and beaten up and dying. Another look told her that this woman wasn't only just nervous, she looked damn right scared.

Suddenly, nothing on the menu appealed to Cecelia. For now, it was not all about food.

'I'll have what you're having,' Cecelia caught this woman's eyes. Again, there was something about the woman which caused Cecelia to doubt her; she was too pretty for something bad to happen in her life. Pretty people have an easy—and then Cecelia saw her eyes. Frightened, she was terrified.

When summoned, their waiter came quickly and took their order; her companion had requested a bottle of good white wine while Cecelia looked on. Wine this time of day with their meal. Now, this was something she would never have thought of, and now she resented this woman for feeling so at ease about ordering it.

At this time during the day, Cecelia never drank. It was a precedent she had set herself. Other journalists chose this method to get the talkers to relax and loosen their tongues. Unfortunately for her, she was not into pressing others to talk if they didn't want to. Which was probably why she wasn't a brilliant journalist? But everyone does things their own way. Perhaps it was because she was more nervous about people than they were about her. In this job, you had to like people, something Cecelia found difficult.

'Well, can you tell me why you have asked me here?' Cecelia asked, well-mannered, polite, ready to listen with the appeal of the intellect. If people wanted to tell you something, they would tell you, you didn't need to get them drunk, intimidate them or even be rude.

'Yes, I suppose I should,' and then again, she giggled. She was nervous.

A few moments passed, and nothing more was said.

Should she tell this woman she didn't have to tell her secrets? No one was forcing her to.

'You could start by telling me your name—and not a false one, your real name, please. There must be honesty if we are going to go into this together.'

'Yes, you're right. I wished I smoked.'

The wine waiter came along and produced the bottle. Would someone like to taste the wine? The woman offered Cecelia to try it, but she refused.

A taste and then a nod. It was good. But did this woman really taste it or go through the motions of it? What did it matter? What did anything matter as long as she got a good story.

A generous amount of almost white liquid was poured into each of their glasses. And then the woman took in a deep breath as if she contemplated running a marathon.

'My name is Angelina Joseph—but you don't need to write that down, or rather, please don't. I don't want any record of this conversation.'

'I'm sorry, but there's a problem here. You know, you're talking to a journalist. I can't listen to a conversation without reporting it.'

'Yes, I understand that, but—it's difficult. Do you have

someone like a source informer—you know. Say you've got it from a reliable source?'

'Okay, that won't be a problem. But you'll have to trust me and let me do my job.' Cecelia frowned. Angelina Joseph was already beginning to make her job impossible.

'Yes,' Angelina lowered her head. 'You're right.'

'So, what happened to bring you to me—oh, do you mind, I have a little recording device?' Cecelia said, taking out a small recorder and placing it on the table.

'Oh, are you going to record my voice?' Angelina's hand went straight to her mouth.

'Yes, it would make my life easier. Our conversation will be more natural and comfortable. I can ask you questions while we eat. It will feel more normal.'

'Yes, you're right,' a small creviced frown had taken residence on Angelina's brow. And then she took her glass and swallowed half the contents.

Hidden strengths are imparted by alcohol, thought Cecelia, as she continued assessing this woman. Her life, until now, had been wonderful. And in some ways, she didn't even know she was alive. At least not until whatever it was happened, thought Cecelia. And now, she didn't know what to do. Were there others who were as unhappy and frightened as herself? Cecelia took a sip of wine, knowing she was being unkind to this woman and yet not able to help herself.

Another deep breath.

'I trained as a midwife, and I'm also a qualified nurse. I love nursing, and I love babies.' Angelina stopped to travel back in reflection. 'But nothing is ever black or white. I used to think I was a feminist; it's the so-called fashion these days. It makes you more accepted.' She shrugged and then leaned forward to Cecelia. 'I believe every woman has the right to an abortion. After all, it's their body isn't it?'

Are you asking or telling me?

'If men had to have a baby, carry it for nine months and suffer all the indignity of being prodded, examined, and then to give birth, I believe they would agree that if a female didn't want to have this hypothetical baby, she shouldn't be forced into it.'

What was this woman going on about? Thought Cecelia? If she called her to this interview to give her views on women's rights, or even that of the unborn fetus, she was wasting her time. Ideas like these were best kept to themselves unless there was a vote on it. Women should be allowed a say on what was going on with their own bodies, and it was a view which she also held.

'And is this the reason you brought me here, just to tell me this?'

'Yes—well, no.' The woman was frustrated.

'Okay, I understand,' Cecelia reasoned. She must give this woman a chance instead of jumping all over her with conclusions based on prejudice. 'Let me ask you one thing? Why did you pick me? I'm not the best journalist going. In fact, some would say I'm one of the worst. I don't have any big stories under my belt. If you've checked out my record, you will find I usually do weddings and funerals.' She was watching Cecelia's face seriously. 'The biggest thing I've done is reporting on the Golden Raspberry awards. I think it would probably be better if you spoke to one of my colleagues. I can give you a name—'

'No—it's you. I picked you because of who you are—' Angelina suddenly butted in.

'Me?' was Cecelia really that dumb she didn't know what qualities she had to impart? 'Why me? I think you'll have to explain what it was you saw in me so I can give my best coverage of what has happened to you.'

'You studied philosophy, right?'

'Yes, that's right,' Cecelia replied, uncertain why she asked. 'I did, but I wasn't a brilliant philosopher.'

'You also tried to join the police force.'

'Yes, that's also true.' This conversation was taking a strange twist. A journey into her own past was not what she was expecting. Who were the interviewer and the interviewee now? 'Look, I think we ought to terminate this interview here and now. I feel very uncomfortable about what's going on. You asked to speak to me, and now it seems you are interrogating me. You've probably found out I didn't join the police because of my record. I had a breakdown. When will anyone be forgiven or given a second chance after they've had a breakdown? One mental breakdown and you're blighted for life. A prisoner serves time for their crimes and is then allowed to rejoin society. But this never happens for someone who has been touched by mental illness.'

'I'm sorry, you're right, but these are the very reasons I thought you would understand.' Her eyes met Cecelia's with the honesty of an appeal.

'Great, a failed philosopher and someone who's had a mental breakdown.'

Angelina nodded and then softly smiled.

'Okay, so now you know all about me. Well, I think it's time you spilled on yourself.'

'Yes, you're right.'

Again, that deep breath of jumping into the deep.

'I have been working for a private clinic—would you mind if I didn't name it for now? I find this very difficult to speak about. You see, it's about breaking loyalties, something I've never done before.'

'Probably because it's the first time you've faced up to the truth.'

'Yes,' Angelina said thoughtfully to herself. 'Yes, it's something I am finding very difficult to accept, but it's also the part I played in it which is haunting me.'

The waiter returned with their food; they waited in silence as he placed the dishes in front of them.

'I didn't fancy the roast or any other meat, including fish. So I thought I would pick the vegetarian for us both. I trust you don't mind?' Angelina apologized.

'No, it suits me. I usually don't eat anything until my evening meal, although I might have a pastry if I'm feeling peckish. But this looks quite delicious and healthy. Bon appétit.'

Digging her fork into the vegetarian casserole, Angelina stopped.

'After my training, I went straight to the clinic—you could say I was selected. In my interview, I was asked what I thought about several things. Such as what did I think about IVF, and what did I think about abortion? I told them what I told you, that I believe it's a woman's right to say what's best for their own body. It's a belief which I still hold today, but I think there are questions now as to these rights.'

'How long have you been working at this clinic?'

'Over ten years now, I am thirty-four.'

She looked good for thirty-four, though Cecelia's looks and age had been affected by her health.

'And you work in a private clinic?'

'Yes, we only deal with the rich and famous. No one else can afford the sort of treatment the clinic has to offer. It's discreet, and you have to sign a paper to say that you will never talk about it, otherwise—'

No wonder this woman looked good, thought Cecelia. A pampered life like hers would undoubtedly take the stress out of struggle.

'Yes, otherwise—?'

'I don't know, or I would rather not say. It's only an assumption, but like anything, if you follow the rules, you'll be safe.'

Something clicked in Cecelia's head. It had a distinctive smell of intimidation; the powerful rich are good at that. Not that she would refuse being rich herself. Being rich was something she hankered after. If she were to become suddenly rich, though, without doubt, her rules for life would change completely.

'Do you have any examples of what's happened?'

'No, not really. It's just my fear,' and then she laughed again, anxiously. 'It could be down to how I feel about myself and thinking about the things I am doing.'

'You know,' Cecelia put down her knife and fork. 'You don't have to go through with this. It can still be your little secret. Nothing has been said, so you're still safe.'

'Yes, I'm safe,' she frowned, revealing for the first time her anger. 'But shouldn't someone speak out about what's going on? It's incredibly wrong. If someone doesn't stand up to these people—oh, I don't know.'

'Okay, I understand, or rather, no, I don't understand. How can I make an assessment if you don't tell me what's going on?'

There was a war going on inside the head of this attractive woman, but was she making her decision based on the few minutes they had sat together? This was Angelina's war, not hers.

'Perhaps we should eat and not talk about it anymore. I'm sorry I wasted your time. If you like, I can pay you for it.' Her hand again went to the glass. Snatching it, Angelina threw the rest of the contents down her throat. In her own polished way, Angelina was disappointed.

'Yes, you've wasted my time, and I should take the money you are offering. But you see, I have standards. I work hard and for a pittance. While you—you have had a privileged life, and now you are complaining about it.' How could she sit there and finish this meal with this spoiled woman? She couldn't. 'I've had enough. Look, I'm going to go back to work.' She stood and held out her hand. 'I had to buy this purse for the occasion—'

'Let me pay for it.'

'No, I suggest you get yourself an analyst and talk to them about your feelings about working in the medical world; it's such a tough life.' She moved from the table before returning with another thought. 'Look, Angelina, a piece of advice. You work in the medical world by choice. You will see things others won't see. Get over it and learn to toughen up.'

It felt good walking away from this spoiled woman. She had empowered herself. Holding her shoulders back, Cecelia power walked to the door. So, she had an insignificant life compared to this smart and sophisticated woman, but it was her life. And she had earned it through her own rites of passage. Two fingers up to her, Angelina had no idea what it was like to be a victim.

2

At home and sitting in the room which Cecelia liked to call her office, the day's memorized itinerary came in all its boring details. Something like depression was setting in to change her world. Sunny became gray, while satisfied became miserable. This was what happened when reality flips over. Course now set for her return to her dark planet.

Why do some people make it to the top while others slip down the drainpipe? Is there something in the genes or the fabric of life that says you deserve a raw deal? She often asked herself this question because of her sense of justice, and the answer suggested was always unfair. Unfair, because if she didn't get into these moods called depression, her life would have been so much different.

And then you meet someone like Angelia Joseph, beautiful and with a career, who on the surface had everything and yet she still had time to complain. If only Cecelia had half her luck.

The telephone rang, demanding to be answered.

'Hello Cecelia, it's me, Angelina. Please don't hang up on me.'

How strange, she had just been thinking of her. 'What, are you bored or do you want to invite me out for another meal?'

'Oh, please be kind to me. I need to talk to you.'

This woman who had everything was asking her to be kind. What a joke. 'What, just like the other time? No, sirree, I've got other things to do with my time.'

'Things have changed. I promise I'll tell you everything this time. Please—'

'And you think I don't have anything important to do with my life?'

'I didn't mean that. Please don't give up on me.'

Not immune to the plea in Angelina's voice, it pulled out an immeasurable feeling of concern that she would do anything to save this other person's suffering. Why should anyone suffer? Cecelia had first-hand experience of this. "Don't," Cecelia could hear the voice inside her head pleading, "please don't." This voice from the past came haunting back to the surface again.

'Why can't you tell someone else?'

'I can't—and I can't explain either why I believe you would understand better. This could be your big break.'

'Nah, that doesn't work for me. I don't need someone to tell me they are doing me a favor. What I need to know is why you really picked me?'

'Because you had a breakdown; because I think you believe in justice. There aren't many people these days who give a damn about right from wrong.'

It came out in one long torrent of words, which meant nothing to this woman but everything to Cecelia. She had lived this life, suffered many humiliations. Learned what she had wanted to believe was not how everyone saw it to finally understanding that in the course of her life, she was often wrong. And it hurt and was painful, but the last thing she needed was for someone else to claim it for their own.

'And you think I do?'

'Yes.'

'How?'

'I can't tell you how; it is something I feel about you. Look, Cecelia, I must be honest. I am desperate. This has taken all my courage to do something about it. I thought you, of all people, would understand. I had been looking for a very special person to talk to, and it's you, Cecelia. No one else but you.'

When Cecelia put down the receiver, it was with mixed feelings. This woman had begged and pleaded to talk to her. Finally, she had agreed, because the desire to help was erasing the face of her depression, and to Cecelia, this was a good enough reason to accept.

SITTING IN A CAB, Cecelia was going to this woman's apartment in one of the most sought-after places in the city. Prepare yourself, Cecelia. Will you be jealous? Probably. Yet, going to see someone else's home always fascinated Cecelia, giving her answers to questions about what these other people had done with their lives. It was a keyhole into their private world.

Yes, Cecelia's private world was a world laid out for inspection. A desk, stacks of books, every single one cataloged and in place. Rooms bereft of character, every mark erased. Someone could enter her studio flat with no problem and start living their own lives. No one lived here, no one of any character. This is what her studio flat said about her.

Everything Cecelia saw was under analysis, which was why she lived her life undercover.

And another thing, Angelina Joseph had asked her to come tonight. Come by cab, and she would pay. Did she have so much money that she could throw it away?

It wasn't on. Feeling insulted, Cecelia told Angelina firmly that she would take a bus and then the Metro. But no, this wasn't good enough for Angelina. She wanted to see her straight away. She wanted to talk to Cecelia, and it had to be now, before she lost courage. And then that same last word popped out, which she always ended her sentences with, please.

Of course, it would be lovely to take taxis everywhere you needed to go, as it would be lovely if she had enough money not to worry about the future. And yes, she was a depressive, which was also unfair. But life was all about unfairness. At least it was for her.

It is hard to walk into another world when the contrast from her stark situation was to one of such luxury, and say, I wish this were me.

There were two uniformed people in attendance at reception, and no doubt there would be a swimming pool down in the basement and a helicopter pad on the roof. They looked up as she approached with the face of readiness.

'I'm here to see Ms. Angelina Joseph; she is expecting me.' Holding her back straight, she gave the impression she was someone of importance.

'Just one minute while I ring through,' said the male receptionist. 'Would you like to take a seat over there?'

No, I wouldn't. His suggestion had come like an order,

but if she thought about it, she knew it was her just being awkward again. Everything is a battle in life, so don't fight it. Instead, Cecelia smiled and walked over to the plush armchairs to the side and stood beside them rather than sitting. There is always a compromise for every event. Good for her. Now she was showing her independence.

'You can go up. It's the first elevator on the right, and Ms. Joseph is on the third floor.'

In life, Cecelia thought while entering the elevator. I will always be in the basement while people like Angelina would continually be rising. That's how life is, she supposed. But one day, when I step in that elevator of life, Cecelia determined, when I press the button to go down, instead, it will take me up.

When the elevator arrived, no squeaks, no moans or grunts, Angelina was waiting. Her beautiful face and perfect features were too lovely to be affected by spots or pimples, and she probably never had a bad hair day. With her income, she could afford to eat well, which meant she was always healthy.

The embarrassing demonstration of being glad to see Cecelia was over the top. It was more of an attack when Angelina grabbed hold of her hands and pulled her from the elevator—over the top emotions, heading towards the dramatic. Is this how Angelina got everything she wanted? It was a thought.

'I'm so glad to see you. Thank you, thank you very much for coming. I'm so sorry about the other day.'

Cecelia was pulled towards an open door, overwhelmed by this woman's display of relief.

'I'm going to answer every question you ask,' she said, dragging Cecelia into her apartment. Her door was open, awaiting the invitation.

This was not the time to be jealous, but for the life of God, Cecelia was, but it was not her place to judge this person, considering she had always asked not to be judged herself. Mental illness claims compassion, and if you want forgiveness, the bargain is that you must first forgive.

The apartment was beautiful, white being the predominant color, with touches of French antiques about the room and the odd French eighteenth-century open armchair. Champagne colored silk with striped patterns was the material covering the seat and back panel. They were there to look at and not to sit on. And matching Champagne colored curtains hung at the windows to melt the hard-glazed light before it poured into the rooms.

'Would you like a drink—oh, first let me give you the money for the taxi.' Angelina's purse was already in her hand.

'No,' Cecelia heard her refusal, which was contrary to what she had agreed with herself before. The other side of her, the one who always looked out for Cecelia's benefit, lost to her awkward side. She was the one whose pride wouldn't be influenced, not by complimentary words, and especially not by money. But this money would have come in handy—and why should she pay for expensive transport when she was doing this other woman a favor? All the wonderful luxuries of life Cecelia wanted, but her vanity overrode her desires by turning her nose up to them.

'You came by taxi, didn't you?' Angelina was now confused.

'Yes, I did.'

'So, then I should pay for it.'

'I don't want your money, and if we are going to argue about this instead of the reason you wanted me to come, then I might as well go now.'

'No, no—I'm sorry.'

Pride, that's what it was. Pride made her refuse, and which also cost her money she could not afford. It was also producing the pained look on Angelina's face. This woman was used to being liked.

'And where shall we sit?' Cecelia looked about her again, noticing the old-fashioned telephone, no doubt an antique, the beautiful receiver balanced on the top like a weightlifter. How she would love to have one of these, but it would look odd and out of place in her rented studio apartment, but not in this woman's place. No, it was clear from how stylish it was that she must have had an interior designer attend to all these details.

'We could sit here?' Angelina offered as she gestured towards the two Champagne chesterfields, sitting opposite each other with a heavy, dark, low oak table between them. 'These are the most comfortable—'

'Do you mind?' asked Cecelia, taking out her recorder.

'No,' Angelina was now timid as the gadget confirmed what she was about to do, blinking quickly and trying to hold back her fears. 'Would you like something to drink?'

'Perhaps in a little while. Now, let's get on with the interview. But can I ask you one thing first before we start?'

A nod.

'Why did you get in touch with me again? You know how I feel about wasting my time?'

'Yes. Something has happened which I can't keep quiet about anymore, not if I want to live with myself.'

Click. On went the recorder.

'Ah, I see. Would you like to tell me about it, or start where you think it's best for you?'

There was a long dramatic pause to make the most impact. The wait was there to gather up the storm of applause. But she wasn't fooling Cecelia. With a skeptical mind, Cecelia waited for the theatrics to begin.

'I have been working at a private clinic for over ten years. We deal with the super-rich, and their private lives are treated with the highest respect.'

Cecelia had heard all this before.

'You could say I worked my way up in the clinic. It holds the highest standards in treatment, discretion, and care. People come to us because they know we are the best. It was something to be proud of until just lately, well, since these last two years.'

She looked to Cecelia for confirmation she was still listening. She was. And then she ducked her eyes back down again.

'I used to take care of the new mothers to be, before and after treatment. These women are always nervous. It's a big step to take when becoming a mother or father. I was there initially to tell them what to expect and to prepare them for the news, good or bad. Do you know anything about IVF?'

Why should she know what happens in an IVF clinic? She had no intention of ever having children. With her condition, she had a responsibility not to pass it on. It would be selfish. But Angelina was waiting for an answer.

'Some women just can't get pregnant, so they need assistance. Although some of these people just want a baby without a partner. An egg and the sperm are fertilized outside of the womb and then returned,' she shrugged. 'Is that good enough?'

She hadn't come here to test out her theories about what she knew of this abnormal treatment.

'Yes, children are gifts. They complete their parents' lives, or rather, they should. Sometimes, people put their careers first to make money to provide for their future children with everything they believe these children will need. They put it off and put it off until they realize that time has caught up with them, and then it's too late. I was very proud to be able to help these people have children. It was my ideal job.' Again, Angelina stopped to consider what she had just said. Was it perfect enough?

But her hesitation to get to the point was annoying Cecelia; she had already judged Angelina as being vain and spoiled, and being a time waster was also now being considered.

'The reason I changed my mind about talking to you happened a few weeks ago when I was given a new client. I will not give you their names because this might be dangerous to us both. It suffices to tell you what this clinic is now dealing in.'

'Yes, understand, but I need more to work with.' Cecelia couldn't keep out the impatience in her voice. If she had no details, how was she able to help this woman? Or, more importantly, how was she going to help herself?

'Do you know anything about the IVF procedure?'

'No.'

'During the first day of a woman's period, several eggs are first stimulated by hormonal drugs, and after three days, they are collected.'

'Why are you telling me this?'

'I think it's important you should know. But to cut the explanation short, the eggs are mixed with the washed sperm for twenty-four hours. The donor of the sperms is usually the husband. After mingling, the eggs are placed back into the womb, and then children usually result from it, but not every time, unfortunately.'

Such a cushy job and all done in lovely settings. Probably there was beautiful and restful music playing in the background.

'On conceiving, younger women normally don't have any real problems during pregnancy until they are around thirty-five. Its nature's little prerequisite for a mother to be young and healthy to deal with the trauma, because it is a trauma and an invasion of the body. After the age of thirty-five, the chances of a normal pregnancy decreases. Which means there is a greater possibility the child may not be healthy. Typically, Down Syndrome is one of the problems which can occur. If there are any problems, we can help them with their pregnancy by eliminating the sick fetus or fetuses.'

'Yes, that figures.' Cecelia was mentally walking out of the door. She had not come here for a lesson in reproduction and its complications.

'I should imagine that you've heard of multiple births.'

'Yes, I have.'

'Good. Then you are also aware there are parents who want to choose their children.'

'Well, it's understandable and not unreasonable. Someone I knew had five boys, but she and her husband wanted a girl. She got the girl in the end.'

'I don't think you fully understand the validity of what I am trying to tell you.'

This came with a spark of anger in Angelina's eyes, which surprised Cecelia. This artificial woman was made of sugar and spice, and the rest of the verse. When was this sleeping beauty going to awake? Too early, perhaps. Cecelia waited for Angelina to continue. But it was difficult not to interrupt.

'Supposing you could have the children you wanted and you could choose not only the sex but their hair and eye coloring. Isn't that power? Would you think this was impossible?'

Again, Cecelia held her tongue.

'Supposing you had, let's say, six eggs implanted into the womb and all of them survived.'

'Yes, multiple births. I get what you're saying.'

'Do you? Do you really get what I mean? What about if you didn't want all six children?'

'Then you abort the ones you don't want.'

A smile. Angelina examined Cecelia's face. Cecelia had won the first part.

'Yes, abort the unborn babies you don't want. But when should you start to abort these fetuses?'

'I heard women could legally abort a child up to twelve weeks.' Cecelia's patience was running out; she was not here to do tests and measure up how clever she was. How to get pregnant was not her territory.

'On special medical grounds, you may abort the still called fetus for up to twenty-four weeks, but this is rarely ever carried out.'

'Twenty-four weeks,' Cecelia gasped. 'But the child will be over five months. Surely that can't be legal with any medical condition.'

'At twenty-four weeks, the baby will be fully formed and be around twelve inches long, and it will weigh about one and a third pounds. At this size, it has a viable chance of survival.'

'You mean?' Gone were the monotony and boredom. Cecelia sat forward, shocked by the unthinkable.

'I was given a new client, as I said before. She was recently married to a business oligarch. He married her because he specifically wanted children. But his new wife was over thirty-six, and she had been on the pill since she was old enough to take it.'

'I'm surprised he picked her when he wanted to have children. Since he was the one with all the money, I guess she readily obliged.'

Angelina licked her lips, eager to carry on.

'It's none of my business why these two came together. It's enough to know she was a failed small-time politician who had an attitude problem. But linked to him, she was suddenly elevated to a newer and higher status. In this way, she became prestigious in the eyes of the world because of her marriage to this man.'

It happens, thought Cecelia.

'She said to me, in an off the wall remark which I didn't give much credence to at the time, simply because I thought she was nervous. She said, "I'll give him what he wants because he can give me everything I want." What do you think of that?' haunted by this memory, Angelina looked down for a moment of reflection. 'Six fertilized eggs had been reinstated back into her womb. This wasn't normal practice, but it happens when partners become desperate.'

Again, she stopped to walk through these memories. They still troubled her.

'The first fetus was aborted after three months by suction. I was with her when the unborn was taken out. Do you know what happens in an abortion?'

'Of course, I've heard things, stories, but really, I'm not that interested in what other women do with their bodies. I'm glad I've never had to make that call. But I believe they do what is called vacuuming? But I shouldn't imagine they would really vacuum out the womb as if they were clearing out rubbish.'

'It takes up to three days for dilation before the fetus can be aborted,' continued Angelina, determined, frowning and being what is called deadly professional.

Already, the gory details were making Cecelia feel uncomfortable.

'It's a big ordeal for the mother, both psychologically and physically. To avoid as much stress as possible, the patient is treated humanely. We like to give them nitrous oxide gas, which puts the patient into a twilight state. To a degree, she is awake but sedated, and tranquil, a very pleasant place to be. Depending on the fetus's age or the mother's age, another sedation can be given, a local anesthetic which is injected into the cervix to make it go numb to cause no pain.'

Cecelia cringed as she imagined this procedure. An involuntary shrug almost became a repellent shudder. What was the point of Angelina telling her this? Was she getting off on seeing her reactions?

'A third procedure which most women prefer is intravenous sedation. This is put into the patient's vein while an anesthetic is injected into the woman's cervix.'

'It sounds so gory.' Cecelia shuddered, now unable to keep the vision from penetrating her mind.

'Yes, but to give birth to a defective baby whose entire life would be one of pain and frustration would be unbelievable. Abortion is by far the best and kindest thing we can do for a life which is not worth living.'

'If you say so,' Cecelia glanced at her quickly. Why on earth would Angelina want to work in this kind of world?

'This woman had suction. The fetus's bones are still soft at this stage, so they are easily sucked out through a tube. The problem after this extraction is to make certain that nothing has been left behind. A tool called a curette is inserted into the womb to search and scrape out any debris left behind. If anything is left from the fetus or the placenta, disease or infection typically occurs. I have to stress that within the twelve weeks, the fetus, although it has everything formed, heart, limbs, and toes, does not have a complete functioning nervous system, so the unborn won't experience any pain.'

'I wish I could believe that.'

'This woman now has five fetuses left in her. But already she had become huge. Five babies at one time could be dangerous not only to the children but also to the mother. Everyone agrees that the mother is the person to be considered first.'

'Yes, yes—can we cut to the chase and tell me the reason you called me here? You've had months—even years to think about all the rights and wrongs of your vocation.'

'Very well—' Angelina appeared flustered.

The face which once knew happiness, who enjoyed her life and career, was not smiling now. Sad eyes had pulled her face into despair.

'The mother is an attractive woman who is underweight. She is also delicately boned. So, when she carries, her stomach protrudes, making her look bigger than she is. The gynecologists suggested that she have all the abortions in one go to reduce the risk to her. But both husband and wife want their children to be perfect, and they don't care about the consequences.'

'Are you saying that she died trying to have her babies?'

'No, she didn't die. They both knew we would do everything to look after her. When you have enough money and prestige, you can do what you want in life, and no one is going to stand in your way. The rich have a different way of thinking from you and me.'

'So, the mother is fine. What happened next?'

'I was told forcefully I should never talk about this to anyone. I said I knew this, and I was a professional so they could trust me. Apart from that, I signed a form stating that I could be taken to court and sued if I spoke to anyone outside the clinic. It would probably result in imprisonment. I told them I understood this and that I would carry out my duty to the best of my ability.'

'Okay, so why are you talking to me about it?'

'Because things have changed. The husband wants two boys, only sons, not daughters. The mother was carrying five boys, and they were, for now, all healthy, but three of them still had to go. Neither of the parents wanted any more than two.'

She stopped to look at Cecelia.

'Do you know what the real problem is with multiple births?'

'That the children will be too weak to survive?'

'Image. The world is full of images. It's not enough to be rich and powerful. People must also believe in you. I have seen how it works and the homages made to these people who conform to an ideal. The rich, the leaders, politicians— they live a life of privilege, and all we ask of them is to comply with our model. If they weaken, they fall.'

'Okay,' Cecelia nodded.

'I thought I could do what was asked of me. Do you understand, to provide an excellent service to help the new parents? It's their lives and their choices. My beliefs differ from theirs, which means I must not interfere. I am not there to judge. I thought by believing this, my part in their treatment would be absolved.'

There is no God; you are absolved, Cecelia wanted to say. But the way Angelina was looking about her, searching for the right answer, kept her transfixed.

'Another abortion occurred in the fourth month. I held her hand even though she was unconscious. Again, she had been dilated for the procedure, and this time, extraction of the fetus would be riskier. The fetus is taken apart bit by bit. At four months, abortion is not uncommon in this clinic.'

'Why do you keep on calling it a fetus? Surely, it's a baby by now?'

'Technically, if the fetus is birthed, it could not survive on its own. And besides, to call a fetus a baby now is politically emotive. It's like saying at this stage, the baby has a soul. I'm sorry, this is the only way I can deal with it. It would be best if you did not allow yourself to get emotional when you are doing an abortion—this procedure has saved many women's lives. And besides, an unwanted disabled child can be a problem for them and society?'

'But the people who you are looking after are the rich and powerful. They want these children. It's a symptom of their vanity to carry on their line. In this way, the rich can rule and always be privileged. And their children's children continuous. A line of rulers with the humble everyone else working for them and serving them.'

Angelina shook her head as if she was clearing her mind of all unsolicited imaginings. She wasn't listening to anything that Cecelia was saying.

'It's unavoidable, but you form a relationship with this soon-to-be mother.'

'A mother?' it came out of her mouth as if she was using a swear word.

'Yes, this woman is about to become a mother, in this case, only to two children, not to the others—shouldn't we give people what they want?'

'Are you asking me this or telling me? But it doesn't

matter what I think. You have a story to tell, and I should be professional enough to listen to you.'

'The trouble is, once you get to know her, you can't help but like her. I can't put my finger on it, but she makes you feel you are the most special person in the world. Then suddenly, you become her greatest friend. You become her family. And she tells you how she feels, and she wants to know all about you—'

'What has this got to do with anything?' Cecelia was now exasperated.

'I don't know. Perhaps it's an excuse or even an apology for what I had agreed to do.'

Impatiently, Cecelia ran a hand down her brow while wondering if she could walk out without listening to Angelia's story any longer. 'And so, you found yourself liking her because she flattered you?'

'Yes, for all she has done and was about to do, I still liked her.'

She looked away from Cecelia's eyes, falling now deeper into the past.

'When the second abortion came along, it was her that told me I would be okay—a patient telling a nurse that everything would be fine. The unborn wasn't a baby, so why worry about it?'

'Couldn't you ask to be put on another case?'

'No. I had to see this through. I made a promise to her. I told her we would get through this together by giving each other strength.'

Was she a fool to damage her mind going through this because of someone else's selfish needs?

'Is this illegal what the clinic is doing?'

'I expect so, but where money is involved, these people can do anything.'

Angelina looked down again. She still had a long way to go.

'It was awful extrapolating the little body. We had to place it together to make certain that all the body parts were retrieved. It's little leg, and little arm; so tiny and yet so perfectly formed. Another few weeks and this fetus would have been a feasible living baby.'

Silence again as Angelina was looking at something only visible to her.

'It was me who had to pick up the little leg and place it against the torso—a crushed tiny human jigsaw, attaching the small arms and the mashed skull on its small neck. The body was strangely still, and there would be no more growth anymore. Its wrinkled face and pushed-up nose looked so peaceful it looked as if it was asleep—poor little boy. Once every part had been identified, the fetus is placed into the macerator. Chewed up as if it had never existed.' And then Angelina tried to smile as if what she had just related became glib. 'But that's what happens every month when women menstruate.' She bit her bottom lip to prevent herself from saying any more.

'Hardly the same thing, though?'

'Yes, I know. Not a good comparison, but one which helps you in your prayers.'

Surely, she couldn't believe in God by doing the job she was doing.

'And after she was gone, she left me a gift,' Angelina began again as if she had awoken from that bad dream. 'A diamond bracelet. It was beautiful, diamonds set in gold, the most beautiful one I had ever seen, and probably worth a fortune. To me, it was, but I expect to these people, its cost was nothing. It felt like a bribe. Do you mind if I have a drink now?'

'No, suit yourself.'

'Would you like a drink? I have everything. You only need ask.'

'Wine would be nice.'

Cecelia watched as she went over to an antique-looking cabinet. She poured out a glass of wine for Cecelia, and for herself, she made a cocktail, then walked back slowly.

'Two months had passed since she had the last abortion. After all that time, I thought they had changed their minds. I assumed by now they were going to keep the three healthy boys, and I was glad. But then I got a telephone call from her saying she was looking forward to seeing me again.' Angelina shook her head in disbelief. 'She was now seven and a half months pregnant. Any babies born now would be premature, but they would survive if they were put into an incubator. She was going to have her babies now, I told myself. I was so pleased they weren't going to go through with another awful extraction until the following morning when I was told to gown up for another abortion. At first, I wondered if they had put me on another case. And then I saw Ruth. She waved to me when she was going into the robing room. "Ready for the last one," she called out to me.'

Angelina stopped. The disturbing memory filled her mind while Cecelia read her haunted face.

'No, I thought to myself, no. You can't be having an abortion now—the baby is alive. It can feel. It can hear its mother's voice and will respond to music, especially when the mother sings. And if she touches her abdomen, its protruding foot will wriggle and delight if she grabs hold of it.'

Oh God, this was awful. Was she reliving this moment again?

'Routine. Routine saves you. I had to wash and gown up.

I believe that's when I went into automatic mode. Scrubbing my hands and my elbows—do you know, every night when I come home, I have to soak my hands in cream?'

How young she looked when she glanced at Cecelia. Innocent with expectation in her eyes, as if she was waiting for her to answer, but Cecelia knew she shouldn't reply. Angelina was deep in reliving the scene, and the horror.

'She was already in the theater when I went in. You know, I can't tell you how many times I've gone through this procedure like walking, eating, sleeping. It becomes a habit, routine. The operation theater is so familiar to me; it's like my home. I think nothing of it. I know this world, it's familiar to me. But not anymore. When I see these doctors, the men I used to respect with intelligence, compassion and understanding. The ones who always made the right decisions. I know they are not thinking about how to look after mother and child; they adding up the money they will make. These men I knew had become white-clothed demons covered up completely with their hands held up as they moved about the theater. They had become awful monsters. At the same time, the silver metal operating tools to aid and cut off pain and fear had become weapons of torture. The child who was sleeping now was going to be destroyed.' She threw her hand to her mouth.

'Is it murder to kill a child at this stage in life? A cesarean would have been the correct way for the baby. But what would you do with a baby when it cries? You can't kill it, this would be murder, but you can pull it out through the uterus bit by bit. Bits of the child's body are acceptable. What are people thinking of when they do this, pulling a living child to pieces so they can work within the law?' Angelina looked at Cecelia with disbelieving eyes.

'Rage,' she continued. 'I had to work through my rage. It

was better to be angry than to give into my feelings. I could have screamed. My friend, this patient, was already prepped up and unconscious. She was not going to feel anything. Everything was cleaned up for her. Her child was not a child anymore. It was now a messy collection of flesh and blood. She was eager to have this thing out of her. How do these people manage to live with themselves? And yet, I have seen this before and slept through it, but this was perverse. This was going right up to the end to see how much they could get away with. I cannot forgive myself.' Grabbing her glass, she took a large gulp.

'My hands were shaking—I was shaking when I took my place with the team, but no one could read my eyes as I could not read theirs. If she had been awake—I would ask of her to please have the baby and give it to me, and I promise you I would look after it, and I would. It was madness, pure insanity. Please don't go through with it, I kept on saying to myself. Don't have this extraction. Let it live and give it to me. But they wouldn't, would they, they wouldn't allow me to have their baby son? They would sooner have it dead.'

She shook her head and stared at Cecelia. In her eyes, Cecelia could see that Angelina had become another woman other than herself.

'I saw the drip keeping her hydrated and sedated. I had to prevent myself from pulling it out to say to this bitch, if you want to get rid of your third child, you should be conscious. It's the least you can do. Be there for your son, just this once. He's been inside you, trusting you for seven and a half months—don't you want to see him to say goodbye?'

Poor grieving woman. Cecelia had to prevent herself from comforting Angelina. She needed to get her story.

'The head gynecologist looked around at us. "Are we

ready?" he asked, calling us to be attentive. Gowned and masked, no one could see that I was shaking and making promises to myself that I wouldn't faint. This was what my job was all about and why I trained. But as I neared her lying on the operating table, her eyes covered with eye pads to prevent damage, I saw her stomach. It was moving. The children inside should have been drugged as well, but now they were moving about.'

Digging her fingernails into her flesh, Cecelia had to leave Angelina inside that dark nightmare until her story was complete.

But was Angelina imagining this terrifying episode? Had she cracked up and from her dreams produced this horror? Could she tell reality from fear? Cecelia knew about anxiety and how it operated with the imagination. Was it possible that Angelina's fears were migrating unreal events to her mind to produce such revulsions? It could not be as bad as this. It must not be this bad.

'But if I should warn the doctor that I had seen the baby they were about to terminate was still alert and alive, would he have ignored it? I don't know. But he must be able to see the children stretching and moving. Mustn't he? If he and the rest of the staff were choosing to ignore the life going on below the flesh, and if I exposed it to them, they would gang up together, and I would be the threat. Put on red alert and certified that I was mad.'

Angelina lowered her head in shame.

'But I didn't say anything. Like a coward, I took my place amongst the monsters. The operation was going to be carried out. Oh, God, forgive me for my part in this infant's murder.'

'The baby was going to be dismantled, his leg caught hold of, twisted and tugged, which meant the bones would break and then be pulled out, piece by piece. Oh, can you imagine the agony?' she shook her head again while her eyes were alert to insanity.

'At this stage, the baby would not be able to cry tears or make any sound in his mother's sack, but he would suffer the dismantling of his body. Can you imagine the intrusion of being grabbed hold of by a cold, long-toothed metal clamp? Impossible,' she shook her head again. 'Impossible to understand the horror committed to the young innocent. Because he would feel everything—'

Cecelia couldn't take her eyes off Angelina. And then she heard her sigh, as if resigned to her part in it.

'Usually, the legs are torn off first before the arms. The head is the last part to come out, as it needs to be crushed first before it's retrieved.'

Horror and the need for reassurance, Cecelia now found she was rocking.

'I was handed his first leg, and now I was waiting for the first arm. I placed the warm leg on the metal dish as I had done before. His body was forming outside of his mother, bit by bloody bit. But he wasn't real, I kept on telling myself, and by now, any breath of life he had would have gone. He is dead, I kept on telling myself. He will suffer no more pain, no more hurt, no more betrayal, and all is peace in his mind. He sleeps now.'

'The gynecologist inserted the instrument again. "I have it," he said as he retrieved the arm. But it wasn't only an arm this time, the baby's head came with it, and it appeared to be still alive. "Quick, get the head," the gynecologist yelled at me. And when I took it, the little person opened his eyes and looked up into mine. I didn't think it was possible. He was looking at me.'

And then Angelina bent over and groaned, her eyes soaked with tears as she sobbed.

'Oh, did this little child so new to life believe that I was his mommy? The poor little child was a mess. His legs had been pulled off, and now his arm was distorted. Yet he waited and suffered to keep alive to see who it was that had done this to him. Oh, what have I done?'

Unable to take her eyes from Angelina, Cecelia felt for the recording device and switched it off. The interview was terminated.

3

Perhaps she was numb. It was difficult to tell how she felt traveling home in the taxi. A luxury that Cecelia knew she couldn't afford, but this was an emergency after what she had heard.

It was late, very late, and how would she be able to get herself up in the morning for work? But there again, how would she now be able to sleep after what Angelina had told her? It was just so horrible and incredible, and something so impossible to believe could happen. But why would Angelina make something like this up? What gain could be had from it? It was now a question of whether she believed her or not?

There are too many questions as there are too many whys. Righteousness always stands out against injustices, but do we choose to ignore it when it's obvious? If we decide to be silent, it becomes a canker, a cancer growing and thriving and waiting to consume.

Now, what was she supposed to do with this story? It was a tale of horrors told through the night, standing tall and gory like an unwanted visitor. But in the hours of daylight, quietly, it became unreal. It never happened; it was just a bad, bad dream. No, go away and forget about it; it's just a terrible nightmare.

Sometimes, the story is only real while it's being told, but then life bubbles through and interrupts and chases the devils away. It's facts which make it real and which stand astride and heaves life into the ephemeral story. But there were no real concrete facts to this story. This woman could have made it up, bore a grudge against the clinic. When they found their name in the paper, who would they sue? The source was where it came from, herself. It was this answer which satisfied Cecelia's need to sweep this dreadful story under the mat.

A night of entertainment had finished with a horror story.

It was late when Cecelia left, and the reason for this was because Angelina couldn't stop crying. She kept on blaming herself for not stopping this procedure.

On that day in the afternoon, Angelina and the team between them had murdered a baby, and it was legal. Everything Angelina had said was now all mumbled. There was no record of the baby; everything which might have been recorded on the register would be deleted once the money was passed over. Angelina knew this because she had looked for it.

The child had been alive, and it had moved and seen the world—it had looked at her and judged. This was life, wasn't it? A young life which had not stopped to live.

It was gone three in the morning before Cecelia left with the promise of speaking to her at the weekend. Angelina was terrified and afraid. Today was Thursday. 'Thursday's child has far to go,' was the adage. But this Thursday's child was not going anywhere, not now. What a mess? But just as she was about to leave Angelina's, the phone rang, frightening them both like the call of death. Looking at the phone, Angelina wouldn't answer it. She was too frightened, and besides, her voice had become hoarse.

Who was ringing her at this time of night? Cecelia walked across to the old-fashioned white telephone and picked it up.

'Hello,' she snapped into the receiver. 'What do you want?'

There was no answer, and for three or more seconds, there was silence, and then the receiver clicked as it was replaced.

'Oh, what the hell?' Cecelia frowned. She had just been through a gruesome story, and now someone was playing dirty tricks. A deep breather probably.

If only. Cecelia's mind was caught in a time trap. If she could turn back the clock now that she had been privy to these events and say no to Angelina's pleas, then she would do so with pleasure. Angelina was behaving like a predator by using Cecelia this way. And now she understood why Angelina had chosen her instead of someone else, or perhaps she had tried someone else, but they had been wise and said no to her. And now, she had brought these ghosts back home.

Hurrying to her bathroom cabinet, the tablets she kept just in case of an emergency were taken off the shelf, her little night-time friends. Sleeping tablets. She would take two tonight to sleep. Sleep away that awful reality. Tomorrow, she would have to deal with the effects of her sleepers.

When the alarm went off later that morning, Cecelia had come to the sensible conclusion that she would not deal with this woman again. Let this Angelina find someone else to unburden herself on, because really, how did she know if what Angelina was telling her was true or one big lie?

A stale headache was accruing its toll from the lack of hydration. She needed to drink and take a couple of painkillers, which meant risking more tiredness. It served her right to allow herself to be manipulated. Stick to what you know—weddings, births, and obituaries. Life's dramatics and its adrenalin were not worth it, not if she wanted to keep her sanity.

Ringing the office, Cecelia asked what they had for her. Her boss told Cecelia there was a demonstration outside a fertility clinic which she could cover.

Such are the coincidences in life. After speaking to this woman last night, the world had awoken to the facts about the lack of control behind those closed doors. Women and their bodies, what rights do they have to impose the word of God from their wombs?

If she could have done, Cecelia would have refused to cover it. But the facts were when it came down to the bitter arguments of need, money kept her going, although, in real terms, it wouldn't be much.

Drinking coffee at double the usual strength, Cecelia collected her jacket and slammed the door behind her. It was a gray day in a gray world. Summer was officially over, and still it was warm, though it didn't feel like it. It felt more like the onset of winter, with wind and rain rubbed into the day, making it colder than it should be. But that was how it always was when she took sleepers.

Catching the bus, it immediately got caught up in traffic. It was that time of the day, but every time now was that time of day. Too many faces with too many thoughts. No one looked at each other anymore. It was safer that way.

Already Cecelia could see the not too small gathering.

Before she arrived at the meeting place, she could feel the anger.

There were two parties at the rally. One was pro-abortion, calling themselves women's rights, and the other side was on the unborn child's rights. Walking through the demonstrators, Cecelia was looking for the right people to ask what was going on. She was looking for someone who looked intelligent from both sides of the debate.

It always amazed Cecelia that people could hold opposing ideas on the same subject. People just didn't talk to each other, each side thinking they were right while knowing the other side must be completely wrong. But nothing is a hundred percent.

It is clear, Cecelia began her piece on the protest, *that as it stands, the woman bearing the child should have permission to do what she wants with her body. This being her only property. But after a certain amount of time, the developing infant also has status and thus must be protected by law—*

Relaxing her hands on her laptop, Cecelia began imagining the baby which Angelina had brought to her through her story. But it was the images of the child's destruction that made him appear much more real by placing that incredible knowledge into her mind. It was strange how this child only came to life because of his horrific death. At least his dreadful death had then been worth something, because there must be some reason for his brief existence.

In everything, the time comes when you must decide if you believe what has been said or not. It was a question in which every wicket of the argument had been touched and satisfactorily verified with one's sense of justice.

Angelina might be right when she related the case to Cecelia. And if Angelina was telling the truth, then something had to be done about it. Angelina's fear about the clinic and what it could do to her if she talked to someone, and it wasn't followed up, was frightening. But if the authorities did, and the clinic was stormed, and all its technicians and management were prosecuted, Angelina Joseph would be a heroine. Otherwise, she and Angelina wouldn't need to go into hiding.

So, why not go and see Angelina tomorrow and explain that nothing could be done to her if she went to the medical overlords?

At last, the place where Cecelia liked to live, where evil had been done away with returned. Where everyone would be kind to each other, and flowers grew in the summer. Where the birds sang and people smiled, and everyone was happy.

She was not going to be angry with Angelina anymore. This woman had not upset her world and way of life. The righteousness will heal the wrongdoers, and everything would turn out all right. Right now, Cecelia would give Angelina a buzz to tell her of her plan.

'Hello Angelina, it's me, Cecelia.'

'Oh,' was all she said.

But this was not enough to put Cecelia off. 'I've been thinking about what you said last night, and I want to talk a bit more about it with you. Do you mind? I can come over tomorrow. I've been thinking about what you told me, and it would make a good story—a seriously good one. But first, I need you to give me names. I know the woman who had the late abortion is called Ruth, but I also want to know the name of the clinic and the gynecologist.'

'I think I might have made a mistake,' Angelina sounded young, so very young, as if she had regressed thirty years back into childhood.

'I understand if you're scared, and now you've changed

your mind because it brings up too many terrible memories.
But—'

'I've been going through a bad time—I just split up with
my boyfriend—'

Holding the receiver closer to her ear, Cecelia began
frowning. What was this story she was telling her now? She
couldn't have made the other story up; it was impossible
because Cecelia had believed her. It was more likely she was
scared and felt threatened.

'Yes, what you told me was a bit far-fetched, but we still
need to talk about it.'

'I'm sorry I got you involved,' Angelina was now panicking. 'I'm sorry, but I've been going through a bad time. What
I should have told you was that it was me who had the abortion. Do you understand? No one else except me.'

'Okay,' Cecelia was mentally ticking off the idea that the
story which had been told wasn't real, but it was more real
now to Cecelia because she believed it. And now she was
excited because this would make one hell of a story.
Angelina hadn't been lying when she told her the story. She
just got scared, that was all. A few kind words would rectify
this.

4

___

First, she would get Angelina's story before telling her editor. Doing it this way would give her control over the story, rather than him telling her what to do and what she could say and how she should go about it. This, in effect, would make it his story.

The excitement Cecelia felt was overwhelming. She had a project that would take her right out of her stale life. A story which would make her appreciated and respected in the world of journalism. True, it was a horrific story, but that's how people make their names.

Finishing her piece about the rally, Cecelia emailed it to her editor. Completion came with a satisfactory feeling, which called for a long, cool glass of wine. She deserved it. What would she do about tomorrow? Why not take the entire day off to prepare, chill out and just do nothing? It would set her up for Saturday.

Sometimes, it's good to take a day off and walk around the city. LA is always beautiful, especially at night. She would catch the bus, then take the tour from 6800 street, and mingle amongst the tourists on the Hollywood Walk of

Fame. Meet all the stars and imagine for that fleeting moment they were there waiting to put their hands and feet into the memorial of immortal cement. Stardust and magic; it was mortals that made them. But it was time and these impressions that would outlive them.

She smiled as she ran for the bus to take her seat next to the window, feeling that she was entering a new chapter of her life. There was hope now when none before had existed. And it was by chance with that one person looking for another on her quest to find the right voice which started it. And it was Angelina who had given her this chance, dusted her with her luck, with Angelina's special luck and blew her the kiss of hope to go with it. It is true, good luck does rub off.

How different, Angelina and she were. Making comparisons with Angelina still made her envious, which was a non-profitable emotion to possess. Angelina had done well with her life. Instead of jealousy, it would be better if she tried to emulate her. Yes, well, that would come.

Beautiful, intelligent, well dressed, you name it, but Cecelia could be as lovely as Angelina, just in a different way. Her long dark hair could be dressed in a new style; she always meant to do something with it. She had never been overweight, in fact, quite the opposite, but some exercising would be a good idea to tone up those flagging muscles. Do it at home if she didn't enjoy going to the gym. Yes, with Cecelia's new style, she could look just as good as Angelina. However, apathy is a powerful force to fight.

At the end of Friday, having walked past Marilyn Monroe, turning into Sunset Boulevard passing the Hollywood Wax Museum. This was a place that both spooked and enchanted her, although she had never been inside.

So rich a city made on the wings of fairy tales. She

counted herself fortunate to have been born here rather than anywhere else in the world. How lucky she was, and how wonderful she now felt because luck had suddenly visited her.

And then home. This is what one does when taking a day off.

From outside her apartment, as the key went into the lock, Cecilia could hear the telephone ringing. Doesn't it always happen like this? By the time she got to the telephone, she knew they were going to ring off. People instinctively know you are either in the bathroom or outside, like she was now. It was exasperating.

Sticky fingers when trying to open the door. Kicking off her shoes, a cardinal rule in this apartment, she ran across the floor and leaned across her small two-seater sofa to take hold of the receiver. On the other end, whoever it was probably sighed and wouldn't wait any longer to hear her answer, hello.

Not important enough gal, but that time when they couldn't get enough of her.

The thwarted call wasn't going to ruin her day. If it were important, he or she would ring back. But if not, never mind. It could have been Angelina. Cecelia smiled; if it was, it was just as well she didn't get to the phone in time.

'I know who it was,' a sigh and a smile. It was definitely, Angelina. She was ringing to say she had changed her mind again, but it didn't matter. There was no going back once Cecelia had made up her mind. Angelina had been right about one thing. This could be her break, and this time she was going to take it.

Excited, this was a new feeling for Cecelia. She was looking forward to talking with Angelina and bending her stiff arm into working alongside her. This time, she would not be overlooked, as she was now on the road to being rich and famous. This chant was a piece of good verbal music humming in her mind.

No hangover this morning from the sleepers and neither had she drank much. She had a good day, and she didn't regret having taken it off as she did not regret buying herself a good meal. She had a cup of tea, brushed her teeth, and brushed her hair. And yes, she was singing, if only to herself. But wasn't life great? And why shouldn't she take a taxi to Angelina's apartment? Well, why not? The good feeling was carrying over in to today. And good feelings are what lives are made of.

Perhaps she and Angelina could be great friends once the story had been released and national coverage had exposed what had happened. Angelina would become a celebrity, someone who stood and shouted out and put herself at risk. And you never know, Angelina's exposure might draw her into the limelight.

Celebrities, yes, why not? People had done even less to become a celebrity. A reality show, an auto-tune screamer, or someone who married a celebrity and claimed it for themselves. These were the new people on the block. At least Angelina and she would be doing something important. They would be the new people that everyone wanted to know, and she would write a book about it which would become a best seller.

Was she going on a high? Possibly, but it was a good high, for there was something to feel good about. Life was speeding along nicely.

Pacing about her apartment flicking the television on for company as she got ready for tomorrow, the television voices were drowning out her thoughts

Just by luck, on the television news, was an item about

Haleigh and his new wife, Ruth. The report said they were awaiting the imminent arrival of their first baby; it followed with a clip of the two holding hands, smiling for the camera, and then was followed by some history of the celebrated couple. Haleigh was born in America forty-seven years ago. His father, born in the Lebanon, left for America in the 70s aware that things were happening. Maheen arrived in America with great wealth still intact. Understanding business, he doubled his money in less than five years. He raised his only son to take over his business when he died. Like his father, Haleigh, whose name was Americanized from Haleb, worked unstintingly to become even wealthier, purported to be in the tens of billions. Now that he had made a safe fortune, it was time to start a family. The happy couple were hoping for a boy.

This Haleigh was not good-looking at all, but what did it matter when you were rich? Switching off the television and double checking her apartment in passing, Cecelia eyed herself in the mirror. Not too bad. Her dark hair was a complimentary contrast against Angelina's blonde locks. Yes, she was not too bad, attractive more than pretty. Locking the door behind her, she ran down the steps and started walking along the sidewalk. This could be the start of a new life, she murmured to herself as she jumped on to a bus.

Every day has the potential to be a good day, Cecelia thought as she skipped off the bus in her low shoes and on to another sidewalk. Did the sidewalks along here look cleaner than the ones down her way? There was hardly any litter drifting in the roads and on to the sidewalk as there was on her side of town. Perhaps she should write a news item on it.

Before Cecelia arrived at Angelina's building, her feet

were already dragging, crippling her to return. A dark feeling entered her stomach. Instinctively, and for no real reason, Cecelia felt rotten with fear. Something was wrong, and it wasn't anything to do with her mood. This was something else, as if she was picking up on some evil vibes. She couldn't say what it was, but she knew something had happened. The road was empty of people. In any street, there would be someone walking and going about their business, but not today. It was as if someone had put up a sign which said, stay away. This feeling was confirmed when she saw a group of people huddled outside the building. If she could only put her finger on it. A hunch—suspicion is not much good when there is no knowledge of what this feeling is about.

Be afraid of what you don't know—be afraid of life. Spook yourself. It's stupid, really, but that's how fear works.

Police officers were milling around in reception, circling around like insects after honey. She stopped immediately. Should she go in or turn around and go out? This would only bring attention to her. Looking at their faces, trying to read what was going on gave nothing. This time Cecelia's skills failed her as she ended up with only guesses. What had happened in this building?

Stepping inside the block of luxury apartments, Cecelia's presence caught the eyes of the receptionist. A challenge for Cecelia to come across and speak to her if only to allay suspicions. The receptionist's interested head cocked to one side and held the expression of what do you want.

'Hello, I seem to have lost my way?'

'What are you're looking for?' the marble face did not smile.

This was not good.

'I was supposed to meet my friend; we were going for lunch. Is the hotel Boulevard near here?'

'It's not far to walk. If you go out of here and turn right and walk for about five minutes, you will come to it. You can't miss it. It's a huge white building.'

She must have walked right past it without having noticed, Cecelia explained. And now she was almost bowing and curtsying to an apartment worker. Sycophant, obsequious, Cecelia was glad to get out of the building to walk in the suggested direction. But this was only a diversion because she was intending to double back to the small crowd standing around.

'Excuse me, can you tell me what's happened?'

A man glanced at Cecelia and looked her up and down, then smiled. He was just three or four inches taller than Cecelia. Dressed in a black tee-shirt and jacket, he looked very smart in a classic casual sort of way.

'A woman living in that building there,' he pointed, 'fell in front of a bus and was killed instantly. An awful tragedy for someone so young and apparently so beautiful. I heard she was a nurse. Sometimes it seems only the good die young.'

Something like a hammer hit Cecelia's chest, as this could only be Angelina. The beating of the dead had happened, and now it was getting louder.

'Yes,' muttered Cecelia. Her lungs withheld her voice.

'Someone said they saw her being pushed. Speculation, I guess, but there's always a certain amount of truth in hearsay. She might have been pushed. She may not have been pushed. Who knows? But for a young woman to take her life just when she is at her best—' He shrugged. 'It's tragic, isn't it?'

A nice man but just an ordinary guy, who once you have

seen him, you would instantly forget him. A bystander who had nothing in life was now filling his day with the happening of another's passing.

'Poor woman,' Cecelia said, frowning and beginning to feel uncomfortable. 'Have they said who she was?'

'No, they haven't,' he smiled, revealing his teeth. 'It's police work. They keep their fingers to their nose, but I have heard she was young, blonde, and lovely, which makes it all the more tragic.'

The world that had opened its day to Cecelia had now switched off its lights. Her vision was failing her, as the world was becoming dark and fuzzy. The strange colors of nausea were perpetrating mauve and black over Cecelia's retina. Daylight had outstripped Cecelia's control. Was it time to say goodnight for a while?

She knew who this person was, and this had become a shock. No one needed to tell her that the deceased person was Angelina. More the surprise because she knew for sure that someone had murdered her. Protecting their secrets, the rich and vain stood outside from the law, and Angelina had broken this trust, and it had cost her her life.

'Are you okay?' another man asked, taking hold of her. Now more than interested in her.

'Yes, I'm sorry, I seem to have something in my eye,' holding her head down to get the blood pumping back into her brain. She needed to get home. Oh dear, it had to happen now. She was going to faint. 'Could you hail a cab for me? I would appreciate it, please.' Where had the world gone? It was swirling away and drawing her into its vortex. Please don't let me pass out here in front of everyone. People take control of you if you show any weakness.

'Yeah, sure.' And her arm was tugged hard as he led her away from the crowd.

Amazing how fear can keep a person alert as danger makes one hang on, tripping and running to keep up and find out what's going to happen next. And now she was shaking. Fear had given into that, who is this guy?

'Taxi,' she heard him call out on her behalf. 'One has just stopped: I'll help you get to the cab—a bit of luck for a change. So now I'm going to walk you across the road. You'll be okay. I'll just open the door for you and help you in.'

His voice sounded hollow as his muscular arms took a hold of her to push her into the car. He was being kind to her as if he knew what was happening, guessing that she had nearly fainted.

'You'll be okay,' he repeated with reassuringly warm breath on her face now he was close to her.

He was very kind, but why was she so afraid of him? This was another reaction.

It was good to sit down and give in to the feeling. She was starting to sweat. He must be able to see what was happening to her.

'Where are you going?' it was a natural question to ask from someone who stayed to assist.

But it was the quality of his voice, and how close he was leaning inside the taxi. So near. So intimate. 'I'll tell the cab driver where you're going?'

'I want to go to—' and then she stopped. It was something about his voice that whispered he was too eager. Telling him where she was going would be a big mistake.

'To the Boulevard hotel. I'm t meeting a friend for a meal.'

'But the hotel is just up on the corner there; it's only five minutes' walk. You could walk it, you know. Come on; I'll walk with you.'

No, a scream rang out in her head, but its power reduced

this to sense and explanation. 'That's very kind of you. I think I'll take the cab. I'll probably be late if I don't take it.'

'I tell you what, why don't I get into the cab with you and make sure you get there—okay?'

'No—no, please, I'm very grateful for everything you've done.' Fear was receding as the colors cleared away from her eyes. His face emerged in front of her, pushed out by the lucidity of reason. 'I'm meeting a girlfriend, and if she saw me with a man, she would tell my boyfriend about it. And I don't want to lose him.'

'No, of course not,' he was moving out of her space. 'Some friend though, if she would do the dirty on you like that?'

He was, she could now see, about five foot eight or nine, square shoulders, and wearing a hat which looked a little like a deerstalker. His hair was dark brown underneath his hat, and it was very thick, bushy even though it was flecked with gray. She judged he must be in his early forties and strong. He walked with purpose to the other side of the cab and gave the address she had given him.

As the cab moved off, he was watching her. His eyes, which had first appeared to be friendly, were now thoughtful, as if he was making notes on her. And while he watched her as the car sped away, she couldn't take her eyes off him. Was he the killer?

5

It was a coincidence, or was it a coincidence? Be honest with yourself, Cecelia. You're not stupid. Think this one through. Was it just by chance that Angelina told you about the fertility clinic and what it was up to, and then three days later, she's dead? I don't think so. I think these sorts of things happen and people don't choose to believe it because the whole thing seems too far-fetched.

People don't want to believe because it ruins their rose-tinted world and places them in danger if they get involved. It's hard work to pursue the path of righteousness. But when the world is not okay, injustice forms a scab.

'I've changed my mind about the hotel.' Cecelia leaned forward to the cab driver as they neared the white palace. 'I've texted my friend and told her I want to cancel. Can you take me home instead?'

The thoughts which sprang so quickly and unhealthily followed on an unsettled keel, flooding her sense of self with its wants.

There goes my story. Forget it. Great. And being rich, what a joke. Angelina would have to be killed now. Just my luck; it always happens to me. This lovely woman who had taken the risk by trusting Cecelia was now dead and gone. Selfish, that's what she was. Why hadn't she taken care of herself—and for goodness' sake, what was she doing going to a bus stop when she was the type of person who either had a flashy car or went everywhere by taxi? Why? There were so many whys.

Now, the only thing Cecelia could think of was, had she lost her chance in this vain seeking and image-demanding world? This should have been her lucky break that she had been looking for. Angelina had given her the story of the forgotten child, although not quite a child, until he was born. Dismembered and horribly mutilated body, whose entire existence for a few seconds was to live as a person outside of the womb. If Cecelia couldn't write about it, then it wasn't real.

Paying for the cab, another expense, which made her angry that she had taken this extravagant way home. The cab driver didn't receive a tip.

'Hi Cecelia,' it was one of the other tenants, Mrs. Rudge, just leaving the building. 'You're a dark horse, aren't you? Not telling anyone you had a boyfriend.'

She was coming back to reality with a crash. Not saying anything, Cecelia tried not to mind the comments. Climbing the steps up to her apartment, she hated this community of shared rentals where everyone was interested in you and your life. Whatever you did with yourself behind the door, they considered it was their right to know, just because you lived in the same damn building as them. Cecelia didn't speak to any of her neighbors unless she had to. The occasional hi or nice day was the passing of shadows, but she even resented these mandatory exchanges. Yet, these busybodies still managed to find out enough about her without her participation.

It was on her lips to say she didn't have a boyfriend when Cecelia stopped, and instead of denouncing this gossip, thought it was important enough to take an interest.

'What did he look like?'

'Quite nice,' Mrs. Rudge recalled the image of the stranger, the one who appeared out of nowhere and was found stalking in Cecelia's life. 'I caught him outside your flat. I think I might have spooked him; I was wearing my house slippers. They're kinder to my feet. Anyway, I took him by surprise.'

'Did he give you his name?'

'No, he just said that he was your boyfriend and asked when you would be back?'

'Did he say my name?'

'Yes, yes, I think so. Yes, he did; I'm sure he did. He said, "do you know when Cecelia will be home?" or something like that.'

'Just Cecelia, nothing more? He didn't say my last name by any chance?'

'No,' now Mrs. Rudge was confused and stunned. 'Why would he call you by your last name when he's your boyfriend?'

'Oh, it's the type of joke we play on one another. We both like to pretend we're hard to get. He pretends he might go out with someone else next week, but I refuse to play his silly games.'

'Oh,' frowned Mrs. Rudge. 'If that's the sort of thing you two like to do.'

'Tell me, just for fun, what was he wearing?'

'A gray jacket and blue colored pants, or were they brown?'

'Oh, Tony never wears blue pants. It's probably one of his friends. He's probably in on the gag.'

'If you say so,' Mrs. Rudge was frowning. She was walking off.

'Thanks for telling me.' Cecelia placed the key into the lock, fumbling to get in.

Once inside, with the door to her back, Cecelia leaned up against it, feeling the heat of fear running hot through her body. She panted.

Yes, she huffed. This was just another one of those coincidences, and she got a boyfriend straight after Angelina's death, someone who she had never met. Now her breath was coming quick and heavy and difficult to catch. Damn it, was she going to have a panic attack? No, it was not going to happen. But the floor was moving away while the walls were running in towards her. Her world had been impinged with ungovernable laws forbidding her to live.

Deep breaths, breathing in and then out. She had to take control of herself through her mind. Think about walking through a field in summer with tall golden wheat, blistering heavy with seeds full of fertility and about to burst and give out. In the background, birds sang while humming, and the winged butterflies stop to land their gorgeous colors blushed. Keep breathing.

Gradually, she was now calming down.

Angelina's death happened because of righteous betrayal. They must have known about Angelina, and had been watching her. Which means they could know about her. This horrifying thought gained ground when Cecelia realized that by listening to Angelina's story, she also was now implicated. Just by listening—or was it by listening and then recording, that she was going to suffer the same fate?

Yet, who would believe this story? There was a tolerance

level where such information like this would shock people into denial. Would she believe a story where there was no evidence but only hearsay if someone fed her with this information? It depended on who the source was. Yet, by observing the way Angelina behaved, this was real.

But she could write a story—a fictional story for the reader to judge for themselves. Often, genuine stories are woven into fantasy. It's one way of passing across information. Facts thrown in one's face can also be thrown away. It's not real; it couldn't be accurate, it couldn't be true, this person must have an axe to grind, fake news. Thoughts though which could enter the big wide world.

It's the norm to have an abortion when the future child is unwanted—already there are too many people populating the world for the planet to sustain them, everyone with open mouths waiting to be fed. One day, this beautiful small world will give out. We are already looking for other planets to populate. Religious values are not about being the best person you can be, but about the God-given right to continue procreating.

And then, for good timing, the phone rang. The voice of reality had demanded the right to enter.

'Hello,' after ten seconds, Cecelia, against her will, picked up the receiver.

'Is that you, Joan?' it was a man's voice, a young man's voice.

'No.'

'You aren't Joan?'

'No, you have the wrong number.'

'Are you certain about that?'

'Yes.'

'But I rang double seven, three, two, one, eight, eight.'

It was her number.

'You have the wrong number,' she repeated slowly, emphasizing each word deliberately.

'I do? Who are you?'

'I'm—' Cecelia stopped herself just in time. This was not a wrong number caller. This was someone who knew who she was and where she lived and now knew she was at home. 'I'm sorry I can't help you. I hope you find the person you are looking for. And now I've got to go; my husband has just arrived home.' She hung up.

Is it wise to panic, believing that someone is after you intending to dispose of you? If they are, then it doesn't matter what anyone else thinks about how you look or behave while you are making your escape. If you are proven wrong and what is happening to you is all in your head, then what harm has been done? You are still alive. But if you are proven right, and people have laughed at you for acting the fool they always thought you were, it still doesn't matter. To act and stay alive was Cecelia's thought as she frantically packed her cases.

Get out of here. Packing everything she could into her case, the one from on top of her cupboard, her life was in peril. Jumpers, underwear, whatever she could fit in. It didn't matter if she had to leave the clothes she couldn't take. What mattered was that she got out of here.

Never did she find her life to be more precious than it was now. Ever since she could remember, she had mocked her life and existence and the pointless reason for her living. What did it matter to others if she was alive or not? It didn't matter to them, but it certainly mattered to her now. And what a shock it was to find this out. She almost laughed at this while she packed. Fancy that, she wanted to carry on living.

Carry on living, yes, but where was she to go? Suddenly,

this was such a stupid question. Cecelia always planned her life, writing every step down she would take. Nothing could be left to chance; this was not her style. If she were to start planning this next step on how to get away, she would still be here when the murderer arrived. That's if there was someone out there wanting to kill her. If this was a coincidence, chances are—

Running away with a suitcase in each hand and a bag over her shoulder, Cecelia flew out of the apartment as if she was on fire. Running, running along the sidewalk, her hair flying behind her, her throat husky with laughter. It was like she was running away from herself and everything that stood as her life. People would think her mad if they did not know she was terrified.

But no one was going to catch her as long as she kept on running.

People in the late afternoon, laden with shopping and chatting to each other, became barriers in Cecelia's path. They had become a great human obstacle course as Cecelia frantically weaved between them. Freedom. She was running to freedom and for the future ahead of her.

But her limbs were heavy, and she couldn't run forever. Her legs were slowing down, bargaining with her to stop at the next block. Where was her energy? What had happened to her power? While the organs keeping her alive, heart and lung were pounding for her to stop. Her arms had become heavy, as if they had been tricked and twisted and were ready to fall off. What happened to the fear which had always kept her alive?

Again, she called attention to herself by stopping and dropping her baggage. Legs were trying to avoid walking into her. Annoyance and frustration, sighing that she had left her presence in front of their lives.

'Are you okay, dear?' another woman had thought her kindness was to stop and help. 'Are you pregnant?'

Such a strange thing to ask.

'No, I'm not,' snapped Cecelia, insulted that anyone should suppose that.

'Shall I help you carry one of your cases to where you're going? Where are you going?'

It was none of her business, and her compassion had become an attack. Grabbing her cases, Cecelia stood up and turned her back on the face of decency. Even kindness had become a threat. With a temper brought on by outrage, she struggled off.

This had become a world that was out to get her.

And then she stopped, her heart causing her to panic. Money. Did she remember to bring her purse? Did she take it out from under her pillow where she slept with it? It was everything she had. Searching her memory for those conscious efforts of retrieving it from under her pillow produced nothing.

Oh, peace now. Trust. Trust yourself that you have taken it. Don't go on that root again into questioning the self with unrelenting doubt. Believe you have collected it. Believe and go ahead with your life.

Her purse, she remembered now, was in her pocket. She saw her hand retrieving it to put it into her case, but then she hesitated; from the case, she put it into her pocket to keep it close by her side, where it would be safer. A quick nod of irony, and then she sniffed and smiled. She was safe, and she was back on the road of escape.

Stopped next to a newspaper stand, she looked to see if there was anything about Angelina? Putting her hand in her pocket, the spare coins which she always kept there came in handy. One dollar fifty, the price of the cheapest newspaper.

She threw her money into the bowl and picked up a copy. A demonstration was being held on Parliament Hill from a group calling themselves *The Baby Evangelists*. Make abortion illegal; the rights of the child come first.

Flicking through the paper, she stood on the sidewalk reading it. People were building up behind her.

'What the hell's going on with you, lady?' A man of five feet ten nearly walked into Cecelia. Bulging eyes almost stalking out of his head.

'Sorry,' she muttered, moving over to the side. She desperately needed to read what was reported.

Why did people become so impassioned about something which wasn't even born yet? It was not a baby, not yet —or was it? Or did it represent hope or the fear that they, as a fetus, might too, have been extinguished if someone had not stuck up for their right? But then, what about the sperm? How many sperm die on the way to fertilize the egg? All those hundreds of thousands of potential voices canceled. And a woman when she goes through her menstrual cycle. Do we have any rights in the deaths of all of those billions of other voices?

But we are here, in the now. Shouldn't we accept the luck from chaos? Shouldn't we just be grateful? Cecelia hastily turned over the pages. Angelina's death was not reported until page eight.

Miss Angelina Joseph, a woman of twenty-three they couldn't get her age right, *fell in front of a bus on Mercy Street. Several people saw her fall; she died instantly. One onlooker was convinced she was pushed while someone said she was seen to be crying. Miss Joseph had not been happy about people demonstrating against abortion. The police are now looking into her death.*

So that was the end of Angelina's life. Nicely tidied up,

parceled away, and would now be forgotten. Is it only Cecelia who thinks she was murdered? No, there was someone else.

Folding her newspaper, she stopped a passerby.

'Excuse me, do you know where there is a good hotel around her, one that is not too expensive but clean?' Cecelia was directed to the local library, the station of information.

Thank goodness for the Internet, the finder of information when you needed something. There was a bed-and-breakfast place called the Regent. Forty dollars a night with breakfast included and, of course, Wi-Fi and the obligatory shower.

With a smile, the librarian assistant passed Cecelia a printout of the directions without thought or curiosity.

STRANGE TO BE SOMEWHERE ELSE, to find you have another bed and that there were people about who don't know you. People who don't care what you do or where you come from just as long as you pay. But the one most important fact that stood up amongst all others was she was safe. No one knew where she was and couldn't get at her. But what was she going to do now? Would she have to stay in hiding forever? No, there was no way she could do that. They would find her as soon as she ran out of money. But, at least for now, she was safe.

At the reception, Cecelia requested an evening meal. At ten dollars, it was relatively cheap. And now that she had showered and unpacked what was necessary, she went downstairs for her evening meal.

The atmosphere was surprisingly nice here as she scanned the dining room. Most of the people who bed-and-breakfasted here through the week had gone home for the weekend. And now the weekend crowd had settled in for their mini vacation, planning what they were going to do, go to the theater, or perhaps see the sites. There was money rolling around to have that good time.

Good manners get you noticed, which was why Cecelia didn't speak but kept to herself and observed everyone else's rules. There were six small tables dressed with white tablecloths adjoined with four seats around them. The guests took their places at each table as if they had known each other for years. With glasses in their hands, they carried on with their small talk. The dining room was bathed in humming and cooing noises, which says everyone was getting on.

And now that they were all seated, it was time for Cecelia to take her place amongst them, but where to sit? There was still one table empty, and this was the one she was heading for. This weekend the bed-and-breakfast hosted twenty-one guests, including herself.

What a relief to have a table to herself now as she neatly sat down to wonder what the meal would be. Whatever it was, she was going to eat it. Money was too precious to be thrown away. Whatever the food was, Cecelia hoped it wouldn't be pasta. She hated it. But chances are it would be, considering it was an inexpensive ingredient that tidied away the hunger.

But no, it was a roast chicken dinner. It had been a while since she had this. A waiter came from behind to place two plates down on the table next to her. It looked and smelled delicious as a generous helping of chicken, roast and boiled potatoes, carrots, peas, and there was a gravy boat left on the table to help oneself and all for ten dollars. This was a feast.

Cecelia overheard that there was going to be apple pie

and homemade ice cream for the pudding. A treat which not only poured balm on the pocket, but promised to be delicious.

'Is anyone sitting here?' a man overshadowed her. 'I've just booked in here, and I thought I would be too late for dinner. Do you mind?'

How could she mind? Looking beside her to see where he could sit or if she had a good reason to say that he couldn't be her neighbor, she turned her attention to the friendly faced man looking down at her.

'Just tell me you're staying here incognito, and I'll take the hint.'

Stretching around, she could see there were a couple of empty places where only two people now sat. If she said no, it would be rude.

'No, these seats aren't taken.'

'Thanks, you know some people at these places can be very touchy,' he was making himself comfortable before returning a thoughtful gaze to her. And then his eyes went to her left hand. He smiled again because she wasn't wearing a wedding band. Available, now that was interesting. At least this was a good place to start.

Usually, she wore a ring even though she wasn't married and never had been. Wearing a wedding ring was a sign for men to keep off; you won't find any interest here, so don't bother.

'I'm new to this part of the world.' The talking had started as he waited, shifting the knife and fork around.

She nodded, but kept her lips closed.

'For letting me sit at your table, I would like to buy you a drink—you drink, don't you? I mean, everyone drinks even if they say they don't.'

When he smiled again, there was the chemistry of

instant attraction. He was charming, and he also came across as being gentle and posing no threats. What harm was there in liking him? In fact, he was reasonably good-looking for someone who looked like he was in his early forties. A wave of dark hair gave him that Latin appearance and his beautiful blue eyes shined merrily. His nose, though, could be slightly too large, but his lips were generous. Yet, this only credited him with character. Something was going on in this head where a beautiful face would leave vacant. Cecelia was impressed with him; he was well dressed. He knew how to enjoy the person he was—dressed in a dark-gray suit with a dark-gray matching tie and a light blue shirt. He looked suave, immaculate—and he wore silver-colored cufflinks, which suggested he was not your average guy.

Her assessment was completed in a couple of seconds. Pleasing, yes, very pleasing. She could not have done better even if she tried. Meanwhile, he had been studying her. She stroked her hair back, tugging it a little to enter the second phase of fate's spontaneous connection. Did he take every chance as an opportunity?

'Will you have a drink with me? I believe they have some decent Californian wine, a Chardonnay. Or if you don't drink—'

'I'll have a Chardonnay. That would be nice, thank you.'

When Cecelia made up her mind, it was instantaneous. Time for action. She would now leap at it, right or wrong. To make a quick decision is always something good. It gives a reason to go forward. Usually, her world had been fractured with uncertainty, but not today, not any longer. Take that opportunity when it comes along. The job of making such decisions puts a whole new perspective on life. She smiled; she was free to go on.

He smiled when she suddenly accepted his offer. The conditions of the relationship had changed. He, too, could now relax. Again, he gave her another smile, which intimated that he also liked her.

Calling for a bottle of wine, they now viewed each other from another perspective.

'I heard it was roast chicken with all the trimmings,' he said, putting his elbows on the table placing his chin on to his interlaced fingers. 'Is that true?'

'Yes, can't you smell it?'

'No, actually I can't smell, well at least, I can't smell things that well.'

'No,' she was openly surprised. A simple piece of news, because they were sitting together at the same table, became more interesting.

'Yes, I damaged my nose when I was a kid and nearly blew off my eyebrows. I was spoiled,' he laughed. 'I was and am that incorrigible kid, unfortunately, my parents' only child, although I had a brother who died from an accident. My parents gave me everything I wanted, and I wanted a chemistry set. I think I must have been a troublesome child to live with,' and then he laughed at the memory again, now instilled on his retina.

Yes, he was charming. She mentally ran her spoon around the pudding, put a hole in the ice cream, and cut through the pastry, now feeling very feminine, very gauche that she was in the presence of a sophisticated man.

She could see his parents and their dismay and how they shook their heads. It was their fault alone that they gave in to his demands. She looked at him and smiled while he was looking at her pudding.

He had a dead brother.

'And what about you—my parents thought I was perfect;

I could do no wrong. I suppose you could say I had a charmed life. There I go again, always talking about myself. Do you have any brothers or sisters?'

'Not really. Well, I have a sister, but she's a lot older than me.'

His eyebrows raised; he was waiting for her to carry on because it was his turn to be interested.

She shrugged; it didn't matter whatever you said to a stranger. Which was why these conversations were so liberating. It gave you the freedom to be who you wanted to be, providing you didn't meet up with them again.

'The age gap. She's seventeen years older than me. I'm from my father's second marriage, and now he is on to marriage number four.'

'Wow, I mean, I mustn't be rude, so how many of you are there?'

'Six going on seven. That was the last time I heard. One each from the first and second marriage, two from marriage number three, and two and a half from number four.'

'I take it you don't get on with your parents?'

'My mother's dead. She died when I was three. By the time I was four, my father had been married again for six months.'

'Wow,' and then he frowned and generously considered Cecelia's face. 'That sounds like a tragedy to me.'

'Not really. I was looked after for a while by my mother's parents. It was okay, but they were old. They both died by the time I was ten, and then, unfortunately, it was the children's home.'

'And your father didn't want you?'

'Of course not. He had a new young wife.' She looked down, still bitter about these hoaxed memories.

'Can I ask you one question—you can tell me to mind

my own business if you like, but is your father wealthy?' now it was his turn to shrug. 'I mean, your father must pay out a great deal on alimony.'

'Well, it depends on what you mean by wealthy. If he carries on paying the alimony, nobody asks where it comes from. But yes, he is wealthy, I suppose, not that this makes any difference to me. Whatever he leaves will go to his last two marriages, numbers three and four. Virginia and I are supposed to be grown up and able to look after ourselves.'

'I'm sorry. However, I had a good life with my parents, being the only star in their sky. I thought every child was treated the same.'

'I'm not grumbling, though. It's just—' and then she stared into space, looking for the next invention.

'So, you have come here for a break—you don't live near here, I take it. No, of course, you don't. Why have a home locally and go and sleep elsewhere? It wouldn't make any sense, would it?'

Half an hour walking distance away, her studio flat sat in the dark waiting. She smiled that obligatory smile that stood for agreement.

'How long are you staying for—oh hey—' he looked up? 'Here comes dinner—now I can smell it. When the wine comes, let's toast to ourselves.'

The dinner and the wine arrived together. The bottle was uncorked, which meant it would be on the bill, whether they liked it or not.

Cecelia watched as the wine tumbled from the bottle into their glasses. She could do with a drink. This was turning out to be a nice evening, and a pleasant end to the day that started out as anything but.

'Cheers,' he held his glass out to her. 'I don't even know your name to propose a toast to you.'

She smiled, but he was waiting for her to supply that name. It was tempting to give him her real name, but that was off limits for now.

'You tell me what your name is first.'

'Okay, why don't you tell me what you think it should be, what sort of person I look like?'

Was this a game? She wasn't sure, but it could be fun.

'Okay,' she said, eyeing him closely and noting his features. 'You look like a—Peter.'

'My God, how did you do that?'

'Is that your name?'

'Yes, how did you do that? Did you go and take a peek at the register? I can't believe it. Most people never guess my name. I've been told I look like a John, and even a Gareth. But you've seen right through me. You know, you've taken my breath away.'

'I don't know. Are you messing with me?' she shook her head. She was as skeptical as he was to have guessed it correctly.

'No. It's true. Peter is really my name. Okay. Now it's your turn. You must tell me what your name is. It's only fair, don't you agree?'

'Clara. My name is Clara.'

'Oh, I knew a Clara once, very attractive, rather like you.'

He knew how to make her smile; she was warming to him.

'So, tell me, Clara, what are you doing here—work or play?'

It was one of these questions that wouldn't receive a truthful answer.

'What are you doing here?' she reflected his question.

He smiled. He understood the game. 'Well, I would like to say play, but it's quite the opposite. Anyhow, it doesn't mean I can't enjoy myself while I work. And now, what about you?'

'Me,' she smiled gently. 'It's neither work nor play. It's a duty. One of my uncles is dying, and I am here for the family.'

'Oh dear, I'm sorry. Now I understand why you want to be quiet. Which uncle is it?'

A spontaneous question, which, again, one she wasn't ready for with an answer to it.

'On my mother's side.'

'And you knew him well?' he was cutting into the chicken with his ears cocked while he listened.

She watched as he popped a piece of chicken into his mouth and began chewing, seeing the movements of mastication fascinated her round and around, mixing up with the saliva. Yet, he was waiting for an answer.

'Not really, well yes, I did when I was very young, but I don't remember him very well except that he was kind to me.'

'Oh, that's interesting. Why didn't he take you in when you lost your mother?'

She had to think fast.

'Well, I suppose he would have done if he was married.'

'So, did he marry later?'

He was beating her with questions, making her struggle to find false answers.

'You know, life isn't as simple as that. When I was sixteen, my uncle got married, and by then, I was too old to be taken in by him.'

'What is his name?'

A piece of roast potato went into his mouth. He was still waiting for her to answer. What was this? A trial? She was becoming angry.

'Does it matter to you what his name is? He's dying, after all. So it doesn't matter, does it?'

'You're right.' He piled some peas onto his fork. 'I can be bloody nosy sometimes. I'm told this is a fault. But really, I don't mean any harm. I'm on my own most of the time. It's my job. You become like your job, don't you? What job do you do?'

'My job has given me three weeks off as a vacation.'

'Well, that was decent of them, I suppose. Are you a schoolteacher?'

'No, what makes you think that?'

'It's the way you look, quiet, keeping yourself to yourself. You have the look of a teacher, intelligent. Yeah, I would bet my life that you are a teacher. Are you?'

'No,' her answer was tight and smart. 'I work for the government.'

'Wow, I'm impressed—are you in enforcement, a police officer? I bet you're someone important.'

'Not really, I just work in an office dealing with people's cases, but I've had to sign a non-disclosure agreement.'

'Oh, really?' his fork was into another piece of chicken. 'So, does that mean you are a tax worker?'

How did it mean that? She was staring at a roast potato that had been lined up for his mouth.

'You should start eating; I'm way ahead of you.'

He was right; she hadn't touched her dinner at all. But when she looked at her piece of chicken laid there so smoothly shaped, the shadows of memory interposed and replaced one for another. The twisted, torn off leg from the baby had been placed on her plate.

'What is it? Are you okay?' he heard her retch.

She had turned white. 'Sorry.'

'No, you don't need to say sorry to me. Are you ill?'

'A bit of a squeamish stomach. It's been an awful day. And this dinner—'

'I can understand, but you must have something to eat. What about trying the apple pie? Pass me your plate. Eat what you can; you can have my apple pie as well if you like?'

He took her plate and poured her dinner on top of his own. There fell the leg onto his plate, cleared of blood, cooked, and ready for eating.

We eat each other in one form or another. Our falling bodies are food for the future.

He had called for Cecelia's pie, and while he continued to eat, she watched, unable to stop her eyes from wanting to see what he did with the chicken leg.

That baby is dead and must be forgotten. He did not know life. The death of a third child.

He ate as if he had never eaten before; his appetite was not suppressed for anything. She wished she could be more like him and live her own life without being influenced by others on what they thought or felt.

A sip of wine might help her relax and provoke her stomach to eat.

6

The morning came without a plan for what she should do. The image of Angelina was still in her eyes when she awoke. Her angel-like features watched Cecelia with the expressive eyes of wonder to what she was about to do.

'I don't know,' Cecelia said, climbing out of her bed and going to the bathroom.

There was a whole day ahead of her, which was already making tracks in her diffidence. And then she thought of Peter and what he might be doing.

As she dressed, she judged his ghost with curiosity. He was the type of person who didn't care about anything. He just got on with his life. A thoughtful pilgrim with many opinions about others. He was nice and easy to like, and she was interested in him. The wandering minstrel of life and happy to be who he was, nothing got in his way or pulled him back. How lucky he was to have this disposition.

It would have been nice to spend more time in his company listening to him talking about himself. He had a lot to say about himself because he was vain. There wasn't any doubt about that. Nothing appeared to affect him. He just got on with his life, maybe because he didn't care.

While the shower water tumbled down, bouncing off her skin, Cecelia drew up his image to play with. Was he, she paused to collect the soap which had slipped down to her wet feet, interested in her? Did he find her attractive? A sigh. Probably not. Was she interested in him? It looked like it. She found herself curious about him.

Like a honeybee, in her thoughts, she couldn't leave him alone. He was fascinating, irresistible. Expensive and sophisticated. Just take a look at his cufflinks. He was a man who knew how to dress. But where exactly had he come from? He was not the typical guy to inhabit a joint like a bed-and-breakfast. She filled her mind with him because it was more preferable than thinking about Angelina and the clinic.

When he hadn't told her what he did in life, she was peeved and decided to pursue him for an answer. Tit for tat, it was only fair; she told him last night.

'You could say I'm a bit like you,' he smiled before plunging another roast potato into his mouth. When he grinned, he had a swollen bump in his cheek like an abscess. This endeared him to her by making him more human.

'I didn't realize how hungry I was,' and then he smiled now that his mouth had relaxed. 'I'm a contractor. I'm called in when accounts and things don't add up. It's me who has to find the missing link and sort out the mess when things go wrong.'

'So, you're not a salesman?'

He laughed; he was astonished. 'No, although I was once into life insurance, I insured people's lives against their properties,' he had noted the disparaging expression on her face. 'Well, someone's got to do it. I was paid well for it—in fact, very well—and I enjoyed it. But like you know, when you are good at something, your bosses want to promote you. And so, here I am going from state to state, county by county and even international. I don't mind doing this job. I'm very good at it as well, and I get paid even more.'

'So, what about your wife? Doesn't she mind you being away all the time?' she had dared to ask him this. The memory made her blush.

'What wife? I don't have a wife. A man doesn't have a wife in this business. It wouldn't be fair to her.'

'But perhaps it would be fair if she traveled with you.'

His eyes said it all. He looked her up and then stared her straight in the eye. Was she proposing?

Yes, in many respects, it appeared she was. The raw embarrassment of desire made her blush as she lowered her eyes.

Oh, gosh, did she like him so much? Yes, she did. Was she going to embarrass herself? Hadn't she sworn she wouldn't get involved with men again, especially after that time ten years ago? Don't go into that anymore. It would pull her apart if she remembered and analyzed it. Everyone makes fools of themselves. It's in the act of forgiving oneself that tests the will to go on. This is the secret she should keep to herself, forever.

But what was she going to do today? You are nobody if you don't do something with this special gift called life, particularly when you're given knowledge. Enlightenment is a gift, but this bounty always comes with a price tag.

Being anonymous was perfect; it meant that she could do whatever she liked. Maybe do something dangerous and then disappear. Life is risky. Whatever one does, there will be a penalty for it. Fortunately, she had always kept a low profile, which was helpful. She would go to the clinic and begin some real undercover journalism. That was her goal now, to be a top journalist.

Nearly every month, a letter from her bank came offering her more money to borrow. I do not borrow money, Cecelia said every time she opened these letters, but now, with no real finances to her name, it seemed like a good time to begin. She couldn't do anything without money, and this was one of those accepted truisms.

To be the part, one must look it. She would buy herself some smart new clothes just like Angelina had, and they didn't have to be too expensive. This was exciting. Change the person she was into someone she could live with. Get rid of that old and embarrassing self, and for now, she could be whoever she wanted. The idea was very liberating.

Ten years ago, she hadn't known what to do with her life when the police department wouldn't take her. Hang on. What had made Peter believe she worked for the police? Was it a lucky guess? Did she look like a cop? Another thought to be shrugged off. But it was a shrewd observation.

Anyhow, being rejected and after a month of severe depression, her thoughts turned to nursing. She would help those people who needed caring for. She had empathy. But such a big step made her wonder if this was the right course to take in life. It was a profession she often thought about taking, believing it to be an honorable one. Yet, in the long haul, she couldn't see herself as being devoted to the sick. But a compromise like becoming a nursing auxiliary would give her a look into the world. It surprised Cecelia to find out that even with this; she needed training.

Ten weeks later, she passed with a certificate to become a Certified Nursing Assistant.

The geriatrics ward at the local hospital always needed

care assistants. At twenty-four, she wasn't too young or too old. It was the best age to start a caring career.

But nursing is not as pretty or romantic as it seems. The qualified nurses thought themselves too superior to do what the care assistants did. In reality, if they could get out of doing the dirty work, they would. But it wasn't the care assistants who got the thank you presents. No, these always went to the nurses. It was a revelation about how two people doing the same job could be treated. Who would have thought there would be snobbery in caring?

Yet, there was another eye-opener. Cecelia saw how some older people were often treated when they had no family or friends. It wasn't right, and it wasn't fair, but it was life. If the elderly patient had someone that was concerned about them, the chances were more significant for them to survive longer. It was Darwin's survival of the fittest. The fact was, there were too many unnecessary people in life. This was another one of those hard found truths.

Two years later, and feeling that she was getting nowhere, Cecelia decided that she had had enough. The pay like the treatment was poor, and when one older man who didn't have anyone, no family, no friends, it was reasoned that his time had come. It was a natural act of compassion; the hospital also needed the bed.

Yes, he was going to die soon, so why keep him hanging on to life? What would be the benefit? This is how the reasoning works. One must have a reason to live, and it appeared to the people going in and out of his life that there wasn't an adequate one. And probably he would agree with them about the quickening of his termination if he had been asked.

Morphine was pumped into his body two milligrams every hour. The machine was hidden under his covers. It was only the slow suck of the quiet machine which told of a life passing. This milk of human kindness took him stealthily further and further from life.

But what did it matter if he should die now or die a month later? Yes, some people could be helped now; she understood or tried to understand. But in her perverse way of reasoning, it still felt all wrong.

What is the price of life or even justice? Who deserves to live, and who is to die? Did Angelina warrant to die? She, who couldn't follow their system, whose own views and horrors at taking the dismembered limbs which had once been healthy, had now been terminated herself. Perhaps if Angelina had gone along with the system, she would still be here now.

The rules are set by the unspeakably rich and now by two people in particular, who are treated as if they were royalty. Whatever they wanted, they would always get. Some people get everything because they demand to be treated as special.

Image. It was down to image and vanity. Celebrated and wealthy people's rights to life were more important than the unwanted child or a single woman. Yet, Angelina was gone, and her history would be erased. If Cecelia didn't speak up for Angelina and bust these people, then it could happen to her.

Should she speak up for Angelina, take her place in the line of fire and carry out what she was going to carry out? It was a thought. In fact, it was a noble thought. And why not carry it out? She wasn't doing anything particular in her life, and this was an opportunity to sparkle.

Unexpectedly, the nursing qualification hadn't gone to waste as Cecelia felt it had. She had the training and experience which she could use. Cecelia applied for a job and sent off the email, giving the relevant information. If it didn't work this way, she would have to find another avenue to gain entrance. Whatever this clinic wanted, she was now determined to get herself in.

But why was she always so constantly tired now?

Tomorrow would be Monday, and some people were now leaving the bed-and-breakfast with their small cases packed, making their way down the stairs. A nod and a smile as they passed, and this was going to be the last time they would see her. A feeling of wistfulness now these holiday people were going back to their everyday lives. The magic time had passed to be secreted in memories. Yet, watching them going out through the doors, a kind of envy enveloped Cecelia; they had lives to return to.

Often Cecelia felt she was filling in time with abstract nonsense while waiting for her own life to begin. She turned away and walked to the dining room. And there he was, sitting at the same table, waiting for her to come in.

He smiled and stood when he saw her, which was very flattering and made her heart flutter. His bright eyes almost winked at her. Who was this Peter, that was so very nice? Quite the gentleman, and in her dreams, a potential suitor.

'How did your day go?' he asked once she had settled herself down.

She smiled and was just about to say it hadn't gone well when she remembered in time the story she had given.

'Sad.'

'Yes, I thought so. It can't be much fun watching and waiting for a person to die. That's why I took the liberty of ordering us a bottle of wine.'

'How nice,' she smiled. Rearranging the cutlery on the table, she moved them about like traffic as she reshuffled her thoughts.

'I didn't think when I ordered the wine that you might not be having dinner tonight. But then I thought, well; if she doesn't come in, then I might as well drink the entire bottle myself.' His eyes were naturally twinkly, like a waterfall of cut diamonds collecting all the light from the sun as they fell.

Shyly, she watched him. It seemed impossible for him not to have a wife. Maybe he was like a sailor, having a girl in every port?

'I'm glad you're here.'

His smile was beautiful. It was the most sincere and sweetest smile she had ever come across.

'I've been thinking about you all day long.'

She touched her cheek as the embarrassment lit up her face and caused her to feel silly; It was like she had a crush on him and had just found out that he liked her.

'Now, this is what I like about you. You haven't lost that engaging look of feminine modesty. Oh, how I hate it when women rebuff you and feel insulted when you open the door for them, or even when you stand to give them your seat. Why are they like that?'

He was frowning, but she was convinced that he saw other women and said beautiful things like that to them.

'Of course, I know that when they are on their own, they can easily do this for themselves. But they're forgetting the graces of being a female, which is theirs alone. It is our vanity to be courteous to a beautiful woman—of whatever age and to treat her special like a lady—and everything else. It makes me feel better when I open a door or offer my seat to a lady. I become their knight in silver armor. What they rob from themselves, they have also robbed from me.'

And then he smiled.

'I do go on, don't I? You should tell me to shut up sometimes.' He picked up his glass and twiddled it around. 'So, you were sad today?'

'A little. Sitting with a dying person is always sad.' She induced this imaginary uncle from the corners of a story she had once read.

'Yes, it must be,' he put the glass down.

'And how was your day?' she smiled lightly. What a nice and good man he was, always carrying the virtues of a gentleman.

'It was one of those days,' he pulled a face, 'if you know what I mean.'

Which made her giggle; she put a hand to her face like a shy schoolgirl who had a crush on a senior.

'The only thing I ask in any job is that they supply me with the correct information. It's not too much to ask for, is it?'

Nodding quickly, she was going to agree to everything he said.

'No, I thought not. The problem is,' he moved closer across the table, drawing her into this joint conspiracy. 'Something has gone very wrong in the company. They suspect a woman of betraying them, and now she's gone into hiding.'

'Really?'

'Yes, really. I'm not angry with this woman—why be angry with anyone when together you can sort out the problem?'

'Should you be telling me this?'

'Perhaps not, but who on earth can I talk to if I can't make my confessions to you? Everyone needs someone to talk to, don't you agree? Even priests must have someone they can make their confessions to; otherwise, it would drive them mad.'

And there was Angelina, half of her phantom body standing between him and her. Angelina had also needed someone to talk to. Someone to keep all horrors at bay. Cecelia was their confessional.

'I know you won't talk to anyone, and even if you did, it wouldn't make any difference. I'm my own boss and always have been.'

He stopped and frowned, looking somewhere above her.

'The problem with this woman is, she has something I need, a code. Okay, I take it she's afraid of what's she's done, and rightfully she should be afraid. She knew what she was doing. But trying to scare her off with what they would do to her, threatening to put her in jail, doesn't help anyone.'

She waited for him to carry on, but for now, he stopped in thought. He looked so handsome in his profound moments.

'Anyhow, all I need is for her to come out of the woodwork so I can ask her a few questions. Do you have any idea how I could get a frightened woman to step forward?'

'No, well, I don't know. Perhaps you could put an advert in the newspaper, something cryptic to say she hasn't done anything wrong, and everything is going to be okay. You know, reassure her. I'm sure she would like this business cleared up as much as you.'

He laughed. 'What a delight you are. You know, you are unique. I have never come across anyone as charming as you.'

She smiled, then blushed. It was like her heart had taken off. This was the biggest compliment she had ever received in her life. She was sparkling with happiness. Caught in a bubble of pleasure.

'This uncle of yours. Does he have children?'

'No, unfortunately, he doesn't.'

'Hang on. I thought you said he did.'

'Did I? Oh yes, you're right, I did. Well, yes, their child died. It was tragic.'

'Your family seems to have a rather catastrophic existence. When you don't want them, they're bumped off,' and then he smiled.

But she couldn't return the smile. In a strange way, he was right. She had just killed off one of her fantasy family.

'You're not laughing.' Uncertain now of her, he worried if he had offended her. 'And I am ungracious at choosing your tragedy for my sport.'

'No. It's not your fault. But it sounds like my family has been unlucky—I suppose someone has to be unlucky in life —even if it's an entire family.'

'But you're not. I can't see you as ever being unlucky.'

'Oh, I don't know—' and then Cecelia remembered the type of person she was trying to be. 'I expect that is why it's been difficult for me.'

Amused, he watched her speak. His eyes alighted on her hands, which had suddenly become very expressive but not too over-energetic. Beautiful hands. People's hands say so much about them, whether they were powerful and grabbed hold of life or whether within those fingers lay talent, music, art, or healing. He smiled, enjoying the delicate details of declarations.

'You know, sitting with someone you know who is going to die soon,' she smiled to make light of the situation. 'Well, it makes me think about my own life and mortality. It makes me think of life and what I am doing with it. Am I living my life well and making the most of it? What do you think?'

'No, I never think about death.' He was adamant. 'It's something people think about others. Death happens when it happens. And it's pointless thinking about it. I trust when it comes, it will come swiftly. Just turn off the lights and you're gone—Oh, here comes the food. I was told tonight it was meatloaf. Now, let's pull the cork on this bottle. I need a drink.'

What were the chances of meeting someone like Peter? Few and far between, by Cecelia's reckoning. Someone you felt you could talk to about anything and forever. It was as if she had come home. They toasted each other and turned to the meatloaf with relish. While Cecelia ate, she was informed by Peter that this was one of his favorite meals. Meatloaf? She never put him down as a meatloaf person. This was followed by plum pie, and again, ice cream, Peter tucked into this with great pleasure.

'I'm going to have to change my lodgings,' he said, scooping up the last of the ice cream, 'or at least get this job sorted out quickly before I become too fat.'

'You're not too fat—' she thought he was joking.

'True, I may not be too fat right now, but with this delicious food. It won't be too long before I have a spare tire. The truth is, I can't afford to put on any weight; it would be detrimental to my work. But you're lucky. You can afford to eat more. I would say you are slightly underweight for your height.'

'Is this you trying to flatter me?'

'No, it's the truth,' he smiled. His show of vulnerability was charming, and it gave him a boyish look that made him more adorable and easier to like.

'That's very kind of you.' She wanted to know how a few extra pounds would impair his work, but it wasn't a good idea to delve too deep into his life. If we penetrate too deeply into the lives of others, then it gives them license to dig up your past. Her past to him was based on the web of lies she was passing over to him.

'I'll probably see you tomorrow,' he said, looking up at the dining-room clock. 'When I work, I try to get to bed early; I like to believe I am professional.'

She couldn't help looking at the clock to see for herself. It was not even ten pm, and he was choosing to go to bed. What was the point of staying up any longer when he wasn't there? She also might as well call it a day and go to bed as well.

7

There was no good in waiting for an answer from the clinic. They could take weeks to reply, and there wasn't all the time in the world to wait for her story or Angelina's justice. She would visit them tomorrow morning and push her luck.

Often, people are impressed when one takes the initiative. But this wasn't the usual kind of interview and one she was not looking forward to. But why think about this now when her mind kept returning to Peter? If anyone could persuade her to change her life and think about having a partner instead of being on her own, it was him.

If she could see her life through his eyes, she was charming and attractive, then this reality would turn into enchantment. The interims of sadness had not damaged him. Life was for living and not grieving, and don't put any power into what fate dealt you. And when it failed to do what you wanted it to, ignore it and move on. This was a better way of looking at life instead of feeling over all the sores and hurts which it afflicts. Yes, life with him could be so different in many, many ways—for one, he had money.

But now, with something else on her horizon, this wasn't the time to dwell on him. When she had done what she had set out to do and made public the sensational story that had entwined in the wants of this couple, then she could pick up her life again and live it for real.

Goodnight, world, let's see what tomorrow has in its bounty to give.

THE DAWN HAD NOT STEPPED up to its plinth when the early morning six o'clock alarm went off. Thrashing her arms around for those few alien seconds to stop the awful noise, Cecelia wondered where she was. And then the ticker tape of memories came falling, settling into place to inform her she was still here in the bed-and-breakfast hotel. It was a strange relief for here she could reinvent herself.

Arriving downstairs light-footed, watching the young dawn dragging itself out of bed, she felt herself to be still young. Today she was going to skip breakfast, she wasn't that hungry, and besides, she had overeaten last night.

How wonderful life is when there is someone else to share it with. Her thoughts went immediately to Peter and how he bemoaned the fate of his growing girth. She smiled at his boyish face. But then her footsteps crashed to a halt. Voices, this time in the morning when people were still dressed in their sleep. It was Peter's voice she heard.

Hi, how are you? And what are you doing up so early in the morning, were on her lips? For they had grown almost intimate. But at this time of the morning, perhaps not. The way he spoke to her was in a voice that he reserved for her alone. But this voice was different, more challenging, and curt. So, what was he saying?

And like a nosy child, she couldn't conceal her interest and the need to listen in.

'Yes, if you don't mind,' he spoke so differently, sharply, annoyed.

Cecelia could hear the huffs of someone in agreement.

'I would like to extend my stay for another week. Will that be possible? I don't mind paying extra if there is any inconvenience.'

'We are fully booked up, sir. We have our usual clients throughout the week. I would like to oblige you if I could. You understand, don't you?'

'Oh yes, of course, I understand. But there is nowhere else for me to go.'

'Yes, I know, sir. It's because of the music festival going on this week. All around here, everything is booked up.'

'What would your price be for me to stay in my room?'

'I'm sorry, sir, but as I said, we are fully booked up.'

He was leaving. Cecelia stood in the jacket of a corner's shadow, frowning and feeling that the world about her had dropped. He couldn't go, not now. He was the only person who gave her hope. The impulse to move from her secret place and offer to share her room was suddenly denied by the sound of his voice.

'I will give you a two thousand bucks for the rest of this week and the following week if you'll let me stay.'

Three seconds of silence or astonishment followed from both herself and the other person receiving his bargain.

'Sir, I would like to oblige, but I can't. I can't turn away a loyal and regular client on a whim. And it doesn't matter what you offer. Some things cannot be bought.'

'Very well. You didn't mind me offering, did you? I had to try?' and then he laughed.

It was the same laugh that gave her pleasure and made her heartbeat twice as fast.

'I would love to accommodate you, sir. But you see the position I'm in?'

'No, don't worry about it,' the stress which had sunk into his voice before had now vanished. 'I'll sort out something for myself. I think I may have a friend somewhere nearby here. But if you don't mind, can I leave my suitcases here and pick them up later when I have somewhere else to stay?'

'Certainly, sir, I am only too happy to oblige. I wish I could have helped you more.'

She guessed the proprietor saw the money in his hands, but it had been denied his grasp because of his sense of decency. He had been tempted. Was he brave, or was he foolish? She knew who she would choose.

'Thank you; then I'll come back this evening and settle my bill.'

'As you wish, sir.'

'Good.'

Peter wasn't even going to tell her he would be leaving. He was just going to walk out of her life. Yet, she must have guessed this might happen, but it didn't make sense. Last night she had seen him happy, but he didn't let on anything was wrong. Was he too proud to share his problem? Or perhaps he was one of those people who doesn't accept reality? It felt like her heart had been broken. And yet, there was really nothing between them except hope. The romance had all been in her mind.

Such was the weight of disappointment that she stood on this spot for nearly two minutes. Her mind was full of confusion, wondering how she could move on with her life without his participation. The door had opened and closed, telling her that now he had gone out of her life forever.

What was she going to do with herself now that the magic had gone? But perhaps not forever. Maybe he would stop and look in on her in the dining room. She would be there for him tonight, and she could give him her home address. But no, that was forbidden. But she could get him to provide her with his.

This is where lying leads.

But the light was still rising, and the day was still hers. It was time to get on with her life. This was all she could do. Stepping out of the shadows, she took three steps towards the door and then stopped immediately. He was still there at the small reception leaning over the desk. Like lightning, Cecelia took those three steps back to conceal herself once again in the safety of the shadows.

'Hello, is there anyone there?' it was Peter calling. His sharp ears had heard someone.

Please don't come any further. Please stay where you are. I didn't mean to spy on you. Cecilia held her breath.

'Is someone there?' he hadn't moved from where he was.

She held her breath and waited.

'For God's sake,' he muttered to himself. And this time, when the entrance door went, she knew he had gone.

Clasping her hand together tightly, she shook inside. This wasn't the time to indulge in her fancy of knowing, but to mind her own business. Not everything you see gives you the right to know. But she could look at what had interested Peter, and why not? There was nothing wrong with that.

Still fearful as she sneaked from the shadows, Cecelia walked to the reception desk. But first, she made sure by looking through the small window panel beside the door. Across the road and walking purposely and quickly was Peter; he had some urgent business to carry out. A businessman who knew what he wanted.

She admired his graceful pace. He traveled at speed, gliding across the road before disappearing around a corner. Farewell, my love, take care. His ghost was still haunting the sidewalk until her mind told her he was gone. Gone perhaps for now, but not forever.

What was he looking at on the other side of the desk? Everything he did interested her now by giving her a deeper insight into his life.

Reaching across the desk, Cecelia found a book. Strange. It was the bed-and-breakfast register of the people staying in this building. Now, why would he be interested in that? Was he trying to find out her real name? Well, he wouldn't find it in there; she had registered herself as Clara Tinder. She shrugged because she was none the wiser. Yet, it was something to ponder when she had the time and wanted to think about something else, rather than what she must do. He could be as interested in her as she was about him. Oh, how wonderful that would be. It was like she had stepped into her own fairy-tale.

Like her, Peter was not stopping for breakfast. Which was something else they had in common? He and she were not too dissimilar.

Cold outside, the long-lost summer had given away its warmth. Even the thought that summer would be back next year didn't give her any measure of hope. The world was passing on.

Angelina again walked into her mind, bringing along with her the poor broken baby. What, what is it you want me to do? In her mantle of death, Angelina watched her. I'm doing my best, you don't have to remind me. You were the stupid one; you should have watched where you were going.

Another dismal day heralded the skimming off of the promise Peter had awoken in her; did she have a future with him? Everything she had kept contained in her closed hands was now running through her fingers like sand running through the hourglass of life. Why couldn't she show him she was interested in him and tell him she liked him? Perhaps because she was not sure if she wanted a serious relationship.

Sometimes being a female was impossible these days. Feminism made a woman poorer and kept men away. Women were wearing too much war paint and trying to be someone they weren't, unreal dolls. She hated these women who took it on themselves to speak for every one of them when they were only speaking for themselves. These feminists that rob the world with their bad attitude have a lot to answer for.

Stopping off to get a newspaper to read on the train, Cecelia viewed the horizon of her life. Last week, if she could have traded in her life for anyone else's, it would have been Angelina's, but not anymore. Who would have thought this woman was destined to die young when she had so much going for her?

At nine o'clock, she arrived at the clinic as the ambulance of life was already going at full speed. People were coming and going, going up and coming down steps with their heads held down and guarded. They had secrets to conceal.

She would have bought herself some smart new clothes, but habit takes its toll on life. Instead, she bought herself some excellent garments which had once belonged to someone better off than her.

New, what is it to be new? New is about how you feel about yourself, even when someone else has discarded you. Look at those women who paint themselves beautiful after a divorce. While still single and alone, she had always felt ruffled and used, believing that she didn't have anything to offer. But to make a difference, you must have something to give, which others want.

Thrift shops have many available items of clothing, and weren't she in luck when she came across a recognized designer outfit. Instead of several hundred dollars, she paid fifty, and with even better fortune, it was a perfect fit.

Walking up to the clinic in a dove-gray suit, she wondered why anyone would give something like this away. It was ridiculous. Some people had money to burn, while other people didn't care what they had.

'Are you Mrs. Chartleland?' questioned the first of the three receptionists, who looked up as Cecelia came towards them.

'No, I came about the interview.'

'Interview?' she frowned at the other two receptionists, who also returned a frown.

'Yes, I sent my resume through last week.'

With quite a scuffle, the receptionists went to their computers and typed in information for new appointments.

'I can't find anything about an interview here. Are you certain that you have come to the right place?'

'Yes,' Cecelia stood her ground and waited.

She was not going to move from here. Someone would have to physically lift her and take her out. Looking at their nails, it would not be one of them.

'Just a minute, please,' asked this first receptionist, who looked like she was in command of the desk and the other two. 'I'll just go and ask someone. Would you like to take a seat, please?'

Nodding, Cecelia smiled. She was playing at being cooperative for once.

It must have been over five minutes before the attractive and well-made-up person arrived back. There was something like a scowl on her face, as if she had been ticked off.

'Would you like to come with me, please?'

Now, this was not like her. If someone had said no to her in the past, her tail would be between her legs, head down and she would hurry away. But not anymore, not until she got what she wanted. Everyone else did that, stood their ground. The next thing she wanted was Peter. Be more like Peter. Angry when it was right to be angry, good mannered when it's necessary, but never, ever allow the other person to walk over you. No, not anymore.

This was the building where Angelina had walked, low heeled and familiar, as if this had been her own home. Where she chatted, learned her job and followed the rules until that one step further she could not take anymore. No, her conscience stepped in and told her enough was enough. It was then she had to do something about it. She could not live with the person she had become. Poor Angelina, the waters had passed over, erasing the steps she had taken. Greed. Don't we all follow greed?

Following the elegant receptionists through the hygienically clean white corridors, Cecelia now wondered whether her bluff would be challenged. She followed the receptionist until the model of efficiency stopped. A heavy rosewood door with a gold plaque inscribed with the name of the person who occupied it—this was another barrier to the top. She knocked and waited.

'Come in,' the voice inside called, not a particularly powerful voice. It was as if he had been affected by his position in life.

He was tall. And even seated, the man was tall. When he stood, he appeared to be as high as the door. Another inch, and he would have a surgical bruise. She was being surveyed quickly but politely as a smile was squeezed out.

'Thank you, Miss Taylor,' he nodded to the woman, who realized she was being dismissed before his eyes turned again to Cecelia.

Us little people against the big man, Cecelia could not help thinking.

'You have applied for a job which does not exist.' Irony smoothed his soft, silky voice. He was pleased with himself. The smug look of satisfaction glowed on his face. A man who had grown big in his own little world, he thought he could do anything. Yet, his taste in clothes alienated him from the rest of society. Was it possible to say his attire described him best? Glasses that were gray with grime and a light blue zoot suit with large lapels piped with pale copper trimming. This could have been a fashion statement decades ago. Yet, this was his image now. He was not only arrogant in his ways, but he also appeared to have never been good-looking although, he thought he was. Perhaps even dashing.

'Doesn't exist; I don't understand?' Cecelia stood motionless and unruffled and keeping strong. She wasn't going to be persuaded by his side of the argument. Stick to the story. Stick to the plot of her own making and believe in it.

He smiled, silently acknowledging that she wasn't going to answer his comment.

'Did you know the clinic was about to request a care nurse from the nursing agency, or are you some sort of psychic? Or maybe another member of staff told you there was a vacancy? I hope they didn't?'

'No, I'm none of those. I just hoped there would be a situation. There is nothing wrong with anticipating a vacancy, is there?'

'No, I suppose not.'

'I sent in my resume yesterday to apply. Have you received it yet?'

'No,' he looked at his computer screen and in the inbox. 'There is nothing here. And your name is?'

'Clara Tinder.'

'Clara Tinder,' he repeated, taping in her name. 'No, there's nothing for a Clara Tinder. I can't find anything for you. Are you certain you've given the correct name?'

'How certain can I be when you say I don't exist?'

He looked up, smiled. He was interested. He liked people who were intelligent but not too smart. Perhaps there was a place for her, if he knew how to use her.

'Well, I'm not sure what to do with you. We need a care assistant—it's just odd that you have turned up just at the right time.'

'Well, if you like, I can go. I used to work in a hospital before, in the geriatric ward. I know what it's like to look after people. They can't be that much different from anyone else.'

'But these people are celebrities, people with money. They definitely need more attention than your geriatrics. Money and age are not dissimilar. Both can be crotchety. You often find that your efforts are not appreciated and often criticized, and we will work you harder than you have worked before.'

Her heart pumped with hope and astonishment. Was he considering her? If he was, then she was fortunate. Under the mantle of Peter, she had become lucky. Amazing.

After a long and deliberate sigh, Dr. Deer regarded her.

'I should consider fate had thrown us a lifeline.' He picked up his pen and squeezed the trigger mechanism, and the nib popped up. 'You will be on probation, and you shall be observed. We value our clients more than we value our staff. Should one of our clients find you not to their liking, you will be fired. Do you understand that? Even if you have done nothing wrong, our clients come first.'

She understood, as shocking as it was, she was in. If you don't ask, you don't get. And it was true; she had done nothing like this before. Life will give you what you ask for. It was like a dream, like one of those enchanting fairytales. It was possible to believe in magic.

8

───────

I t was just like following the same path in a story which Angelina had taken and told her about. Forms had to be filled in, requiring every detail about her. Photographs taken, and references of her previous jobs were requested, which she was making up as she went along. By the time they would have found out that these references were fake, she would be gone. True, it wouldn't bring Angelina or the little dismembered body back. But it would, though, secure them justice. The natural justice of life demands that every death must be avenged.

With a red-colored pen, Cecelia signed the clinic's official non-disclosure document, and then her eyes traveled down to the small print, which warned her about the penalties for her actions if she went against their rules. She would be struck off from the medical registrar, followed by imprisonment. Shocking punishments, yet not so difficult for Cecelia to accept because she had no plans to work in this profession again.

But there wasn't any clause which said anything about losing her life. Like the unwanted surgical clothes, Angelina, too, had become discarded. So, she had been disposed of. A push, and she was gone.

After being shown around the clinic, its wards, and the equipment department, Cecelia was introduced to some of the staff she would work with. The reception from the others was not kind; they looked at her as if she was a threat. A very sobering idea to remember while she was taken on her tour. She considered this on her journey back to the bed-and-breakfast.

Under the guise of good manners lay the threat of fear. They had looked at her and then at each other as if they knew something. No one even bothered to smile, but why should they smile? People had to work to keep themselves alive; it wasn't in the contract to like the person who you were working with. Yet, in their suspicious looks, they believed her to be a spy.

Most of the staff were women except for the doctors. Young women were easily managed. No one was older than their late thirties. There could be a reason for that, or it could be just one of those things. As someone once said, don't read too much into things. All these things she was considering. Are these the sign of an excellent journalist? To doubt and question?

It was almost like a smell. That's the only way she could put it. She could detect something, the uncomfortable feel of suspicion. As soon as she walked into the hotel. What had gone on? Because something was different about the bed-and-breakfast place today. It didn't have the usual casual atmosphere, where people came to meet and unwind after a day of work. People stood around in bent head conference, shaking their heads and glancing at Cecelia as she passed. They choose to ignore her usual salutation.

She had not changed. The person who left this morning

was the same one who returned. They were withdrawn, yet polite. The look in their eyes was the same as ones at the clinic. What did they know she didn't? Or was there something about her? Cecelia nodded to people. Returning the nod and smile, they turned and hurried away to speak to one another under the hush of secrecy.

What is it with this suspicion? Created and conjured up by misinterpretation, Cecelia felt angry for her past and present reputation, questions to be asked of herself first before launching a likely attack.

Such unnecessary hard work; the politics of people.

But was it because she wasn't one of their small group? Those who traveled from another area too far to travel to work in the city came together in fear. Keep the enemy out. She was new; she must be part of the enemy. Surely, it could not be so petty, but you never know with people.

It's true that people are strange. Cecelia climbed the stairs to her room with thoughts of comfort herself. Clicky and snobby, they weren't like the weekend crowd. But she couldn't worry about them; she needed to get ready for that chance meeting with Peter. Oh, please be there. Surely, he must stop off to collect his luggage and then come and speak to her. They were friends, if nothing else.

Oh God, please help. Yet, going downstairs, Cecelia knew their table was going to be empty. Please let him come into the dining room and at least tell me where he was going from here.

It was two minutes before seven, and the room was already lively with voices. She stopped to listen for those few seconds. Pushing open the door, her decision next was based on self-protection. It was easier, for now, she could pretend he was sitting there in his seat. Sitting there and waiting for her.

What would she do if he wasn't?

Passing the tables, she smiled at a couple of people who didn't smile back. Ignorant pigs. She might as well not be there, judging by the way they dismissed her, glancing away to get back to their important conversation. Was it about her?

He wasn't there. Cecelia knew this before she got to the table. Time to face up to it. He was gone, and she was already forgotten by him.

'Are you going to walk right past me?' it was Peter's voice. 'Have I done something to upset you?'

'Peter,' she gasped, grabbing hold of his shoulder. 'It's you.'

'Yes, of course, it's me.' He looked puzzled. 'Who else would it be?'

'But I thought—' he didn't know she had overheard him early this morning. So now, what could she say to his question? But she was so pleased to see him. 'I had a real awful dream last night.'

'Why don't you sit down and tell me,' he gestured towards the chair opposite. Now in a different smart gray suit, with a light blue shirt and a darker gray tie; he looked immaculate. And handsome, and his blue eyes sparkled.

She looked at him to make sure he was real. She looked at the chair while her mind and head were all over the place. But when she scrambled to her seat, her legs, unaccustomed to her hesitation, broke free from her hips and nearly pull her over.

'Careful,' he said, leaping agilely like a cat catching her. He held her in his arms tightly while his sparkling blue eyes looked deep into hers. 'Have you been drinking already?' he still hung on to her body, while his eyes traveled quickly around her face before gaining entrance to her heart.

Please hold me forever, ran through her mind.

He embraced her against his chest so tight that she swore she could feel his heart beating.

'Are you coming apart, Clara?' he was carefully sweeping her to her seat. And then he stopped. His face read surprise as he sniffed the air. 'What is that awful smell? It's the smell of disinfectant, the smell of hospitals. It's your uncle, isn't it? Has he taken a turn for the worse? I can't stand that smell of pending death.'

Gaining her chair, Cecelia's now refreshed eyes flew across the table to land on his. How would she explain her story to him? She touched her chest, and then to her face. Would he in the future forgive her when she told him the truth? Never had she behaved like this, silly and feminine and all over the place, and all for him.

'Oh, it must be the nurse. I was there when she came today. I don't know if she was as blind as a bat because she almost walked through me. It was probably then when she rubbed her antiseptic perfume all over me. The smell was very strong.'

'Poor child, you've had a rough day today. No wonder you are confused. It would be better for everyone if he died now.' And then he took up his table knife to examine it. 'People hovering in and out of life. It's very selfish of them.'

In the blade, he had managed to catch his reflection. One eye and then part of his nose were disconnected from the rest of his face.

Her uncle was only imaginary, but even so, he meant well, Cecelia thought.

'This dream you had. Was it about me?'

Another lie. So far, their relationship was based on lies and it was ruining her sensitivity. Heat seethed into her cheeks, running like a defeated warrior to expose how lost she was. She was lying to him, but only to a part of him, only to his brain and not his heart. In his heart, she would always be loyal to him.

'Oh, it was just a dream,' a smile of admonishment. 'Sometimes, when you awake, it's hard to get out of the dream—has that ever happened to you?'

He smiled lamely, but he wasn't going to answer. She continued.

'Well, in this dream, I thought you had gone.'

Peter put the knife down and then leaned forward. 'Gone? Gone where?'

She shrugged. 'I thought you had left this place, this bed-and-breakfast place.'

'And that mattered to you?'

'A little,' she lowered her eyes, hoping this answer would work.

'I'm flattered, and I'm flattered that it made a difference whether I was here or not.'

And what do you think about me, she wanted desperately to say, but of course, like everything else, this was drugged into silence.

'So, how is your uncle?' what was that look in his eye? It was as if his natural course had diverted him to stop and look at her? She puzzled him. Like he couldn't quite make up his mind about something to do with her.

'Oh, you know, he's still hanging on.'

'And what about your auntie? What does she think about this?'

'I don't consider her as being my auntie. I don't like her. I think she's only after his money,' Cecelia said with vehemence, and this surprised her.

And then Peter broke into laughter, which caused everyone in the room to look at these two.

'You tell it as it is, don't you, Clara?' his laughter was diminishing? 'I love your sense of humor. Well, your nightmare hasn't come true. I'm still here, and the world is still beautiful.' He smiled to himself, amused by what she said.

'How long are you here for?'

'Until my job is done.' A smile changed to curiosity; he leaned his head to one side.

Was he trying to make his mind up about her? What did he think and feel when he looked at her?

'And how's Victoria?'

'Victoria?'

'Yes, your sister. Is she coming to see your uncle?'

Now he was interested in her fantasy sister. Oh Lord, whatever was the matter with her to invent so many people in her life when they were few and very infrequent.

'No.' she frowned. Had she called her sister, Virginia?

'Don't tell me she's dead as well?'

'We are a dysfunctional family. We never talk to one another, never see each other either. It's as if we're dead to one another.'

He laughed again. 'That sounds like my kind of family. You know, I like you and your family more and more.' He looked about the room, searching for something. 'Dinner's late tonight. Why do you think that is?'

'I don't know,' she shrugged. 'Everyone here has been behaving strangely.'

'Yes, they have. I agree with you.' Then he, too, fell into silence.

He had forgotten about the wine until the kitchen door flipped open, and out came the hot plates, feeding the air with the aroma that it was cottage pie tonight.

'I just love cottage pie.' Peter poured out the wine. It fell, tumbling and sparkling into their glasses. 'It reminds me of my time in England.'

'You went to England?'

'Yes, I've traveled all over the world, but there's nowhere like home.'

'Yes. Thank you,' Cecelia took the glass he passed to her, took a sip, and then waited for their plates to arrive. There is an order to everything.

The people next to them were being served first. Politely, and sitting with their backs straight, the two at this table waited.

'It's a tragedy,' said a woman to the proprietor, standing in as a waiter. 'And so young. Forty isn't anything these days. He had a wife and two daughters, I believe?'

'Yeah, I spoke to his wife earlier,' said the proprietor, catering to the audience with a show of respect. 'She's in shock. It was awful, absolutely awful. And so sudden. She asked me to keep his things. I was packing them away for her. It was the least I could do. We forgot the time; that's why dinner is so late. I must apologize.'

'No, please don't apologize. You have been very good. Very good. A decent host, which is why we always come here.'

The landlord was now between the tables. 'She said she would come and collect his things at the weekend. I told her not to rush. Her head must be all over the place.'

'Yes, poor thing—what was it he was supposed to have died from?'

'A heart attack. Apparently, it came out of nowhere. He was someone who looked after his body, you know, exercised two or three times a week. He was a charming man, friendly, well-mannered. It's unfair that it should have happened to him. He was one of our favorite guests.

Followed the rules, always polite and never raised his voice. We are going to miss him.'

'Yes, I know. It's such a tragedy.'

'Look, can we get our dinner before it's tomorrow, already?' Peter had been listening and now had lost his temper.

'I'm sorry, sir,' said the landlord as the waiter turned to look disapprovingly at Peter. A death deserved some respect, and he should know that. 'I think everyone's suffering from shock here, sir. But I'll fetch your dinner right away.'

Cecelia felt strange. Someone in this bed-and-breakfast had suddenly died and without warning. Why was everyone dying about her? Death had become a plague or the new fashion.

'I know, I'm a pig. My attitude stinks, but honestly, why should I be upset about a man who I didn't know?'

'Someone died here at this bed-and-breakfast house?' Cecelia appeared dazed as she looked at Peter. Did he know more than she did about the man who now would never go home? Death, for some reason, bothered him more than it should have. Why was he so touchy about the death of a stranger?

'No, he dropped dead out in the street. No one really knew him here. I don't know why they're making so much fuss.' Peter's cheeks had turned red from annoyance and anger.

He picked out a cracker from his dish and broke it in half. Cecelia looked at this symbolic gesture and wondered.

'I suppose it happened right out of the blue?' she replied in a dull voice. Another question she couldn't help asking. It was as if she was taunting him.

Was Peter angry because someone couldn't help dying?

'It frightens people when someone they know disappears out of their life just like that,' said the owner, now standing beside them. Could this be the grim reaper here to remind them they could be next?

'Well, then. They should thank their lucky stars they're still alive and teach them to make the most of it while they still have it. Because if they continue to gossip between the —oh, hell, what does it matter, I'm not hungry anymore—' Peter stood up, swallowed his glass of wine, and then without saying anything more, he walked out of the dining room.

What had happened? Had she or the owner said something wrong? She was so pleased to see him, and she wanted to know how he had got on with his day. She wanted to know everything about him, like the young woman he was looking for. But Peter, she realized, didn't like to hear about death any more than anyone else, or perhaps more so.

When two plates of cottage pie were brought to their table, Cecelia's smiling excuse told the waiter that Peter had just gone out for a breath of fresh air, and he had been agitated by all the talk of the other boarder's death. Calming the waters for what she hoped would his swift return. He would be silly if he didn't.

'Yes, well, the other man's death was Mr. Thornton's gain. If Mr. Jonaway hadn't died, Mr. Thornton would have had to board somewhere else,' the sad faced proprietor said as he duly placed down the hot dinner plates. 'Funny how things work out like that.'

'What do you mean?' Cecelia was now confused.

'I mean that Mr. Thornton was fortunate, that's all. He pleaded to keep his room, but I said no; we do entertain scruples here. I hope you enjoy your dinner.'

Now she understood what was wrong with Peter. Guilt. He felt terrible that he was sitting here in the other man's place while the late—whatever his name was, Jonaway was now lying in the morgue. Well, he wasn't to blame for that. And he wasn't to blame for being upset about his feelings about death. It was a shame that Peter had to suffer by having nothing to eat, and why should he? She knew what she would do; she would take his dinner to him.

'Do you mind if I take this plate up to Mr. Thornton? He was very upset about the death, very upset. No one realizes how sensitive he is.' A smile is often a way of apology; it usually gives license for thoughtless actions or speech.

'You can do as you please,' shrugged the waiter.

'Do you know which room he is in?' She wasn't going to get upset by this man's ignorance.

'Eight, he is on the right as you turn the corner.'

'Thank you,' Cecelia emphasizes with courtesy.

Why should he dine on his own? It just wasn't right. People were jealous that Peter was single, in a good job, and probably receiving a very healthy paycheck. He had every right to good manners, the same as the rest of them. Should she be cheeky and take her plate with her and offer her company? Would he mind if she brought his dinner with hers, hoping to cheer him up? There was only one way to find out. She would take the initiative; it was part of her new persona. Be brave. What could she lose?

Stairway to adventure, Cecelia knew she was being watched as she walked out of the dining room with two plates in her hands.

Let them talk; she smiled to herself. Let them think whatever they want. This was her life and no one else's. I'm too important to worry about what they think. Throwback the unkind whispers peeping inside her head. She was a celebrity or even royalty; she could do what she liked. She was not imposed upon by others' values or rules. She didn't care what they thought.

Yet, as she climbed the stairs, the manacles of other people's thoughts twisted heavily on her ankles and wrists. Disproving, and perhaps even getting together on a petition; we don't want people like him and you in our hotel. She cocked her hips from side to side as she climbed the stairs. Give them something else to be disapproving about.

Her room was on the left side of the house, number seventeen.

But what if she read him wrong to find that he didn't want her? Just because you were attracted to someone did not automatically mean they were attracted to you.

Standing outside number eight, she wondered for a moment if what she was doing was the best idea? Lost in indecision now, whether to knock or return to her room. Can't turn back now. Everyone had seen her walk out of the dining room, and the proprietor was probably confirming it.

Take the plunge. Cecelia kicked the door and waited for an answer.

There was a scuffling sound from behind the door, something which she couldn't make sense of. Was he undressed? Oh dear, bad timing. Now she was worried about his privacy because she didn't like it when anyone poked their nose into her life.

'Who is it?'

'It's me, Clara. I'm sorry.'

'Clara?'

Long strides to the door, and it was wrenched open.

'What are you doing here?' and then he saw with astonishment that she was carrying two plates of cottage pie in her hands. 'My God, what are you doing with those? Is this your intention to feed me up with two plates of food?'

'No, I'm sorry. I knew it was a big mistake once I arrived at your door. But I thought you had been upset about the man who died today. And I didn't want you missing out on your dinner—but, you know, it wasn't your fault for what happened to him. It was one of those dreadful coincidences which you had nothing to do with.'

His eyes grew bigger and bigger as he listened to Cecelia talk, and then he burst into laughter.

'And you brought my dinner up for me, and yours as well?'

'Yes, I thought we could sit together. I spend most of my time eating on my own, and although you can do what you like when you eat alone, sometimes it's nice to have company.'

'What am I thinking of?' he stood back from the door. 'That was very considerate of you. Would you like to come in, and we can eat our dinner together before it gets too cold?'

Once more, her heart bounced in her chest as she followed him into his room. This was the sacred chamber. She smiled to herself while taking potshots of judgement on his room, and if it was better than hers. He was neat, very, very neat. The covers on his bed were drawn tight. There were no clothes left over the side of chairs or anything else left to wander while the curtains were drawn closed. His room was probably tidier now than before he moved in. Some great habits here.

Now to his face, she looked for things in his expressions. Was he pleased to see her? He was pulling the table over to his bed and pulling another chair around.

'You know, as soon as I walked out of the dining room, I knew I'd been a fool. But pride stops one from returning, don't you think? Put the plates down—I should have taken them from you. Sit down, sit down on the chair.'

'Oh blast, I've forgotten the knives and forks. I only picked up the spoons.'

'That's how I like to eat,' he laughed. 'I'm a class one pig if I'm allowed to get away with it.'

I think you're lovely; she thought as she passed him a spoon.

He was now staring at her, and his merry blue eyes contained glee.

'I've got a bottle of brandy, only for medicinal purposes,' he said grandly.

'Oh yes, brandy is the best drink to have in the house.' She couldn't help nodding enthusiastically.

'Do you want a glass—I'm having one, and I recommend you having one also?'

In a gesture of hugging her shoulders, it confirmed that she was game if he was.

'Brilliant, just wait one moment. And I'll get madam her drink.' He moved to the other side of the room, where there was a cabinet. Squatting, he opened the door. 'I have everything under control,' he said with his head almost in the cabinet. 'I am in charge of my fate. And things always work out right.'

She smiled. She could see them together. A lovely little house with a white wicker fence, going on trips to other countries and even to England, a place of enchantment. People would look at them and wonder how much they loved each other. They wouldn't have children; children would come between their love for each other. Yes, she was a dreamer, but that was okay as long as you have someone to dream the dream along with.

'I found one glass,' he called to her. 'And now I know

there is another glass. I've seen it somewhere, because I remember seeing it on the day I arrived. I believe he must have been a secret drinker. And I bet his wife didn't know that about him?'

His wife, Cecelia, repeated to herself. What wife was that? Like a ball which had been hurled without a thought, had now made its mark on her. Of course, it had to be Mr. Jonaway. He who had walked into this room and probably rang his wife on his cell phone, who had taken his meals down in the dining room. She rubbed her nose where the impact had landed. Yes, just a few hours ago, he was enjoying his life. She turned her head away to the side.

There, on the floor to the base of his single bed, was Peter's briefcase. This was the reason for the rustling. Papers had been hastily picked up and tossed into the case.

'I think I've found the other glass. Yes, I have. The owner said he had taken away all his things, but he missed some of them—and for us, the most important one.'

Was that a photograph? Cecelia pushed herself forward to look. She could see a pair of black-and-white eyes looking back inanimate at her, and yet just as real as if they had been in life. Was this a picture of the woman that Peter was looking for?

'There you are.' Peter placed the glass in front of her, followed by the sound of the brandy bottle being cracked open. 'Let's have a drink. I think we damn well need one.'

Looking down at the glass now presented before her was a healthy tot of brandy, half a glass full.

This was nice.

Sitting down opposite her, he took up his glass while looking at her. 'Cheers, and here's to life and the living of it. And here's to money, which makes everything worthwhile.'

He waited for her to clink glasses. The satisfying tinge

of agreement again provoked another one of his smiles. This was something that should have made her happy, but it didn't. In the present flush of the evening, she felt despair.

Had anything changed with her? Would she always find her faith and belief in rejection and suspicion, preferring that instead of hope?

Over her glass, Cecelia watched Peter gulp down his brandy. He was a professional drinker, yet he knew his capacity, and now he was waiting for her to complement his thirst.

This thing between them would never work out. What did he see in her but someone to pass the time with while he worked away from home? Look at him. He had everything. Handsome and intelligent and obviously, he had plenty of money.

Impeaching her taste, Cecelia took a sip. Brandy and whiskey were two drinks she disliked, even though this one was better than most. She glanced shyly at him. The romance was over.

'You are such an angel for bringing my dinner to me— no one has ever done that for me before,' he began pouring himself out another glass. 'Mind you, I've allowed no one to get that close to me.' He stopped and smiled at Cecelia. 'Except you.'

She found herself staring at him, wondering what on earth they were doing together. Her life had stepped into the bizarre. Where was she in her head?

'You know, you've affected my life, and I'm not sure whether it's for the best. A person like me doesn't have any time for others, but I've been thinking all day about what you said. You know, about a wife traveling with me.'

'It's a very nice brandy,' she rubbed her lips to erase the

taste. Brandy, as she saw it, came from sharp pipped stems while wine clung juicily on family vines.

But somewhere inside his heart, he was listening and seeing and entertaining his dreams, or perhaps he was just playing with her.

'I've got the impression that you've never been married?'

What a question to ask a woman who was now in her mid-thirties. It was almost rude. Biting her lips, she lowered her head.

'I thought so. I thought you'd never been married. The same here. I've never contemplated it. My life, I told myself, was to live it on my own. I'm not like anyone else. It's something to do with my job. I have to pick up luggage and go to wherever and whenever I'm needed.'

Who is the woman in the black-and-white photograph in your briefcase?

'I'm not husband material. Yes, I've had affairs—I'm a man,' and then he laughed. 'And this is delicious, but you're not eating yours. Come on; I can't sit here and eat on my own. Eat up, or otherwise, I'll eat yours.'

She was ruminating on her thoughts and not on the food that sat on the table. Yet, had he worked it out why she had become silent? No, he was busying himself with what his future was now, guaranteeing that he didn't notice her voice had given in its notice and gone to bed for the night.

'Tell me something more about yourself,' he asked, sweeping up some mashed potatoes with his spoon.

'There isn't much to tell. Except that I'm a bit like you.'

Yet, had he heard her because he picked up his glass and took another swig. 'Was I correct when I guessed that you worked in the tax department of the IRS?'

'Yes, you were right.'

'I knew I was.' He punched the air like a conquering

warrior. 'Are you going to drink the rest of your brandy, and then I can refill your glass?'

'I've suddenly got a headache.'

'Well, it can't be the brandy. You only get headaches and hangovers from cheap booze—and I never drink cheap. Like I normally never stay in cheap hotels, except for here. I earn enough money to have the best.'

'Did you find the woman you were looking for?' Could he be looking for his wife? Wasn't it true that she was his wife in the photograph?

What a change to his mood. From a high to a low in less than a second. Holding his glass, he rolled his lips and looked uncomfortable. Yes, and we know why.

'No, but I will. No one ever escapes, except perhaps you. I take it that the headache was to leave me?'

'If you don't mind. I think it was seeing my uncle like that today. I remember when he was young and strong.'

'And that's how you should remember people. People should never be allowed to get old. I'm never going to get old. The grim reaper will have his way someday and find me before I find him.'

He held the door open for her as she passed by. Looking at her as if he were considering something. The gentle smile lay on his lips, but it could have been the brandy.

9

———————

It was true Peter had a wife, she knew, and there was no use in him trying to deny this. It was something she had to accept. There were those little give away signs, his familiarity with women, absolutely everything. Just because he didn't wear a wedding ring could mean that he took it off because it suited him. Not everyone wore rings, Thomas didn't. How mixed up she was becoming towards Peter. She hated that there could be anyone else in his life other than her. Her jealousy was all-encompassing and corrupting, turning her once stability into murderous thoughts. If he had anyone else in his life, she knew she could kill her.

Please don't let there be anyone in his life. Cecelia, returning to her room, avoided the patterns woven into the carpet.

Every look he showed her, the turn of his chin, the way he crouched, the clothes he wore, even the smell of his aftershave was collected and stored inside a temple in her heart. She would never release him. He was hers. But to keep him, she had to be careful. Not like the first time. The first time drove her to the threshold of madness. Down in that dark and bottomless gully, the screams of confusion echoed, but didn't receive any answers.

It was summer; these wonderful incidents always happen in the sunshine, and was it really ten years ago? It was just another day when she came out from the office at lunchtime. Her mind had been on how she had been treated by Chris, two years her senior. Now she could not remember what had been said, but she had been upset. She was thinking of chucking the job in, but she knew she wouldn't. Walking along the sidewalk, Thomas suddenly walked straight into her and knocked her down. All her papers and books went up in the air and scattered on the ground.

'What do you think you're doing?' she yelled, now feeling embarrassed. It seemed like everyone had stopped to watch. This day was getting worse. But like the hero in a fairytale, his hand went around her waist to help gather to her feet. Her skirt had flared out to expose her underwear. She was angry not only because she felt humiliated but also because he was grinning as if he found her distress funny.

'Don't you look when you're coming out of a building?' she yelled at him while he carried on grinning.

She brushed herself down while pushing at her skirt because it had betrayed her. Who was this rude man who could laugh at her? She stole a questioning looks to his face while admitting that he was attractive.

But he just carried on grinning as he collected the rest of her papers and notebooks to present them to her like an awkward and bashful schoolboy who had taken a great downer on his teacher.

Even from this awkward start, it was written on the cards that she had fallen for him. Compared to Peter, he was one of those irresistible guys who could do no wrong. He had charm. Instantly, she liked him.

'Well, aren't you going to say something?'

'What's there to say? I wasn't looking where I was going, maybe, but you are prettier than the girl I was following.'

She was angry, and she was what she was holding on to it. She had no intention of smiling, but with one look at his handsome boyish face, she knew she was his. Instead of him apologizing to her, she was now apologizing to him.

'It's my fault. I saw you as you walked out of the building, but I thought I could get past you before—' she shrugged. 'Sorry.'

'No, I'm glad we bumped into each other,' he grinned rather cheekily. 'But let me make it up to you, would you? What are you doing after you've finished work?'

She had never made a date like this before. She wasn't cheap, but his boyish face and those beautiful hazel eyes told her to quit this doctrine and get herself a life. Women that passed on these opportunities and never took that extra look were losers. It was not because he had tumbled her, but because he was good-looking.

Did anyone refuse him? No, they didn't? This was a test. Should she play hard to get, but if she did, she might lose this handsome man?

'I suppose I'm doing nothing.'

'Great, then I'll meet you here, outside this place at seven?'

Just as soon as she said, okay, he was off.

At five to seven, she was waiting outside the building. At five past, she was still waiting. She had been stood up. At seven-thirty, she knew she had been dumped. Turning on her heel, she started to walk. Never again would she put herself into this situation. It was demeaning and stupid.

'So, you weren't going to wait for me?' his long legs, golden hair, and handsome face were walking towards her.

'I've been waiting here for over half-hour. Where were you?' how handsome he looked, just as if he had walked off a beach.

'Busy,' he said, casually picking up her hand while continuing to walk.

If she wanted to be with him, she had better walk.

'Man, isn't this a lovely day?' his head was high in the air, dreamy eyes looking at something that only he could see.

A couple of young women walked past and fluttered their eyelashes at him. If she didn't want him, they did. But Thomas didn't even look at them, yet by the look in his eyes, she knew he knew he had been admired. It was something he'd got used to and accepted.

So, where were they going? He was holding her hand and taking her in silence. But where was he taking her—did he have a plan? He was breathing the air, enjoying everything while feeling pleased with himself.

'Where are we going?' she asked at last, out of exasperation.

He shrugged. 'Just walking. We don't have to go anywhere to feel happy with life.'

He was pleasing to look at, but she didn't know him. How can you commit to a stranger when you haven't passed through those questions? What sort of things do you like to do, the books you read, the food you eat, and how do you feel about this or that?

One must have a plan in life and know where one is going, and here she was, walking along without any direction. Was he safe?

If there was one thing Cecelia hated, it was indecision. Every question must have an answer, and there must be no room for emptiness or surprise. So, what on earth was happening? As handsome as he was, did he have a plan? He seemed to know where he was going.

They were heading to Hermosa Beach and The Strand. It was a while since she had been to the beach. The people who went there weren't the type of people she mixed with. The golden people who thrived on the beach, filling their days with beach sports. Sunshine's eternal children. These were his type of people. Their uniform was their golden tan, which he also decorated himself in.

She liked him, but he wasn't saying anything. They were walking along, hand in hand, as if they were ethereal and in love. Was he showing her something about his kind of life? Showing and not telling, breathing and not speaking, feeling the energy of life, and not thinking? Was he someone who should have lived in the sixties?

'Do you think we could sit down somewhere? I've got the wrong shoes on.'

'Well, take them off.'

Take off my shoes? Why? Sure, the sidewalk would be cooler on the eve of the evening, but this wasn't like her. She needed her props, her bits and pieces in life to know who she was. But then, it was as if something clicked in his head because he dragged her onto the sand.

'You can walk on sand; it's better for your feet,' he was now taking off his shoes. He wore no socks.

Reluctantly, Cecelia slid off her heels and found herself several inches shorter. He had grown considerably, or rather, this was how he always was, a tall man in a tall world.

They carried on walking for a while.

'I just love the sea,' he said, taking his shirt off and walking towards the blue waves.

'What are you doing?' she was trying to run on the soft

and uneven surfaces to keep up with him. Unsure as to what was happening, she didn't feel like smiling. She was an alien in his world.

'I'm going for a swim,' he called over his shoulder.

'Why?' what was she supposed to do while he was swimming?

'Come and join me,' he was now taking off his pants while still carrying on his approach to the beckoning Pacific.

'But I haven't got a swimming costume.'

'Free yourself from the constraints of life and come and join me. You should do what you want whenever you want. This is your time. Don't allow anyone to tell you what to do.'

'But I can't,' she stood stunned, staring after him.

'You can, babe. You're wearing panties and a brassiere, aren't you? No one will know any different. I'll see you in the water.' And then he was running towards the big blue.

Bewilderment, she didn't know what she should do and never had she been put into this situation before. In the distance, she could hear him whooping and laughing, enjoying himself. It was a choice of whether she wanted to join him or stay on the perimeter of life. Unbuttoning her skirt, she let it fall into the sand. Leaving it in a huddle with her shoes, she ran towards him.

Splashing into the sea, Cecelia was wading towards him. Twisting and turning from one leg slowly to the other, this was the only way she could move through the water. He turned around and smiled at her. With his arms outstretched, he waited to take hold of her. She was in his arms and up to his still warm chest. Pleased to see her, he kissed her, then removed her bra, followed by her panties. She had become naked in the water.

'What are you doing?'

'You know what I am doing. I am freeing you from the

restraints of life. You don't need them, babe. Look at you. You are doing so well. You are beautiful, you must remember that.'

How breathless she was and how vulnerable she had become. He had access to every intimate part of her. Her cover had been taken away, and she had nowhere to hide. Yet he liked her better for this. He approved of her; this was how he wanted her to be.

Holding hands, they waded out from the sea, two beautiful creatures. They were going to be this way forever. How natural, how wonderful, how free.

On the beach, he made love to her. She didn't consciously know if she enjoyed it, being aware that several passers-by were watching at a distance as they strolled along, but it was an honor to be mounted by a man like this.

'I could sit out here all night and watch the surf.' He was staring at the ocean as if this blue-moving body was his lover.

'I don't know your name,' she had dressed straight after the lovemaking.

An inward laugh, as if knowing the other person's name was the least important thing for anyone to know.

'Thomas,' he volunteered, still staring out to sea. Ignoring the minutes and hours which were ticking by.

'Do you want to know my name?' she frowned, staring up at his dispassionate, nonchalant face.

'Yeah, ok, what's your name?' he had turned to her, taken by her curiosity.

'Cecelia.'

'Ce-ce,' he grinned, turning back to his mistress in the waves.

'Shall I see you tomorrow?'

He held his head upwards, feeling the spray from the

sea. A seagull flew past, an aimless stranger so like this Thomas.

'I could meet you again outside the office building at seven.'

'Sure.' Speaking it appeared was not his first language.

This was not the sort of guy she usually went for, but they spiritually joined after the lovemaking.

Now they were officially going out together. This was a day to remember for the rest of her life. Important and wonderful, their first memory had been formed.

Difficult, trying to be like him, relaxed, laid-back, and just so, but it wasn't natural for her and took a lot of working on. Surprisingly, for a good-looking man like him, he was an excellent lover. Gorgeous men are never any good in bed, not that she slept around. It was just something she had read. This was going to be a new way of life for her. Were they always going to make love on the beach? She wasn't an exhibitionist. But these were the rules, his rules.

Yet, inside her mind, she was making plans for them both. April was an excellent time to get married because they would have the summer together. They would buy a house instead of renting by pooling their money together. Although there was nothing wrong with renting, having a place together suggested their relationship was more concrete. And at twenty-three, if she intended to have children, it was better to start early and enjoy their children together. After thirty-five, it really was too late for women.

He never asked questions about her, which meant she wasn't to ask any about him. This is what she understood from his silence. Rules which were felt but not said. She wanted to know many things about him, and it was difficult for Cecelia not to have any answers. The few times she asked little things like where he was born and lived, silence always answered her questions.

Why wouldn't he talk to her? What was all this secrecy about? Was he ashamed of her? Or was this the person he was? Whatever it was, it took some getting used to.

They met every weekday and headed straight to the beach. They would walk forever, then strip off and go for a swim and then make love. But it was not enough for her. With Thomas, life was very simple, but she wanted the tangible arms of commitment. She wanted to know how he felt, the politics he voted for, or if he ever took the time to join the committee of the majority of people. Why wasn't he curious about her? Something which bothered her; one thing she had already found out about him was that he didn't like questions. But questions were what made relationships possible.

What did he do with himself on the weekends? She wanted to know but didn't dare ask. She felt if she did, he would drop her. Yet she knew he loved her. No one made love like that if they didn't love you.

They were in love, and this was their time.

It's amazing how you can find out the answer to your questions yourself. Friday evening, and after the lovemaking and staring out to sea, the sea by now had just become the sea. The time had come for the night world to come from under its bedcovers. For Cecelia, it was time for the inevitable sleep. Her arm was now linked through his as they retraced their footsteps back to the lights of the town. It was ten-thirty.

Time to say goodnight and see you on Monday. A light kiss, a smile, and their fingers drifted apart. A few steps in her direction, and then Cecelia stopped. This time, she was going to follow him home. She had to know where he lived.

She needed to know everything about him to make him real.

Hanging back as far as she could, Cecelia dogged his footsteps, only stopping when he stopped. He caught up with a few guys and stopped to chat for a while before bumping their fists together before parting. Everyone he met liked him, yet who could not like this kind of guy?

They had been walking for an hour. From 6th Street, he headed towards 8th street, and he still carried on walking, not knowing or caring if she was behind him. And then he stopped and turned into a front yard. Taking out his keys, he headed to the front door. He was very sure of himself. He had access to the house.

So, this was his home. She stood for a few seconds staring at it, trying to memorize the details of the house.

So, this was the house where he lived, but it was not how she pictured it. A bungalow style house in an ordinary street. This automatically said family and domestic. It all appeared so strange as she got closer to the house. Where had the bohemian gone, doing what he wanted to do and dismissing all the rules? An enigma? Perhaps he had stopped off to visit a friend? But Thomas had the key to the door, which said this must be his home.

Thriving in her imagination had been the idea he was the lead singer in a band; he played the guitar and smoked dope, especially when he was doing a gig. He said peace, not war. What was he doing here?

Moving towards the windows and blinking in and out across the shadows while walking on soft mowed turf, Cecelia kicked something hard. Bending, she found it was a child's toy. Thomas lived in a house where there were children. Young legs and arms and smiling faces. Her heart was beating frantically with the word no. This could not be his home.

Knowledge kills as it answers. She ran to the house and looked through the windows. Thomas was just about to switch off the light when she saw he was a man, a father who had children. Everywhere around were the articles of their living. A pretty doll, a cuddly teddy bear. Who would have thought these things could be dangerous?

'What the hell do you want?' he said as he opened the door to her thunderous rapping. Not the laid back Thomas who she had just had sex with.

Their eyes met, and the illusion was destroyed. His anger turned to sarcasm because she had spoiled everything for them, for him, and then for herself.

'What the hell are you doing here?'

'What do you mean, what am I doing here? What are you doing here?'

'You're on my property, and I want you gone. You're not invited.'

'You led me to believe we were going out together and that we were in love. You did, I know you did.' She was panting. Fear and denial were mixed with incomprehension. He couldn't be doing this to her. He couldn't. We are in love—we love each other.

'I led you towards nothing. You wanted to follow, you wanted to believe.' He was angry, his eyes had turned into the devils.

'Thomas, Thomas, it's me. Your Ce-ce. Please don't do this to me.'

'Who's that, Thomas?' a woman's voice came from the dark, switching on the lights and now walking towards them.

A woman who was in no way attractive was now

standing beside Thomas. She was plump and plain, and even shorter than herself, but she was beside him, and now she was staring at Cecelia. Was this the woman who owned him?

'What is it you want?' she asked, staring at Cecelia.

They were both staring at her. Cecelia looked at this pudgy woman's hand, trying to understand what had happened. Yet it was her hand that the band of gold was on and not on Cecelia's. Thomas then put an arm around his wife.

'You two are married?' Cecelia asked incredulously.

'As you see, and we have three children. Now, what is it you want?'

'Thomas is mine. We are in love. We've been having an affair.' This last minute desperation was directed at the woman claiming to be Thomas' wife.

'Oh yeah, well, I know all about you. Thomas told me you were following him and offering yourself to him. You ought to be ashamed of yourself, going after other women's husbands. Why don't you get one of your own instead of trying to steal mine? Haven't you any decency? You're the kind of woman that disgusts me.'

'But it was he who came after me.' Standing with the awareness of a child, Cecelia was lost.

'Yes, a very nice story which you would like to tell yourself.'

It was there in that woman's face that she wouldn't believe anything wrong said about her husband. Adamant, strong, the lioness claiming her mate. Her loyalty to him was stupid—or was it? There was nothing Cecelia could say to make her ever feel that she had been betrayed.

'We go to the beach every night and make love,' said Cecelia, staring at the wife to see what you thought of that. Now she should understand how she has been betrayed.

'Yes, of course you do. My husband goes every night, and you've been following him. It's his break, his release after working, but every weekend, he's always with me. You think I don't know my husband is handsome. Of course, I know, as I know, he will always attract the attention of women like you.'

There was a lazy dry smile hanging on Thomas's face while he gloated at her, trying to fight for a man which is not hers.

'But I love him,' cried Cecelia.

'You don't love anyone except what you see and what you want. Leave my husband alone because if you don't, I'll get the police after you. Do you hear what I'm saying? Do you understand me, girl? Come on, Thomas, let's leave this trailer trash outside.'

'Thomas, Thomas—please don't do this to me. I gave you everything. I gave you my heart.'

'As my wife said, go home and get out of our lives.' He was closing the door. 'You wouldn't leave it alone, would you?' he whispered. 'You had to have more.'

'I can't believe I was just an affair to you—Thomas, please, don't close the door on me. I love you.'

What could she do? Where should she go? He had become everything to her. She couldn't believe he would do this to her. What they had shared was special, something he couldn't have with his wife. You have to fight for what you want in life. She would get him back. She understood why he was doing this to her; it was because of the children. He was staying with his wife because of the children. It wasn't possible for him to love his wife—just look at the state of her. But when he divorced and married her, they would take custody of the children. And she would love them as if they were her own because of Thomas. If he didn't have his wife anymore, she knew he would come back to her.

Now when the memory of this whirlpool pulled her back, swimming in the agony of embarrassment, she heated up. Her shame burning up on her face made it impossible to disown this episode because it was her's alone. The humiliation of her actions for weeks and months afterward weighed heavily on her that not even a restraining order could stop her. She had gone insane because of him.

But she wouldn't do this with Peter. She would not go through the same humiliation and anguish for a second time. Let him make the advances. This was the only way she would feel sure about him.

10

———

T he shift started at eight in the morning and finished by four, but the conditions were that she would have to stay later if they needed her. It wasn't an imposition for Cecelia; she welcomed it. Work defined who she was to herself.

Being conscientious, and as this was the beginning of her employment, Cecelia arrived early. At seven-thirty, she walked through the door and into the clinic. At reception, her arrival was recorded in silence. She didn't want to put a foot wrong. A cellophane bag contained a white uniform eradicated from dirt and germs, and this was to be worn only on duty and left in the clinic at the end of her shift.

Before dressing in their uniform, they had to scrub up, and all hair was to be tied back from the face. No one was permitted to wear jewelry, which included rings, and nor was perfume allowed. Short nails, no nail varnish. In fact, there was to be no sign of personality. No one was over-weight because this was a sign of unhealthiness. Their shoes were flat, no heels permitted. No one could frown or look upset. The best look to have was a neutral expression.

An all-female crew, and as she found out later, they were all single. Nothing unusual about that; here was a place which expected dedication, and the management paid for it.

Once Cecelia discovered she had the position at the clinic, the tiny camera she had bought two years earlier was going to come in handy. But with no pockets on her uniform, no belts, or even wristwatches where devices or personal items could be stored, a hiding place was going to be difficult, but not impossible. Like the other members of the caring staff, she was to wear a deaconess nurse's hat. An ideal place to secrete her camera.

But today, on her first day, she was expected to work with another staff member to get to know the duties. Her name was Samantha, Samantha Mantle. Samantha was in her mid to late thirties, and she was still a flawless beauty. Long golden colored hair and with her large blue eyes and a smile which lit up her face. Like Angelina, every hair was impeccably kept in place, smoothed, and coiled up in a bun at the back of her head.

They were not to hold or touch hands for the obvious reasons or to be intimate in anyway with clients. There were other ways of getting one's point across, and that was eye contact. Gravelly looking at Cecelia, Samantha ran her eyes over her.

'Loose hair is frowned upon,' Samantha said, her voice was without humor.

'But I tried to scoop it up,' said Cecelia, about to touch her hair, but then put her hands down by her side.

Touching herself was also not tolerated.

'Make all your excuses to Dr. Deer, not me, and then see what he has to say. Now follow me. We cannot go in there,' Samantha pointed to the heavy-duty double hospital doors.

'That area is banned from us. If you go in there, you risk losing your job on the spot.'

'What's in there?' Cecelia was tempted to peep through the small window.

'You are not to ask or to know.'

'Are you serious?' Cecelia showed her incredulity.

'If you want to keep your job. You have to abide by the rules.' And then she stopped to face Cecelia.

'We are not paid to ask questions. That's why the money is good. Do you understand? No one here asks any questions because the person who answers them also faces being fired. This is a clinic where only the very rich frequent. These people are vulnerable to the eyes of the public. It is a serious offence to break your trust and secrecy to the papers or to anyone else. We have been sworn to secrecy, and to look after these people to the best of our abilities. If you can't hold your mouth, then you shouldn't be here.'

It was the sharp, cold slap of comprehension applied to Cecelia's face for the staff didn't have a private life; once they took the pledge, their lives belonged to the clinic. No wonder Angelina was terrified.

Silence and fear kept this clinic working. If she didn't understand this from the start, she was out. The cult conditions of the radical prevailed.

Her tasks were not important, but they were necessary even though menial. Undressing and dressing the clinic's clients, taking blood pressure, weighing and measuring them. They were not too far away from the treatment of slaves, except the nurses get to go home at the end of their shift.

Altogether, three gynecologists were working at the clinic. It was Dr. Deer who was in control, being the senior partner. Cecelia saw him come out of the forbidden zone, talking to one of the other gynecologists. He didn't see her, or it could be he didn't notice her because of the discreetness of her opaque uniform. Gowned, Dr. Deer wore the traditional dress of a surgeon, suggesting that he'd just come out from surgery.

'We do not talk to the gynecologists,' warned Samantha. 'They are the royalty in this clinic, as well as the patients. You don't need to bow to them, but you must stand out of their way. They are to feel our presence, but we are not to be seen or heard. Do you understand me?'

Cecelia fumed silently to herself.

'If this is a problem, then I suggest you quit the job right here and now.' Seeing Cecelia's show of rebellion, Samantha was angry. She didn't like those who disobeyed these rules.

Hygiene ranked top alongside keeping the patients' identity private. Staff recognized themselves as being inferior. This went against everything Cecelia felt about herself, but she had to forget about her feelings and hide behind this job if she was going to find out what was happening here.

Only half an hour for lunch, and everyone had to eat in the clinic's canteen. No one could bring food in, and if you had an intolerance or allergy, you simply could not work here in the first place.

The food provided was healthy and tasty, no fault could be found in the meals. And while cheerful talk continued as they ate, Cecelia saw security officers walking between the tables, listening in to the conversation. Did no one mind being screened?

This is why the money is so good. Cecelia heard the voice of reason. But to Cecelia, there wasn't enough money to bribe her mouth shut and suppress her feelings of right and just.

Again, what did it matter to her? If she wanted to get her story, she would have to forget the bullshit this place represented and blend in like the rest of them.

'Now we have to go to the bathroom and wash our hands,' said Samantha, who had been sitting opposite Cecelia, watching her while they ate. 'Remember, germs and bacteria kill.'

Don't, Cecelia warned herself, question, argue or comment on anything, just lie low, do as you're told and blend in.

Another break at two-thirty, which was for five minutes to go to the bathroom, drink some water, wash your hands and then be back on the floor again. It was when coming out of this break with Samantha and walking to her unit that she stopped.

Two figures, husband and wife, had arrived from the clinic's back entrance and were now walking along the sterile white corridor. She had seen these two before on the news, and now they were padding towards her dressed in reality.

It was Ruth and Hadleigh Blaine, the billionaire royalty of business, the dealers of weaponry. The leaders of every tinpot country courted them. They had the power to make these countries winners or losers in war.

'Oh—hi,' Ruth stepped ahead of her husband, holding out a straight hand as if proposing a salute and with a smile to a face she thought she knew. With her head lowered and leaning to one shoulder, she had the pose of a shy forty-one-year-old child. 'How are you?' a sweet comment to no one in particular, or perhaps to someone who would respond? That orchestrated smile said I'm a nice person. Be careful what you say to me and especially what you do, or everything you are or what you do in life will be wiped off the map. Now, that's power.

Impossible for Cecelia to take her eyes off Ruth. So, this was the face of power. Not exactly beautiful, but reasonably attractive. A slight person with dark brown eyes, which when she smiled, it wasn't noticeable that her eyes were offset. Yet, she had quite a large nose that would look abnormal on someone else if separated from the rest of her face. But Ruth's generous lips and cheekbones counter-balanced these defects. Money makes anyone beautiful, and even the camera set at the correct angle pleases the face.

'Stand back,' said Samantha under her breath, warning Cecelia. 'When she passes, lower your eyes and do not speak to her for any reason.'

Although Cecelia had heard Samantha's advice on respecting this special person, it was impossible for her eyes to obey. They were transfixed on Ruth's abdomen. This was the birth and death place of the third child. While this famous origin bereft of several was now being shown to the world. Conception had happened, and their lineage would be continued. It was a time of rejoicing for everyone.

Black stilettoes stopped at Cecelia's white-shod feet when Ruth dropped her black purse next to Cecelia's feet. The gauntlet had been thrown, and someone needed serving. Immediately, Cecelia went down to retrieve it for her, and as she stood, Ruth's curious brown eyes were on her. Returning her purse, Cecelia unconsciously made a curtsy. A remarkable feat, which was rewarded by Ruth's A-listed wonderful smile.

'Why, thank you,' Mrs. Blaine said, staring at Cecelia. 'Aren't you sweet? You needn't have done that. Hadleigh, did you see what she did?' Ruth called to her husband. 'I want her. I want her to be with me. You will be my friend, won't you?'

Samantha turned to Cecelia with a mixed up look of danger and warning in her eyes. Ruth saw this with annoyance, that she should be challenged. My power is more significant than your power, and my power outranks yours.

'Come with me,' Ruth said, walking ahead again. 'I want to have as many friends as I can around me.'

Cecelia looked at Samantha for an answer, but she turned her head to the front. Pulling in her temper, Samantha ignored her.

This was Cecelia's lucky break in every way. On her first day on the job, and now she was selected to be with the top people. The silent advice from Ruth to this new courtier was, you either take it or leave it. I have given you an invitation to fly with me to the top.

Cecelia quickly recognized her offer and hurried to catch up to Ruth, always mindful of her position in this strange situation. She had heard the whispers on social media, the history which had by loyal others tried to quell, but which appeared now and again shared by other people who hated this Ruth. Secrets which said she had slept herself to the top, dropping her two husbands ruthlessly. No one was going to topple this woman off her throne. Now she was here. This madam was going to remain.

'What's your name?' Ruth's smile was beautiful. It had the power to make everyone feel special, loved, and needed.

'Clara Tinder.'

'Clara Tinder,' repeated Ruth. 'What a pretty name. Do you think we two could be friends—and please, forget who I am? I'm no one special, just an ordinary person like you who just got lucky.'

'Oh no, you are special,' hushed Cecelia with awe. 'I see

you on the television—and your charities are famous. You are an amazing person.'

Ruth smiled and blinked. 'You are so kind. I think you're amazing too. We all do the best we can in life,' she said absentmindedly with a sigh. 'But I will be so happy when I have my babies. I hope I will be the best mother ever, but now I'm feeling so tired. It seems I always have to be on show.'

'Well, that's understandable,' said Cecelia, buttering up to the royal. They had now reached the forbidden doors.

The doors swung open, and Dr. Deer was looking down at them, but especially at this nurse, Cecelia, with disapproval before he recognized what was happening.

'Where are you going?' he was looking at Cecelia.

'Dr. Deer, are you forgetting yourself? This is my new best friend, Clara Tinder, and I want you to be good to her because if you mistreat her, you'll be doing the same to me.'

A smile to Ruth and a frown to Cecelia. It seemed Dr. Deer had no choice. Cecelia had flown to the top on the wings of a powerful woman, and he had to let her pass.

'Hadleigh, be a darling and stay outside,' said Ruth. 'I've got myself a brand-new friend, so I don't need you for a while,' and then she grabbed hold of Cecelia's arm. 'We girls should stick close together,' she cuddled up, hanging on to Cecelia's arm as if they had been great friends for all their lives. And it was friendship which she needed as they walked through the forbidden doors together.

Power is given to a few people. It is a beautiful coat which forces everyone stop to admire it. And the one who wears the coat and knows its value will remain beautiful. And Ruth was wearing her coat well. Wherever she looked suddenly sparkled. A dull day became a sunny day. But she was selective with her choices, and they had to be the right people who would take care of her and speak well of her, because she had become one of the untouchables.

Charm was something Ruth had studied before she got to where she was. She had watched others with absorption, the people who had already made it to the top. Making notes and then aping these perfectly in front of the mirror. That little look which said, oh really, how interesting, while another expression suggested she understood sadness, and to respect the suffering of others. And all the time with a fixed smile which said she was the Madonna. Yes, she was well versed and well-practiced.

Paying attention and mimicking what these achievers had done in the past was nothing to sneeze at. Copying was the veil over a calculating woman. She was just your common tart, which was a degree smarter than those with scruples, which was why she was able to sleep her way to the top. But it didn't matter what anyone said, because their words now were only splashes in the ocean. Ignore these critics, and they'll go away. These weren't the people who joined her circle. They were frozen from her reality, and placed in line to be easily dismissed when they were of no further service in helping her up the ladder of power. The new law was, she was stunning. People who spoke against her were jealous, callous, and prejudiced.

But isn't this true because, in the end, everyone is envious of those who succeed?

When she was a child, Ruth understood this, and the way to success meant you had to have no values, no ethics, or morals when you're struggling on the ground. These were the things that would come later when you got to the top. Once you were there, you could relax a little and do what others expected from you. Yes, it had a price. And if you could live with the price, you will enjoy the freedom of the gods.

But Ruth had an image and vanity. She had learned quickly that not everyone was in love with her. Sometimes, she would fall out of love with them when they didn't have anything more to offer.

'We must be friends for the rest of our lives.' Ruth was still hanging on to Cecelia's arms. 'I instinctively know when someone is good. We should keep in contact all the time. I love my husband, but I also love my friends. Oh dear, I have to get undressed for another one of those examinations. Will you come into the dressing room with me, Clara?' Ruth's smile was wistful and hopeful. How could Cecelia refuse?

'Oh, I know I'm a nuisance and although being pregnant is lovely and all that. It would be nice sometimes if the man carried the baby.' And then, placing a tightened hand to her mouth, she giggled.

Angelina had been correct in her estimation. Whatever the world said about her, it was difficult to dislike Ruth. She had a way of looking at you, childlike and sweet, vulnerable and innocent. Even though Cecelia's logic told her it was false, the crazy arm of charm kissed the temper away to say, "what does it matter?" This was how she was with people who could do something for her.

Do not be seduced. For underneath the veil of sincerity and friendliness, Cecelia knew there was a snake ready to strike.

In the warm, well-lit changing room where the mirrors discreetly flattered, Cecelia helped Ruth undress. Her hand was flattering and gentle to the pop-bellied mother, who was nearly ready to launch. As Cecelia's hand stroked lightly over

Ruth's irregular-shaped body, she couldn't help staring at her abdomen. It was still huge for just two babies, which once had contained six. And then they moved. A kick, then a push of a limb, then two, a little leg ready to strike the world with life.

Putting her hand to her mouth, Cecelia gasped with surprise and shock. Ruth looked down and then grinned.

'Yes, he's alive. Do you want to touch it?'

'I can't,' Cecelia still had her hand to her mouth in awe.

'It's amazing. The first time it happened to me, I felt like I had a parasite growing in me. I've always wanted children. Go on, feel it.'

Almost trembling, Cecelia stretched her hand across and touched the fleshed veneer across the child. This is how all children are born, developing, and growing inside the womb's warm cage. This was where the magic of all life began.

And then they both smiled at each other.

'I wonder what sort of person he will be,' said Ruth, looking down at her belly. 'I hope he doesn't become anything like his father or grandfather. All whiskers and beard,' and then she laughed. 'Of course, I love Hadleigh until someone else better comes along. Well, we girls have to keep our options open.'

Ruth had got to the top, but it still wasn't high enough for her.

Cecelia stepped back to take the gown she was to dress Ruth in while Ruth's interested eye fed off her.

'Tell me something about yourself, Clara,' asked Ruth as Cecelia placed the gown around her to tie at the front.

'There isn't much to tell. I'm not as important and interesting as you.'

'Do you have any brothers or sisters? Are you married,

divorced, or single, and more importantly—do you have any children?'

'No, to all of that. I live on my own and keep myself to myself. I try to be a good person,' she shrugged, reluctant to say anything personal about herself. 'You know—'

Ruth's attention was now riveted to Cecelia's answer. If this was a loser, well then, she didn't want her, but maybe, just maybe, she might come in useful.

'How sad your life sounds. Well,' she placed her hand around the still moving child. 'I will say my prayers for you. I know what it's like to be alone, and if I can find love, then so can you. You are a beautiful person, but you must believe it. If you believe in it, it will come true. Look at me. I got to where I am, all by myself. I had no help from anyone—none whatsoever. So, if I can get to the top, so can you. Just believe in yourself.'

How many people can get to the top with self-belief if there are only a few places open? But it was a delightful idea, Cecelia thought on the way home. But what had happened to Ruth had not come out of sheer luck. She had plotted her route to the top by putting herself into all the right places.

Nevertheless, when you get to the top, it doesn't mean you have reached ultimate happiness.

Perhaps it is for some, but for others whose goal is to prove to those who had discriminated against you as inferior, who left you out of their sonority because you weren't born in the right class. Yes, and not forgetting those who always looked down on you and spoke about you when you passed, and were now suddenly your friends? What do you say to these people? Remember me? You thought so little of me, but I have exceeded you. You bow to me now instead of me bowing to you. When I had acknowledged you, you turned your backs on me. Now fortunes have reversed.

Ruth had become a door to these people. An entry for them to pass through into the same world of success. But what sort of door was this? Revenge sometimes comes in the shape of a trapdoor.

Will this person ever be satisfied? Cecelia reflected? Remember, be careful what you wish for.

She had nearly forgotten about Peter when arriving at the bed-and-breakfast. And now she was late coming back because Ruth had needed her. Ruth had suddenly made Cecelia her best friend, and as an honor, she had given Cecelia her phone number and made her promise that she would telephone her tomorrow. This woman completely overwhelmed her. Like a vacuum cleaner, Ruth was sucking every bit of strength out of her, and she didn't want to share Cecelia with anyone else, especially with Cecelia herself.

It was gone seven o'clock when Cecelia arrived at the inn. Peter was sitting in the corner, waiting for Cecelia to make an appearance. He had had a frustrating day.

'Where've you been? I've been worried about you,' said Peter, now stood as she came through the door into the dining room. 'It's your uncle, isn't it?' he was watching her face for any details of a demise.

'It was a close one,' she managed to smile, still blinking with surprise to find him waiting there for her. 'But he's survived the worse, and now I'm wondering if he might actually pull through and live.'

Peter smiled and reckoned with his thoughts.

'Well, I've managed to save you some dinner. It's pasta, which I understand you don't like from what you've said.'

'Well, I suppose I'd better eat it. It's healthy enough, I guess...'

'Look, and this is only a suggestion which you don't have to take. Would you like to come and have a proper meal with me at a decent restaurant?'

'Oh, I don't know.' This invitation was a great surprise, and more so because she found herself fluttering her eyelashes.

'Say yes, please. It would make my evening as I've had such a pointless day. Nothing is working out the way I want it to. Usually, I never have problems with my clients.'

'You mean you haven't found that woman?'

'Not yet, but I will. And I'm not sure if she is even in this country anymore. How can a person disappear like that? She thinks she has done something wrong, but she hasn't, and now it has become very complicated.'

'Okay, I'll come with you for a meal, but only on one condition and that I pay for myself.'

'Are you always so difficult to please?' Peter was frustrated. 'What's wrong with women these days? Can a man not look after a woman without anything else going on? Be friends with me, please.'

'We will still be friends even when I pay for my meal.'

With exasperation, he stared at her.

'Look, I get paid a great deal for what I do. You know, I have so much money I don't have the time to spend it. In fact, you would help me enormously if you would let me treat you—just for tonight, please.'

His sparkling blue eyes reached imploringly into hers, which made her feel strange. Dare she admit to herself, delighted as if it were safe to be feminine. Yes, it was nice to feel like a female. Relationships with men after the Thomas affair had made her very wary, especially after the humiliation. For she had believed he loved her, the way he kissed and the other things they did together. Which was why she couldn't believe he was married to such an unattractive woman whose face had been the inspiration for many famous gargoyles. Of course, this other woman had deserved to be loved, but by someone of her own kind, not by someone like Thomas, a god tossed out by the deities. How the humiliation still stung at the thought even now— even after all this time.

Running after him and pleading with him, she even offered herself to him. If only he would be kind to her. But he became a pig. He scorned her. Oh, if only she had left it alone, he told her when she found him walking along their beach with someone else.

'You were stupid, Ce-ce,' he told her in front of Merrilee, his new gal.

Who looked at Thomas with questions, the answers to which she eventually supplied herself. She could have this man as long as she didn't question him. So, now ends this lesson for Merrilee.

But they were the dark days that should be canceled and forgotten.

'Okay, that would be nice.' Cecelia suddenly remembered that Peter was waiting for an answer.

'Good.' His hand for a second touched her arm in a gesture of happiness.

'But first I need to change. Give me twenty minutes to shower and dress.'

'Yes, I can smell you. The same nurse again?'

'Yes, the same nurse.'

When she reached her room, she put her hand to her nose to smell herself. The odor of the clinic was barely noticeable, yet he could smell it. Something terrible must have happened to him in the past to be affected like this.

11

Sitting in the restaurant together was like having a holiday from life. It was wonderful to catch a cab together and be helped from the car as if she was a princess. She took his hand when he offered and felt herself to be very special.

The restaurant's specialties were swordfish and other seafood, especially lobster, crab, prawns, and oysters. Cecelia looked down at her thrift shop dress and wondered if the original owner might be here. She might even be here right now. And if her eye should fall on Cecelia, would she look with puzzlement, identify the dress as being one which she had previously owned? This was filling her mind so much that she didn't notice the beautifully decorated interior, which was probably just as well as she would undoubtedly have hesitated to go inside.

Peter escorted Cecelia as if she was his queen. Holding her hand up for the entire world to notice. People could not help stopping their conversation to look at these two together and make that comment to themselves that whoever she was is worth knowing. And in that contest of being special, Peter purposely ignored the maître d who hurried over to suggest a table. Ah, it was not to be, but he carried on walking behind these two enigmatic people enjoying their wave of speciality.

'I want the best Champagne you have,' Peter said to the man who was waiting at the side of the table.

'Yes, sir; I'll get your waiter to serve you.' With that, the very trim man of medium height, looking dapper in his sharp dark suit, walked brusquely away. With his hair slicked back, this proud and elegant man with an expensive nose left the table with it seriously put out of joint. He knew his job, this was his life, and his world and he had been offended, but of course, he showed it with elegance.

'Can you see anything on the menu you would like?' Peter asked with courtesy, wanting to make a good impression, and wanting Cecelia to recognize how important he was.

Cecelia's eyes were more on the prices than what this restaurant offered. 'It's very expensive,' she said at last, after looking for the cheapest dish to eat.

'I think what you mean is that time is expensive. It's the only genuine item of value we own on earth. My time and your time are much more expensive than anything on this menu. So, please, if you can't choose anything, would you allow me to select you some dishes?'

Shrugging meant she would be pleased if he took the responsibility from her. Taking up the menu, he scrutinized it seriously.

For both, he ordered lobster for main. Everyone likes lobster upon seeing the price. This was to follow a starter of caviar. And finally, Crepes Suzette.

'So, what do you think?' asked Peter, holding his glass of sparkling champagne.

Cecelia, though, had been totaling up the price of the meal. What he was about to pay for one meal could easily keep her going for a month on groceries and even rent. Yet, there was one person who Cecelia knew would appreciate these settings. While she looked at Peter, Angelina awoke from her grave in Cecelia's mind. Her silent face said nothing except she was waiting to see what was going to happen next.

'It's very nice here,' Cecelia's smile was followed by a gesture of discomfit, a quick glance about her, and then to Peter. This was a very different world from what she was used to.

In the middle of the restaurant was a heavenly chandelier, a rain of sparkles which suspended as if every soul born and died and been captured in its circle of constraint. Perfect. To the side, there were columns which could have graced and furnished Rome two thousand years ago. But was this all real? What people spent so much on décor, and how could they afford it? And then she remembered the price list.

While leaning back in his chair, Peter was pleased with her and her answer. He was appreciating her more and more while sipping his wine. She was the type of person he could get along with. She looked good, and she was aloof, which was something which also appealed to him.

'This is the style of life that I could easily get used to,' he smiled happily, chin and eyes towards the ceiling. 'I am rich, you know—not fabulously rich in the fashion of kings, but nor am I very far off it either. I could live my days in comfort, doing very little. I have enough money to keep us both and still have plenty over.'

He leaned across to catch her eye. 'The reason I work, is that I need something to occupy me. The devil makes work for idle hands, so they say. But if I have someone to share my life with, then I wouldn't need to work.'

'Everything becomes a habit after a while,' she smiled; she didn't know what else to say. She was in beautiful surroundings and felt way out of her comfort zone. But even to her ears now and on reflection, her answer sounded glib. But had he heard her? It seemed like he didn't. Had she heard him? Sometimes she knew that she only heard what she wanted to hear. This was such a lovely evening.

He was now staring at Cecelia evocatively.

'I have been doing a great deal of thinking, particularly about you.'

At last, he had attained her full interest. She tilted her head to one side, still dreaming.

'We get on well together, don't you think? I enjoy your company, and you mine, I hope. From what you've told me, there doesn't seem to be anyone significant in your life. You are on your own, like me. Do you like me?'

This was true, so why did she suddenly feel uncomfortable with what he said? They had been spending their evenings together ever since they had met at the bed-and-breakfast. Her hesitation to his question caused him to elaborate on what he was about to propose.

'What started me thinking was what you said the other day. For the first time, I considered alternatives to my life. From that point, I considered I had got into a bit of a rut.' His smile was vetoed by seriousness. Changing one's life should be done with grave prudence. 'I've been asking myself, do I really want to do this all my life? But the trouble is, I have never done anything else—' he scratched his head. 'But I could change. It's not impossible. We could enjoy our lives and travel the world together. I find I have a growing passion for art.'

Cecelia was still smiling after she had listened to his new passion for life—it was her. What happened here? Had he said what she thought he said? Yes, I believe he had. It was a shock to hear his thoughtful wants and needs. So much so, it impacted her head with vibrations and consequences. True, she had given birth to fancies and daydreams, but somehow, not anymore, or at least not yet. While his career was showing he was in a rut. She, on the other hand, felt differently. Nearly ten years of living on her own gave her thoughts to independence. His suggestion was sudden, and it came like an avalanche on to her quiet composure. And just when she was now deeply involved in her own pursuits, he was making an offer. *Come live with me and be my love*, but Peter was no Marlowe.

'Think about it. Would you like to travel the world? You're alone like me—and we get on well together, isn't that so? You care about me because, why would you bring my dinner to my room after I quit the table?' a frown poked between his brow as he continued to regard her, noting her looks, the shape of her figure, and how well she would do on his arm.

'Think about it. Once your uncle decides to die of his own free will, you will be available to go. And let me guess, I don't believe you are enthused about your job. I have been watching the anxiety on your face. From what you have told me, I don't believe that life has been kind to you?'

'Well—'

'At the moment,' he interrupted her. 'I have to finish this job, but I won't be on it forever. I know that quite soon, I'll get my lucky break. I can feel it. It's always the way.'

Her smile he considered meant she was thinking about his offer.

There was a great deal to think about, and while they ate

their lobster, Peter conversed with an admiring Cecelia about all the places he had visited. The exotic names like Istanbul, London, Milan, Paris, and even Russia. Visits that had nothing to do with sightseeing. This had never been his primary goal, but it would be nice to journey there with her and fill his head with the culture of other countries.

In her quiet way, Cecelia was noting everything he did. He was a gentleman, respectful and thoughtful, educated and eloquent; she could, Cecelia realized, not do much better.

In the light of other people's eyes, their togetherness could be seen as romantic. Two people who met by the whims of fate had found a gentle relationship between them. It might be their last chance. Who knows, for what were the chances of that?

When he saw her yawn, he thought she wasn't enjoying his company. He was peeved and suddenly irritable. For a handsome man like him, he was strangely insecure.

'I didn't sleep very well last night,' she explained, seeing the frown growing across his forehead. 'I'm not particularly doing anything, sitting there and watching, and when my uncle is conscious, I talk to him, but the morphine makes him sleep more. And the more he sleeps, I find myself also wanting to nod off. It's very—'

'Contagious,' Peter supplied the word.

'Yes.'

It was a relief for Peter because he laughed after she made this confession. He liked her more for it; she was refreshing, and she held every virtue he admired. When he totaled the bill, his eyes turned to Cecelia; she was worth it.

Another early night wasn't so bad. Ten o'clock was a reasonable time to turn in. He had a few places to go to tomorrow, and he wanted to make it to every one of them to complete the job. It was better to do this sooner rather than later. Did she mind? No, in fact, this would suit her well. It appears they really thought alike; it is what is called —harmony.

They took a cab back soon after that. There were people by the small bar chatting and drinking; they could see them from the window as they climbed the steps to the door. A couple of people who were by the dining-room door turned to see who it was when Cecelia and Peter entered and passed. These two together were undoubtedly going to be talked about. This was a story that they liked to spin out of proportion. True love, who knows?

Should she kiss him goodnight? Cecelia wondered when they stood on the landing before parting? Was he going to make that proposal and kiss her? Yet, despite what he projected to Cecelia, Peter did not appear to be very romantic. If there was to be a relationship together, it might not be a conventional one. But what are relationships all about? A friend in your life, someone you could talk to who you knew would be on your side.

As they were about to part, Peter, going to the right, and she to the left. They both stopped for a count of three seconds. Didn't he want to kiss her? It then struck her that perhaps he didn't know how to kiss.

'Well, goodnight,' she twisted. 'I'll see you tomorrow morning,' she said as she walked smartly away, wondering what was going on with him. Still, he was a nice man; she repeated this idea to herself. A gentleman, a man one could settle down with. A tame man—and there is much which could be said for that.

'Where were you?' said Ruth, answering her private line the next morning. 'I've been up since five. The baby keeps me awake.'

'I don't usually get up till six.'

Cecelia had a smile on her face when she answered the call, but not anymore. Ruth's familiarity knew no bounds. Back to work and back to reality, even though she was still at home, and even for her, her morning had not begun.

'Excuse me a moment, Clara. My husband is asking me who's calling?'

'Are you going to say, who called you?' the panic button had been pressed.

'Why, you, of course? The problem when you're A-listed and wealthy, everyone needs to know where you are, who you are seeing, and what you're going to do. It's security. It's very claustrophobic. They're frightened I will be kidnapped and held to ransom. And with Hadleigh's business as an arms dealer and provider of weapons to the world, they see it as dangerous when it concerns me.' And then she chuckled. 'He would give them anything they asked for to have me back.'

'You're not going to give him my name, are you?'

'Well, of course I am. Whose name can I give?'

'Someone else's name—please don't give him my name.' If she were going to be researched, then her cover would be blown.

'What's wrong with me giving your name? Aren't you to be trusted? Have you done something wrong?'

'No, it's this. You know I told you I had no one in my life, no family who I keep in touch with. Well, I do—did have a boyfriend, and he was obsessed with me. He told me if I ever had any thought about leaving him, especially for someone else, he would kill us both.'

'Is he nuts?'

'I left him nearly two weeks ago, and I'm trying to remain incognito. He's a police officer. Security and the police often move in the same circles, if you see what I mean. The likelihood of him finding me through your security is probably nil, but there is a chance—and if he does—'

'I understand what you're saying. But I've got to give a name. Someone who is real and exists. What name do you suggest I give?'

Thinking quickly, only one real name came to Cecelia's mind.

'You can say that I'm Samantha Mantle. She works in the clinic. You probably saw her yesterday. She was standing next to me.'

'No. I don't notice anyone unless they're important. Okay, I'll do this for you. But, after this, you've got to be honest with me about everything. I have to trust you. If you must choose anyone, it has to be me. I'm taking a risk for you.'

'Yes, of course. Thank you, Ruth. And now, for a while, I can still live safely.'

'Why didn't you go to the police about him? Oh, I know, he's the police. What's his name?'

'Why?'

'Because that kind of person can be sorted out. Now listen, I've got to go to my charity today for unmarried mothers. These women really need support.'

It was a strange charity to choose, considering her own pregnancy, but maybe this was her way of alleviating her guilt. The birth of Ruth's child or children must be soon.

'Has Dr. Deer told you when you are due?'

'No, I told him. I want the child to be born on the twenty-fourth of November, the birthdate of Dale Carnegie.

I wanted Cornelius Vanderbilt, but he wasn't born until May, so that ruled him out.'

TODAY WASN'T such a late night at the clinic for Cecelia. When Mrs. Blaine wasn't there, Cecelia was back to her old position. The part-time high life she had hadn't done her any favors with the other members of staff.

No one appreciated her sudden rise to the top while they were overlooked, including Samantha. Her popularity, if she had any, had sunk, but this was a job which she was not taking seriously; a means to an end.

When she said hello to Samantha, Cecelia was ignored, and for some reason, Samantha's attitude bothered her. She liked Samantha very much. Cecelia respected the rules Samantha had set for herself. Her dedication was honorable. No one was overlooked who she cared for when she was on duty. She was respectful and honest with everyone she had dealings with. It was the virtues of the old world. As well as that, she was also classy; she reminded Cecelia of an older version of Angelina if she had lived a while longer, but possibly without the problematic conscience. Poor Angelina could not turn a blind eye.

'I'm sorry,' Cecelia came over to the table with her tray in her hand, looking to take a seat beside Samantha. 'Please don't do this to me. It's not my fault what happened. I didn't set it up so I would be picked.'

Samantha looked up from her dinner with an expression of tired resignation.

'Go on, take a chair next to me. You're right, of course, but just try to understand how we felt.'

'I do, and I felt awful when she asked me to come with

her. Believe me; I would sooner be here with you and the others than with her.'

'Then you're stupid,' laughed Samantha, who appeared to have a sense of humor. 'If I had the chance like you did—especially on the first day. I wouldn't want to come back to this. I've kept my head down for over five years. I've worked hard and studied to improve myself. But I guess it's more to do with luck and who you know that helps you get on in life. Don't worry, Clara, I'll tell the others to get off your back.'

Happy to be back with the other staff and to make herself more popular, Cecelia thought she would confide in her friend Samantha. When she began discussing Ruth's annoying parts to Samantha, she was quickly stopped by Samantha's raised hand. Other ears were listening, and Cecelia could be reported and fired. It was the act of a good friend. A client's personal life should not be discussed, and this was a lesson Cecelia had forgotten.

Again, with admiration, Cecelia regarded this beautiful woman. With her looks and her qualities, what was she doing here working in this clinic? She must have some idea of what was going on with these illegal abortions? But perhaps she was one of those people who kept herself to herself, who preferred not to know and decided that she would be the best she could be. Unfortunately, Samantha was one of those rare finds, which in this day and age were dying out quickly.

But it takes all sorts to make a world.

Pleased now to be going back to her lodgings, and pleased that she had made friends with Samantha, a strong person who she admired, Cecelia felt relaxed with her wise advice.

Taking the Metro back to her lodgings, Cecelia thought admiringly about Samantha. She was the kind of person who you knew you could rely on and trust. But the irony was, and as Samantha had said, "there isn't any reward in being decent and honest, the more crooked you are, the faster you get to the top. But it's who you are to yourself, which is the most important relationship you will ever have." And this was true. It was something to think about and to keep on remembering.

PETER WAS on a high when he came into the dining room. His day, Cecelia worked out, had gone well for him because he came up to their table with a bottle of excellent wine.

'Well,' she asked eagerly. 'How did your day go?'

'At last,' he said, taking the seat opposite her. 'I found her, and she was in a real mess. I told her everything would be fine, and all she had to do was trust in me and tell me what had happened. I'm so pleased it's over. I've only just got back myself.'

Pleased for him, Cecelia was glad that at last, he had found the woman who he'd been looking for. This was a different mood she saw in him. It made him look young and boyishly handsome. She liked this side of him.

'So, everything has worked out for you—and the woman you were looking for. How is she?' she asked, feeling good that this handsome man was interested in her.

'She gave me the details and her opinion of what had happened. Of course, I have taken it with a pinch of salt on who said this and who said that. It's what they all do to save themselves from embarrassment. But in the end, it worked out well. And now she's gone.'

'Yes, did she say where she was going?' Cecelia felt the excitement like Peter. His high was infectious.

'I didn't ask. But now I'm free to get on with my life. A life of being happy with someone else.' He was looking pointedly at her.

'I haven't decided yet about what you're asking me.'

'Oh,' he was disappointed.

'I've got a lot on my mind right now, my uncle, you know.'

'Well, of course, you have,' some of his anxiety eased her answer. 'Your uncle must always be on your mind. I never got to know any of my relatives.'

'But I'm considering your proposal. It would be nice to travel the world and be your own boss. But I would still need my own money should you ever decide you have had enough of me.'

'Then we should get married. And when we are married, I shall put half of my money into your name. But why should we part from each other? I can't see myself doing so, and I expect the same could be said of you.'

She smiled at the talk of plans for their future, and the idea was working on her. The hardest part, she was starting to realize, was making that commitment. It was like glue; once joined, they would never part. Once they had overcome the acceptance which they had made, everything else from then on would be nice and easy. Why was she hesitating? Looking at him, he was everything she could ever want.

12

———————

The gentleman in Peter had offered to take her out for their evening meal. It was tempting, but she needed to get up early for Ruth's chat. Ruth had this thing of telephoning early; it was almost as if she was keeping her on the ball or trying to give her a nervous breakdown. But while Ruth could go back to bed later in the day, she couldn't.

These early nights that Cecelia was now advocating pleased Peter; he saw this as a wonderful trait and a good presentiment for the future. His eyes were now engaging on her with proprietorship. A critical analysis was being made perceiving her good qualities, and as to the bad, he could see none except perhaps with the way she dressed. But that could be remedied with some money; their tastes would soon attune to each other. And how much he had to tell her about himself, his thoughts on life, what he saw and felt. Yes, having a mate in life would be rather perfect.

While in her room, Cecelia went about collecting her clothes together for the following day, while her thoughts were on Peter. It was becoming a reality, and a potent factor in her life. Carefully, she was maneuvering herself into the idea that they were going to spend their lives together. Was this a risk? Of course, it was. They hardly knew each other. But what is there to know about a potential mate except that she liked him, and he was a gentleman who would treat her well?

At five after five in the morning, she rang Ruth, who this time had a better reception voice. She was especially pleased, because Cecelia was learning how to accommodate her.

'I thought I was nearly going to give birth yesterday—and by the way, I thought you would ring me yesterday evening at seven—I know we said nothing about it, but I still thought you would.'

It felt strange to apologize to Ruth when she knew she hadn't done anything wrong. But apologies are trifles in life; if it is all it takes to appease another, then just do it and move on. There are many more important things in life than to get bogged down by another person's silly whims.

Arriving early at the clinic, it became apparent that the starting time of Cecelia's duties had changed by subtle acceptance. Why would you arrive early if it wasn't for work? Being taken advantage of was understood by both parties, for what else did she have to do? She also reasoned that it was better to be useful with her time than wait for the eight o'clock contract to start. What did it matter? It was only thirty minutes.

Thirty minutes of being useful, thirty minutes of being unpaid. Was that the reason the clinic only had single women working for them?

During the lunchtime break, Dr. Deer came into the dining room with another member of the staff. Their faces were white with anger; something had severely upset them.

The two security men stood beside them. It must be something terrible, whatever it was, that had happened. The team fell silent, recognizing something awful had upset him, and he was set on blaming the people here in front of him.

Cecelia looked about to see where Samantha was, but she was nowhere to be seen. Which was strange? Last night, when Cecelia called out to her to say goodnight to Samantha, her reply had followed with, "See you tomorrow," and then she waved. Samantha only lived five minutes from the clinic, while Cecelia had nearly forty minutes and then a long walk.

Dr. Deer waited until the room was quiet enough for him to be heard. No one must cough when he talked.

'It's Samantha Mantle. She's dead.'

The room was struck by lightning as everyone froze on the spot. Except for shocked gasps, nothing else was said.

'Who was the last one to talk to her?' Dr. Deer asked, looking furiously about the room. His eyes, seeing Cecelia, stopped at her. 'Was it you?'

'I said goodnight to her when we left the clinic.' Terrified, Cecelia felt she was to blame.

He turned his eyes away to choose another one to blame. 'Does anyone know why she would kill herself?'

Killed herself repeated throughout the dining room.

'Well,' his eyes were hunting for the one who knew of this tragic vendetta.

Like everyone else, Cecelia caught up and began shaking her head. It was unbelievable that she would do such a thing—and now Samantha was dead.

'As you know, when someone is late, the clinic rings the person,' began Dr. Deer, narrowing his eyes for the criminal. 'If someone takes time off because they don't feel like coming in, they are immediately fired. When someone went to see her, they discovered Samantha had hung herself.'

A huge round of gasps once again flew about the room. It could not be true not to anything, but for Cecelia, the impact of Samantha's death hit her chest with a thud. It was a sad and ghastly day that followed, and as no one could speak about it, the oppression became even more rigid. Who would have thought that Samantha would have taken her own life and in such a way? It was so shocking to think about, mostly as there was no reason given as to why she would have done such a thing.

Like one of those nightmares that you never awaken from, everyone, including Cecelia, walked out of the cafeteria. That smile that was required made Samantha's sudden passing feel incomprehensible and bizarre. How can someone die like that when only yesterday she was relaxed and happy and warm?

'Do you mind,' said Cecelia, seeing Peter waiting for her at their table, 'if we give tonight a miss?' how she managed to get home, she didn't know. People on the train and thoroughfare were too bright and gaudy. It was painful to look at them. This was a second death that had come so quickly on the first.

'It's your uncle, isn't it?' Peter anxiously read her face and had come to his dramatic conclusion. 'He's dead, isn't he?'

'No,' her voice sounded like she was far away from the world and disconnected from humanity to protect her from any more pain. 'A good friend of mine died.' She could not bring herself to say that she had hung herself. It still didn't seem real.

'A good friend?' his eyes were searching her face for clues. She was robbing him of answers.

'Yes.'

And because Peter kept this vigil on her face, wanting to know every little detail about her and wondering how she had a friend he didn't know about? She had suddenly become alien to him. He was the only friend she had in the world, Peter thought, and now there was competition, even if they were dead.

'I meant to keep in touch with her,' she shrugged. 'You know how it is? A card once a year at Christmas, always promising to see her—'

'So, it's a she?' he looked relieved. Glad that it wasn't a he, Peter forgot Cecelia was still in a state of grief and shock. 'How old was she?'

What did it matter how old she was? It mattered that she was gone and in such a mysterious way. The one person Cecelia could never imagine would take her own life was Samantha, and she couldn't tell him the real story.

'I've got an awful headache and no appetite for food; would you mind if I went up to my room?'

'No, of course not.'

'I can see you've brought a bottle of wine for your celebration, and I'm sorry. I would have liked to have celebrated your success with you. You deserved to be happy. But it's one of those terrible coincidences. You've found the woman you were looking for while I've lost one of my best friends.'

'Never mind, there will be other times, I'm sure.' Peter looked at the bottle and smiled. 'I tell you what; I'll save this for another time.'

'Thanks, Peter, you are a wonderful person. I'll say goodnight.' She put a hand to her brow to show she still had a headache.

He understood because he nodded. But as she was about to move, a buzzing sound came from Cecelia's purse. He looked at her bag; guessing it was her cell phone, he diverted his eyes back to her.

'I'm just going to ignore it, whoever it is.' She had understood his scrutiny and knew this was another betrayal to him.

'You could answer it now,' he suggested almost aggressively.

'I expect it's from my work—'

'Your work,' he interrupted quickly, jumping suspiciously at what he thought was going on.

She had forgotten herself. The story she had given him looked like it was in jeopardy. 'Yes, they're probably ringing to find out when I'll be back.'

'But they know when you'll be back.'

'They should do; they're probably hoping I will come back to work sooner rather than later.'

'Well, you can't. You can tell them you're never coming back. Answer your cell phone now and tell them.'

Although she smiled inside, Cecelia felt the spear of worry cleaving through her chest. This was ludicrous. He offered a demand and not a suggestion. 'I'll talk to whoever it is tomorrow, but Peter, give me some slack. There's been a lot of things going on in my life which I am trying to deal with. I'll give you an answer next week, by then—' she left the rest unsaid purposely.

Without a doubt, his eyes were watching her leave the dining room. She could almost feel them. Oh god, don't say he's one of those people who is controlling and suspicious of everything. This might be the reason he's still on his own. Someone as good-looking as him should have been taken years ago.

This would be her luck, wouldn't it? Yep, she shook her

head up and down. A man with everything that she could possibly want, but he had to be possessive and jealous.

Going towards the staircase, she knew that all the other guests' tongues would be flapping. But for now, leaving the dining room, she didn't care. A thumping headache had, in reality, reached her temples. The oblivion of sleep was calling her; she needed to lie and down and forget the world.

In her room, she checked her cell phone to see who had called her? It had been Ruth.

At five past five the following morning, Cecelia was ringing Ruth as per instructions. It had been a dreadful night filled with interrupted sleep. Three o'clock in the morning was when it hit her, making Cecelia sit up abruptly. Someone had whispered into her ear, telling her that this was no coincidence. For two people working in the same clinic to die within ten days of each other was no act of chance. These two women had been targeted.

But just what was their connection to each other? If they were specifically targeted, wouldn't it damage the clinic's reputation and bring the law to their doors? But money buys silence and control.

Cecelia thought of Ruth Blaine and the fact that her husband feared for her life and had her under surveillance, as he did with everyone else who came into her circle. She was carrying his precious cargo, his children, and the line of succession. But was she more loved for what she could produce rather than for the person she was?

So, Angelina had been murdered, as had Samantha. But where was the connection between the two except that they worked in the same clinic? Only Angelina knew about the abortion of the babies even though they should be thought of fetuses, but her voice wouldn't be heard now.

There was a connection between these two women and it was completely to do with them working in the same clinic. Or was it? The answers had to lie in Dr. Deer's office. It's there he would have kept notes on his very important clients. Up to now, nothing was making sense. She was looking for the right answers in the wrong place. What she was looking for had to be right in front of her if only she could see it. Until then. The riddles were in what she asked her, so why had Samantha been murdered? And had Angelina just taken that jump into the next world? Was this all about grief and somebody else to blame?

'OF COURSE, YOU WILL BE TIRED,' Cecelia told Ruth the next day when Ruth decided she needed to see Dr. Deer again. This time, she came alone except for her bodyguard. 'My goodness, I would be tired if I carried as much weight as you are.'

'I am not complaining about Hadleigh, but sometimes. Sometimes—'

'Yes, I understand what you mean. If men had the babies, everything would be different.'

'Oh Clara, you do make me laugh. My poor baby must be bouncing up and down and wondering what is going on with his mama.'

'But at least he knows that his mother is happy.'

'Should be happy, but Dr. Deer is determined to bring the birth forward, which is not what I want, although I do want to get rid of what is inside of here.'

'Then, perhaps it is for the best. And then you will be able to hold your baby in your arms.'

'I have no desire to hold the kid; we have people to do

that. Oh Clara, I know you are like me. I can read your mind, Clara, and I believe that you have never wanted children. Now tell me if I am wrong.'

'Yes, you are correct, although I would do no harm to a child.'

Which was the wrong thing to say to Ruth, but she was not paying too much attention to what she was saying

'I have done everything Hadleigh wanted for his image.' Ruth complained to Cecelia, with a freedom she had never used before. Anger and frustration had made her liberal with what she said.

In her distress, whatever it was inside that sacred place, the womb, must be moving.

'I think we might be distressing your child,' said Cecelia. If she was there, she would have put out her hand to placate the bouncing fetus. But this concern fell on deaf ears.

'I always look good; I always say the right things, and I'm an excellent host to all his disgusting friends. Where is my life? You have no idea how dull and boring this life is. If we go to any parties, I have to behave myself and not dance. It's ridiculous. I'm the wife of a very wealthy man and not heir to a throne. But if I was an heir, I know royalty are still be able to enjoy themselves. I'm still young, while he is trying to make me old.'

Patiently, Cecelia listened to this spoiled woman. It could be said it wasn't Ruth's fault, as everyone had given her everything she wanted, and she had become used to it.

'Try not to get yourself upset, Ruth,' for her baby or babies looked to be doing somersaults, but still this sound advice fell on empty ears.

Ruth had found herself a listening board, Cecelia was the only one who paid any attention to her.

'I've undergone examinations—do you know how many

fetuses were impregnated into me? Have a guess. Six. I have no choice in what the child is going to be. It's been Hadleigh's desire all along. I wouldn't mind if he found himself a surrogate. What does it mean to me if there's a child or not? I don't care. But he doesn't want anyone else to have his child except me.'

Her voice whined on. She did not seem able to stop now that she had started. It was very difficult for Cecelia to feel sympathy for her. After a while of the same repetitions, Cecelia switched off as again her mind drifted once more back to Samantha.

'I know what I'm going to have. It's no secret to me. Hadleigh made it quite clear about the gender I would have. I'm going to have twin boys so that Hadleigh's line can be secured and carried on. He said twins to make certain that at least one will survive. I'd sooner have none. Twins are acceptable, but certainly not three, four, or even six. The sixth one had to be aborted, and that wasn't my fault. It's been a terrible imposition—and of that I'm certain you have no idea. I had to come into the clinic now and then to have the three others aborted—you promise you won't say anything to anyone? Because if the newspapers get to hear about it; I'll leave you to guess what will happen next.'

'What do you think?' Cecelia quickly and curtly replied. She had not been listening until Ruth said newspapers. Her thoughts had been entirely on Samantha. Why did Samantha hang herself? Why had her life become so intolerable that she spontaneously needed to kill herself like that? She had forgotten the dead conversation that she was supposed to be having with Ruth. The word 'newspaper' winged her back to where she was supposed to be.

'What do I think? What do you mean, what do I think?' Ruth repeated. The snake was now coiled up in anger and astonishment. 'I think you're being extremely rude to me. I could have you sacked right now, or maybe something worse. You know you would never work again.'

What happened? Was this a threat? If not, it came very close to it. Don't ever underestimate a woman like Ruth. She hadn't got to the top of the power stack without some dangerous fighting.

'I'm sorry, Ruth. Of course, I won't say anything. My head has been everywhere since yesterday. I've had some bad news.'

'Yeah, so what's the bad news then?'

'I'm not supposed to say anything either, but one of the staff I work with was found dead.'

'Well, we all have to die sometime. Anyhow, you probably didn't know her that well, but you're forgiven. I'll see you tomorrow then,' and then she hung up. No one gets to speak to Ruth like that and expects compassion.

Cecelia sat on the edge of the bed, looking at the chair in front of her. There was a frightening coincidence concerning Samantha. If Ruth had given her the name she was using, Clara Tinder, would it have been her now that was lying in the morgue, cold and still? No. Because Samantha had hung herself, which was something that she would definitely not do. Stupid to think like this, and yet probably natural when young beautiful women seemed to drop like flies.

Yet, in the horrible darkness of her thoughts, a web had been spun, and it was being drawn tighter and tighter. But who was the little spider in the middle? Someone was picking at the strands and making connections. If she had something to fear, Cecelia knew she should now start being afraid. Was it worth risking her life to get this story?

It was something Angelina had said which hadn't held

much value at the time, but now it had obstinately returned. Rich people had to consider their image and the face each of them projected to the world.

What is the price of an image? Is this what it's all about? Did an image mean death to those who tried to distort it and tell the truth? Starting with the aborted unborn. Yet, children are dying all the time because of where they are and who they are? Is it that important that we kill our own children to protect and save our image? But why not? In our children, our lives are carried on. For tyrants, and even the sick and insane, will have children. We will be remembered in our children, but in what way? The future history is not ours to even speculate upon.

We take our lives and our rights for granted, but changes happen, as do values in every era. Not everyone has a right to life, but those who do must appreciate those who have been sacrificed. Those who are privileged and in power must cherish those who gave up their lives and rights to keep them where they are.

But those who stand at the forefront of life, do they deserve to be where they are? If they do not honor their posts and show the values expected of them, someone else will usurp them and take their place. This is where image comes into play. They don't have to live the part, but they must create the illusion they are moving towards perfection.

Though for now, big money and power rules. This means they must set the example and be seen in the right places, and support one new idea over another. It doesn't matter if they believed in it or not. Just to be seen to care by saying the right buzzwords that were now fashionable, and the right words were now feminism, equality, and the rights of the minority. But for the powerful, the one and only thing that matters is themselves.

Interestingly, the most significant power comes from the bottom by people who just wanted to get on with their lives. Yet, one flick of their opinions and the top topple down to the bottom. The unhappy actor, the indiscreet politician, or the person in the wrong place at the wrong time, their lives are over. It doesn't matter what they've done before or how noble or kind they were—or even how much they say sorry. One mistake, and they're out of life's game.

These were Cecelia's thoughts for the piece that she was going to present to the world. The story of this game was taking shape for Cecelia, and she was compiling the right words to say. It was the death of an unborn that had started it.

Joanna, Cecelia knew, had been good friends with Samantha. Now why didn't she think of that before? These two had always been found together, chatting and smiling, although friendship here was frowned upon. A conversation with her might shed light on Samantha's death or give some understanding as to what had happened. But how would she approach someone she'd never spoken to before?

It was four o'clock in the afternoon, the time for the evening staff's changeover. The evening staff needed to know what had happened while they were away. And as she was the daytime staff, handover was also meant to be part of her duty. Although up till now, she had always been at Ruth's disposal. But today was her chance. Cecelia took the opportunity to sit next to Joanna.

There was no significant news to pass on at the changeover, except what new persons had arrived and left the clinic during the day. After the meeting, the staff made their way to the changing rooms.

'I still can't get over Samantha killing herself,' Cecelia caught up and was now walking in line with Joanna.

Joanna felt Cecelia's presence, but she refused to look at her.

'Well, it's something you must accept. She's gone, and there is nothing anyone can do about it,' Joanna snapped. If this new woman, Clara, should ask if she liked her, she would have no hesitation in telling her no.

'I shall miss her; she was a lovely person.'

'Yes, she was,' Joanna, frowning, didn't want Cecelia hanging on to her. The rather dull Joanna didn't take to people kindly, and especially to this over-friendly Clara. Only a week she had been here, and now her friend Samantha was dead. She wouldn't put it past the clinic to hire a worm to determine what their staff thought about them. As far as she was concerned. It was Clara's fault that Samantha was dead.

'To hang herself is so dramatic. I wonder what the last thing she thought about was when she tied the noose around her neck.'

But Joanna was remaining mute. This dark-haired, brown-eyed beauty was not as generous with her friendship as Samantha was.

'Joanna,' called Emma, catching up with them both. 'Are you going to Angelina's,' and then she stopped and acknowledged Cecelia. She was another one who also didn't trust this new stranger.

'Yes,' Joanna said, while eyeing Cecelia. They had to keep guard; she was an intruder who couldn't be trusted.

'Can I come?' Cecelia piped in, seeing this as her opportunity.

'Come where?' Joanna turning to the invader with fearless aggression.

'To Angelina's funeral.'

'How do you know about her?'

'Samantha told me.'

'I don't believe Samantha would discuss anything about Angelina with you.'

'Samantha was my friend. I asked her about Angelina—it's not a secret. I read all about her in the paper. What a tragic accident. I said I would like to go along to the funeral. It was appalling to die so young. But if you don't tell me where it is, I can find out for myself.'

Two pairs of hostile eyes stared resentfully at Cecelia.

'It's tomorrow at two in the afternoon at St Edmund's.'

'Thanks.' Cecelia's eyes brightened. 'I'll be there, and I'll buy her some flowers.'

'Suit yourself,' the two friends walked off together.

Puzzled, Cecelia strolled to the changing room. She had never come across such hostility before. Sure, people kept to themselves, and if they didn't want to talk to you, they moved out of your way. But usually after a while, they befriended you. But these two were extraordinarily belligerent, like they had something to protect and something which made them afraid. Cecelia had a strong feeling that the staff here talked about her behind her back, but she took their hostility and cold shoulder with a little touch of disinterest. They could say and do what they liked with her because she was only going to be here as long as the job lasted.

But tomorrow, she would be there for Angelina, a person she had only met twice and hardly knew. Another blonde earth angel who was certainly sweeter than these last two. And tomorrow would be her first weekend off.

'How are you feeling today?' Peter was waiting for Cecelia again on her return.

She had gone shopping for something to wear for tomorrow's funeral. He saw the bags and showed interest. Was she going to show him?

Strange how she forgot all about Peter when she was at the clinic; it was like he was a part of another life that she had compartmentalized in her mind. One side was for work, while the other side had Peter in it. Something to think about for the future.

It hadn't surprised Cecelia to find Peter waiting for her in reception. In reality, she hoped he would be there so she could show him what she had bought. In her bag was a new black dress for tomorrow's occasion.

'I've bought myself a dress. Would you like to see it?'

This invitation meant she was inviting him into her life and he knew it because his eyes beamed with pleasure. That awful sulk and suspicion he was wearing yesterday had dissolved and disappeared, like the early morning mist.

'You should have said you wanted a dress. I would have been pleased to buy it for you. I have more money than you, and it would give me great pleasure to spend it on you.' In his correct and incisive mind, Peter had already worked out that this dress was for her uncle.

'You are too kind,' for of course, she would not allow him to buy her things like clothes. And yet, in her thoughts, she was already spending his money on the possessions she would like, but could not afford. Such daydreams are inexpensive and really do no harm.

'Tell me,' began Peter, 'how long has your uncle got now?' He was hopeful, possibly counting the days and even the hours, and probably looking forward to the time when she would tell him her uncle was dead.

Though this uncle didn't exist, it still surprised Cecelia that Peter should be optimistic about her uncle's death. But this uncle's supposed death depended on finding out if the dismantled baby had actually existed, and for that, Cecelia needed proof that Angelina's story had been real.

And it all depended on Ruth. But Ruth had admitted to having had abortions, but information about when she had them was existent only in the misty times of the past.

Yet, it still was a shocking notion that people with money enough to buy an entire country could execute their child to satisfy their vanity and with no consequences. But what can anyone do to the parent when it was their child they had terminated? Did you put the mother away when she was cutting out her own flesh? So, when did these fetuses' rights kick into life when they didn't have a voice? And who would miss them if they didn't have a name?

Somehow, it seemed to diminish Cecelia's own status and rights to life compared to a woman as powerful as Ruth. An incomprehensibly wealthy person could decide that if they didn't like you, you could be sentenced to death with one word. The past warning to the future of the consequences of what happens if you don't listen to it. Torturing and illegal deaths, 3,257 people had to die for the vanities of Marcos in the Philippines. And there are many others. Many, many others.

More extraordinary was the fact that it could be covered up with the help of their friends. An association of like-minded people who will look after your back for you with the promise that you will look after theirs when they are in need.

This was not Cecelia's world, and she didn't recognize anything about it. The gains and profits of selling your soul to her were a world of insecurities. One day you could be on top of the world, the next day quite the opposite. These people's radar maps were selective. It was like joining a club where everyone followed tribal rules. In fact, it was unreal, and yet, it impacted everyone's lives. People in the middle who finished up in the middle of nowhere.

'So, what are you doing with yourself now?' she asked Peter while they once again dined on another meatloaf.

'I've been looking at houses.' He stopped eating now that she had asked. Elbow on the table still holding his fork for this subject was more interesting. 'Somewhere for us to live. I don't know about you, but I would prefer to live in the country and away from the noise and drama of city life.'

It was all so strange for Cecelia to think about, because honestly, she hadn't thought about it. Since their last conversation, this had not crossed her mind. To get a house together for her was way up in the air. This additional fact that she was going to spend her life with someone she barely knew came with the new idea that she was to spend it with him in the countryside. When she had always lived in the city.

Would she be lonely or, more alarmingly, would this man turn into a control freak who, once he had got her away from everything, could turn her life into a living hell? Sometimes, handsome and wealthy don't tick all the right boxes. This conversation with herself was surreal.

Coincidentally, these were the complaints that Ruth had about living with her very wealthy husband, Hadleigh. Would Cecelia also find this out for herself when or if she lived with Peter? He was very handsome, but was this enough?

'I have never lived in the countryside,' Cecelia said shyly, hoping that Peter wouldn't think of this as a criticism.

'Well, I used to live in the countryside when I was a boy.

It's all right. There is plenty of hunting to be done, as we'll have our own estate. We can rear our own food, kill it and eat it. Hunting is a wonderful sport. I would recommend it. It's wonderful to know that you can provide for yourself. Yes, it's the height of majesty.'

Killing her own food? She had lived in town, and her meat had come in hygienic packages. There were no feathers or fur. To see their eyes open and alive with trust, and then to witness their death, especially by her own hands. To know that their hearts had stopped beating as the creature slips to the ground from something she had done. No, she couldn't do that.

But in a fashion, this had happened to Angelina when the unborn's torso lay helpless in her hands. It must have appeared like it had waited for this moment to open its baby blue eyes to her. First and last look had been impregnated on her mind forever. If this had happened to Cecelia, she didn't know if she could ever delete this image from her memory. The impact of such innocence would walk every step with her, each and every day of her life. How would you deal with such a memory? Would you contemplate killing yourself?

'What are you thinking about?' Peter was now smiling, trying to peep into her mind. She had gone somewhere without him being there, and he didn't like it. He, too, had been doing his own thinking and musing and had concluded that he didn't want to be on his own anymore. It was a shocking fact that he had just owned up to.

'I was just trying to picture you as a young boy living in the countryside. Somehow, I could never envisage it.' She was trying to save herself.

'I know.' He was gazing into the distance. 'It's something that I, too, find difficult to believe. A time when I was innocent. But life can be cruel to the innocent. It takes everything away which you would like to keep,' and then he laughed and looked at Cecelia. 'I'm so eager for us to start our lives together that I can't help hoping your uncle will die quickly. Do you think that's wicked of me?'

'No, my uncle is nothing to you. It's as if he doesn't exist. So, no, you are not wicked. I can understand.'

'Let me come with you tomorrow?' he took hold of Cecelia's hand. His plea urgently needed to be fulfilled. His excitement now was overwhelming. She was the one he had been hoping to find for all of his life.

'No, I can't—I'm sorry I can't,' she was panicking. 'My uncle is frail, and seeing you with me might kill him.'

'Ah, I understand.'

Smiled Peter, but it was the smile of the devil; it was easy to guess what was going on in his mind. What was she doing with the dead when she could so easily walk into his life and into the living? He would undoubtedly be shocked to know what was going on in hers.

While Cecelia in her own mind worried constantly if he would understand what she was doing when she told him later? Already, she had broken the first trust of their delicate relationship. Lies. Their relationship had this far been based on lies, and then more lies. Sometime later, when Angelina's story was set in print. Would he understand when she explained she had to do it this way?

13

—————

When the gray Saturday finally arrived, peeping over the top of midnight and sinking its yellow-gray jaws into the young milk of the day, Cecelia met Peter at the breakfast table and was astonished to see that he was dressed in a mourning suit.

'An explanation,' Peter said, sitting down at the table. 'I thought I should visit the family's grave since you won't allow me to come and visit your uncle. But when you see me tonight, you shall see a different me and it will be a time for celebration. I think we should both go out tonight. It's Saturday night, which makes everything okay.'

Again, she hadn't been listening to him. Occupied in Cecelia's mind was how she would wear the black dress without Peter seeing it? She might just have to take that chance or wear another dress on top of the black one, just in case.

'Give my respects to your uncle, and wish him well,' said Peter, shaking his head.

'My uncle will never get well. He is on his deathbed.'

'What exactly is wrong with him?' asked Peter, taking the time to be interested.

'Nothing very much except old age, I suppose. Everything is packing up on him, but he has had a good life and has lives to a grand old age, which is all we can ever hope for.'

'That is a fine way to die,' Peter frowned and was just about to pick up his cup when something else occurred to him. 'I need to start living my life; this job of mine is not one I can do forever. A grand old age, you say. Getting old is something I have never considered. Yes,' he nodded again. 'To live to a grand old age would be something.'

Talking with Peter was never about small talk. If there was something important for him to say, then why say anything else?

'So, we must meet for this evening, don't forget your promise. You need to be cheered up, and that honor has fallen to me. I feel we have been in this relationship for far more than a couple of weeks. Don't you feel like we have known each other forever?'

She was not too sure if this was true for her and yet it seemed impolite to disagree with him, and so she smiled, which seemed to be enough for him.

Cecelia excused herself after breakfast to get ready to go visit her uncle. That surprised and gentle look on Peter's handsome face showed how touched he was with her devotion to such an old man, although he did not know how old Cecelia's uncle was. As for himself, Peter told Cecelia that he was going to stay down here in the dayroom where the bar was. It had just come to his attention that this is where the hotel bought in several newspapers. And as he had not interested himself in what the rest of the world was doing for a few weeks, he thought it would be a good idea to catch up on the world's current situation.

Upstairs in her hotel room, changing into that black dress, Cecelia sat and waited until enough time had passed. Two hours would do, surely, but she sat there for another hour just in case while making some notes on this future piece for the papers.

It was the telephone call from Ruth which had unsettled Cecelia on this of all days. Last night, Cecelia had explained that she was going to a funeral; it was her day off, which meant that she was entitled to do as she wished on her break. The subtle message was not quite appreciated or respected when the phone call screamed out on her cell phone.

'Are you at the funeral yet?' Ruth asked in a voice which was definitely disconcerted.

'No, Ruth, not yet, but I shall leave in a little while. What is it you want?'

'I have had an argument with Hadleigh. It's the first real argument we have had and me this pregnant. How could he do this to me?'

'Perhaps he's nervous as you both are becoming a first-time parents?'

'No, it's not that. Something has gone wrong with his latest business acquisition, and it's like he is blaming me for it. I swear he is going to kill someone—you must tell no one what I talk to you about because if you do, I cannot guarantee your life.'

'I promise you—swear to you I won't.' A conversation like this was enough to alert Cecelia to unknown dangers.

'Hadleigh is becoming paranoid; he suspects everyone. He is even suspecting me. I said to him, Look Hadleigh, I am like fifteen months pregnant. What do you think I am going to do in this state?'

It was a case of trying to calm Ruth down. Women in her condition are prone to exaggerated emotions, but usually this happens through the first trimester and not near the last. Being in this state of panic and terror would not do the babies any good as well as herself. Blood pressure for one. Unusually, Cecelia felt sorry for Ruth, who appeared to be going out of her head. Eventually, Cecelia said all the things to be said, and when she hung up, Ruth was in a better place in her head. But not so Cecelia, as her thoughts now mirrored Ruth's. A criminal minded billionaire would have no problem getting rid of the people who stepped in his way. This was what could have happened to Angelina and Samantha. She must watch where she was going and what she said.

At half-past twelve, Cecelia left her room. Surely Peter must have left by now. If he was still here, she was going to have to brave her way otherwise, she would be late for the funeral. It was another one of those heart stopping moment when she went from the stairs into the foyer. Peter, though, was nowhere to be seen as Cecelia's approach the door. A quick exit outside and a walk to the Metro, no turning back to see if he was there and watching her. Relief came when it now seemed like he had already left the bed-and-breakfast for his own strange rendezvous.

So many secrets she was keeping from Peter, and too many to count in the way of deception, but it was all for his own good. If he should know who she was, and what she was about, then that perfect image he had of her would certainly be destroyed. Dear Peter didn't know anything about women and what they were capable of. Men, they either want to destroy or put you on an impossible pedestal.

Once out of the bus station, she was given directions by someone who wasn't too much in a hurry. His pointing hand was all over the place as he tried to be as quick as he could. But it was a big church which couldn't be missed.

When she arrived, a large crowd was already waiting outside to go into the church. Busy with their lives and opinions as to what happened to Angelina. A lovely girl, but she was often too trusting. Cecelia mingled and listened, wondering at the different facets of a personality and how everyone viewed the same person so differently. She found that even going to a funeral was fascinating.

Everyone was dressed in black except for the people grouped to the side, and almost hidden by bushes next to the church, Cecelia could recognize her own kind anywhere. Journalists. The necessary evil, to give their version of the truth.

The way they were hankering to the side, they knew they didn't belong there invading on people's grief, but they had to do a job. This is what she told herself. News, news is what makes the world go around; we need to know to keep in contact with our fellow man. Life must be reported, and history must be recorded. The toll of the innings of wrongs and rights had to be rung out. It was part of life's cycle of justice. A voice suppressed is a wound that will never heal. But theses voices often change to fit the views and slant of the people reading it.

But why were they here with their big flashy cameras, an overstatement to show how powerful their work was? Although she knew this type of person, by their cameras, even by their clothes, these people at the church were ones she didn't know personally. It was fortunate because this meant she could ask them what they were doing here.

Relaxed as if she knew everyone, Cecelia wandered off in their direction, and when she approached, she smiled.

'You're from the press, aren't you?'

'Yes, mam, we are.' At least he took the trouble to dress in darker colors. 'Are you attending this funeral?'

'Unfortunately, yes,' she could see his paper and pen coming out. She had better hurry and ask them before making her getaway. 'Why are you covering it?'

'With a beautiful woman like that, her sudden death has made the news.'

'But it was a tragic accident. She fell in front of a bus.'

'It was tragic, that's for sure, but our boss believes differently. He thinks she was pushed. But that's his choice. Either way, it's still tragic. How did you know Angelina Madison?'

'Oh, you know,' Cecelia turned with a smile and walked away.

These men wouldn't pursue her, not at a funeral. Despite what they say about reporters, only the lousy media guys get the worst kind of coverage. The profession usually gets invited into an event because they want others to know how well they've done, who they are being seen out with, and other festive things. But they're only wanted when life is going well.

Drizzle slipped through the air, making this affair all the sadder. It was as though the world was weeping for its loss. On this gray Autumn day, Cecelia saw the other people from the clinic huddled coldly together. They were waiting for Angelina's body to arrive. Black dressed bodies flocking united in a conspiracy of grief, whispering to each other that this was a tragedy and ever mindful that one day, their ends would come.

Strange how the departed becomes the crowd's possession when the soul and body are separated. She was once identified as an entire entity. But not anymore; poor Angelina had gone away, released from the compound of her flesh. If people really had spirits, would she now be looking down on them and feeling pity?

A large black car, a shiny polished hearse, was now approaching slowly. Inside lay Angelina, her eyes closed in her eternal sleep, while she waited to be delivered to the ground. It was one of those disturbing moments filled with unutterable somberness and sorrow. One day, we will each make that journey. This was the thought which entered the minds of everyone waiting.

Now, as the hearse approached, the chill from the waiting flock spoke a word of respect, the hush of reverence. It stuck in your heart how sudden and sad this slow movement from life to death bore its passing.

Moving to the congregation's side, Cecelia needed to witness the car coming down the church's drive. It was her acceptance of what had happened and the beginning of closure. But then she stopped to catch hold of her breath, for watching and waiting was the unexpected figure of Peter.

It was Peter, wasn't it? The same brown hair, dark overcoat and suit that she had seen him wear this morning, to even the way he held his head. So decisive in his bearing, so sure of himself knowing that he had every right to be there. He should not be here, she was sure of it, but neither should she. Yet, her eyes would be more forgiving than his. And if he saw her, would he question her reason and then her honesty?

Quick, get out of here, Cecelia warned herself, seeing their eyes meeting ahead in the future. He must not see her because questions would be asked, and she had a great deal more to conceal than he did.

Keeping her face masked and away from his eyes,

Cecelia used other people's bodies for her camouflage. Yet, if he should turn now, he would catch her running out of the churchyard, a lone figure on an unforgiving landscape before she reached the black iron gates.

Then came that question, which stopped her and made her hide behind one of several mausoleums. Why was he here? If she went to him now to ask him why he was here, their answers might be similar. But why give him any information about herself? She had the advantage, and it was a good idea she kept this secret to herself.

Once the casket had entered the church, people started their walk silently in behind it. From the mausoleum, Cecelia watched Peter analytically moving among the crowd of black-draped mourners. It was as if he was looking for someone. Discreetly, he looked from side to side to inspect everyone's face before they went in. It was almost like he was making sure their feelings were real and wretched enough before going into the church himself. Yet, before he went in, he took one last look about the churchyard as if he was making sure about something.

Quickly, as Peter's eyes survey the church perimeters, her head jerked back to her hiding place. Had he caught sight of her? A whisk of her hair or the shape of her profile to answer his question—was she spying on him? Had he seen her? Would he turn back and cut across and catch her watching?

He didn't.

What was going on? Why was he here when he said he was going to see his family's memorial? Was Angelina a relative? How awful if she was? Yet, he had mentioned nothing about Angelina and the grief he bore. The only thought that made sense was that she must be one of Peter's cousins?

Perhaps her death was too painful for him to talk about.

Poor man. But should she mention she had seen him at the funeral? And if she did, what would be his question to her? Why was she at the funeral when she said she would be somewhere else?

Back at the guest house, Cecelia picked up her cell phone, which she had purposely left behind, and found that Ruth had rung her four times. This was an order, not a request, which meant she better call her back now.

'I'm in the clinic,' Ruth said, her voice frightened and panicking. 'I think I might be going into labor. Where've you been? You said you would be there for me when I give birth.'

'I'm sorry,' Cecelia begun. 'I was at a funeral.'

'Oh, a funeral. I suppose it was your friend again. Well, she's dead, and the dead can bury themselves. You need to be here and now. Damn it, Clara, get here now. I'm afraid. I'm going to give birth to two boys, and I have this fear they are going to be monsters. You will come now, won't you?'

'Yes, I've just got to change, and then I'll be there.' With her other hand, Cecelia was dismantling her dress by undoing the buttons.

No wonder Ruth believed she would give birth to monsters after the destruction she had done to her body. Too late now for regrets. Out of the black and into the yellow The color of happiness, and she should be happy now she had hope. Cecelia's skin and dark hair could take this color. Though for most of her life, she had chosen to wear black or gray.

Her finances were being stretched, and her limited supply of money was draining quickly out of Cecelia's pocket; it was wicked because she didn't command much. But again, she had no choice when the need demanded her to act straight away. Cecelia took a cab to the clinic.

'I've come to see Mrs. Blaine,' she ran exhaustedly

through reception. 'She's asked for me.' As she ran, she hoped that Frank, the receptionist, would know what she meant and not detain her.

In the elevator, Cecelia was carried to the third floor where the delivery room was, and she was still running. The children of the damned were about to be born.

'Stop!' Dr. Deer called to Cecelia. 'Where are you going?'

'It's Mrs. Blaine. She has been calling for me. She needs me by her side.'

Hate sat perched in his eyes; he stared down at her as if he could murder her. 'You can't go in there until you're washed up. If you contaminate the child, you could kill it.'

'I understand, sir.' Thankful for his lack of interrogation, Cecelia made her way to the changing room where she intended scrubbing up and putting on her clean uniform.

But other thoughts were stealing her movements because Cecelia stopped to watch Dr. Deer walking away. Something on her mind urged her to do something and not put it off as she kept on doing. This became her opportunity while Dr. Deer was occupied with something else. From the visit two weeks ago, she knew where his office was, the place where he had interviewed her. Turning right instead of left, no one was about. This was her chance.

Hardly anyone came to this side of the building. There was no need to. It was the business side of the clinic, yet Cecelia was still nervous because what she intended to do was illegal. Rules had been set down, mandates followed. A person in charge could do this sort of thing in their clinic, cover up, and lie. But where were those rules when it came down to the justice of what was right and wrong? Justice came with investigation, and the answers which were found from those meddling questions.

Upon reaching Dr. Deer's office door, her heart hit her

chest with a thump, her ears hearing sounds that weren't there. But blast, she should have credited him more than she had because she found his door was locked. For a few seconds of frustration and anger at the door, Cecelia moved away. Everything she did was without a plan, working on impulse, not thinking ahead; it was as if she was allowing life to do anything it wished to her. She always working on her emotions and never with her brains. Did she have a death wish? When, from around the corner, Mr. Blaine was walking, beating his feet on the washed vinyl floor towards her.

Their eyes met in passing. But he didn't stop; he didn't stop for anyone. Regarding her with interest, as if it was his right to know what she was doing there. Lowering her eyes, Cecelia continued walking away, determined to keep to her own beat of life, but hoping he wouldn't say anything to Dr. Deer and then wondering if Mr. Blaine would call her back to question her.

These few seconds followed on with an ecstasy of fear. The challenge of terror comes when it has no power. Mr. Blaine held every currency when it came to the supremacy of control, while her need to run out of the building was great to protect herself. What on earth had she got herself into? Was it really worth losing her life for this, even though people had died for less?

It was now that Cecelia understood how ill-equipped she was to write a living story, and it was also now that she blamed Angelina for choosing her instead of someone else. Why had she done this? She, a broken-down person, broken in the mind from the severing of strings that gave confidence, love, and advice. Is it your right to take part in life? Cecelia had lost that right many years ago.

That was over twenty years ago. Even so, the bitterness

seeps through, as all that she tried to forget was again raised to the fore.

Now she had nothing more to do with her mother. She didn't even care if she was alive or not, not after what she had done to her father. People accept that a woman is the victim of abuse, but they failed to accept so readily that it can often be the man. And Tina had abused him badly, not by striking him, but by humiliating him while he still carried on loving and caring for her because she was his wife.

Cecelia could never understand why her dad didn't say anything against his wife when she targeted him with her bullying weapons. Why hadn't he told Tina to stop it or accuse her of the same things? Like she was stupid, useless, who nobody else wanted. Why hadn't he defended himself? Cecelia listened, and watched, and waited right to the end, right until she couldn't take anymore. So, she accepted he was everything her mother said he was. It was true. If he didn't defend himself, then it must be true. So, why should she be surprised that the inevitable happened?

This last time, it had been her fault. Completely her fault. She deserved every bit of blame for her acidic tongue throwing scarring acid at her father during those last few weeks. She had listened and watched throughout all the years how her mother would taunt him and mock him. It always happened, and later, after Tina's terrible words, Cecelia would creep up and comfort him. She would put her arm around him to tell him she loved him. Cecelia knew it was her love for him which kept her father going.

Year after year passed with her faithful love, her mother's taunt was canceled by Cecelia's love. And then, one day, when she reached thirteen. The little girl was becoming a woman. Puberty that awful sin of adolescence, when a child's eyes close and a woman looks out. Suddenly, she was ashamed of him. Angry at how he allowed himself to be abused and frustrated that he never tried to defend himself.

"Why don't you stand up for yourself," Cecelia, as a girl, shouted at him. He looked at her and smiled so tenderly that it almost melted her. "I love your mother. How can I be cruel to her?" he had said. "Do you know how embarrassing it is to know that you're my father? I'm ashamed of you." It was the voice of her mother talking, and the power that came with it was liberating. With anger, Cecelia wanted to hit her father. She hated him for being weak, but then, alternatively, she tried to hug and protect him. If he could only stand up for himself and say just one angry word to her mother, her mother would back off. But not once had he spoken critically of her. "Cecelia, I am so sorry I've been a disappointment to you, but try not to judge me—or your mother too harshly. I can't do what is not in me to do."

Anger built up in Cecelia's face. "Then you're a fool, and I don't want anything more to do with you. You make me sick, and my friends laugh at you. They call you a coward and a wimp. They all laugh at you." This wasn't true; her friends knew nothing about her family except what Cecelia chose to tell them, which was that her mom and dad allowed her to do whatever she liked. "I'm ashamed to have you as my father. Why don't you do yourself a favor," she said, walking away feeling powerful, pleased that she showed her father how angry she was with him? Perhaps now he would pull himself together and act like a man. But she hadn't meant that he should kill himself. No, she hadn't meant that at all, and that's what she kept on telling herself for all those years. What she had meant was that he should divorce his wife. Didn't she? This was what she meant; she was sure of it.

Years later and this same argument continued. She had wanted him to stand up for himself just that once. But the stupid man didn't understand this. He strangled himself in the woods with a rope where no one could see to stop him. And she had killed him. This awful memory rang deep in her head. She felt she had killed her father because she told him she had stopped loving him. No one could ever love her like her father, and she had killed the person she loved the most. The arsenal of vindictive words is crueler than the sharpest dagger.

But what did this mean to her now? If only she could return to that day and repair the damage. If only she could grab hold of him and hug him. If only she could have been on his side to tell him all would be well and he could divorce his wife and she would live with him and not her mother. If only—But he wouldn't do that; he wouldn't leave her mother. How stupid was that? How stupid and cruel is life?

Unable to forgive herself for her part in his suicide, she felt it better to be glad he was dead. Yet, this too was also a lie. The conversation continued with who was to blame, but it always ended up being her.

The strength of remorse carries a life sentence. When would the time come when she could say to herself she had suffered enough? When can she make peace with herself and allow those demons of the past to make their way home? Perhaps never. Or maybe accomplishing acts of goodness would outdo the wrong and give her peace. Cancel out the cruel with overwhelming love. Or maybe she must change the nature of herself to understand life.

With the unborn innocence and Angelina and now Samantha's spirit, these three were free to find their peace. While for Cecelia, forgiveness came in appeasement by giving balm and justice for their wrongs. It was on the surface of knowledge and wisdom where she would find it.

While Mr. Blaine passed by, knowing nothing of the war going inside her head. She went to the changing room, where she scrubbed up and gowned herself before hurrying to the delivery room. In the distance, she heard Ruth's frightened voice crying from inside the birthing room.

'I'm here, Ruth,' Cecelia, calm and refreshed, rushed across to Ruth's white, drained, forever tanned face.

'Oh Clara, I'm so scared—take out the babies like you did the others. Give me something for the pain.' She was looking about the room for Dr. Deer while still holding on to Cecelia's hand.

'You'll be fine,' assured a low platitude voice to his suffering wife. Behind a white mask, it was still clear who the bullish, ugly man was, even dressed in the gowns of a white-clad religion. Mr. Blaine was not a handsome man and even scrubbed up and covered by the dress of amputation. It couldn't conceal the structure of a tank. Yet, his grotesqueness became beautiful when bathed and dressed in wealth. Taking no interest in Cecelia, he stood over his wife as if he was inspecting a new weapon.

'Just calm down, Ruth. We don't want anything to happen to our sons.'

A quick glance of cold eyes of indifference to Cecelia made her remember she wasn't there for him before he turned his attention back to his wife.

No affection for this woman who was to provide his life with pride. What was about to happen now was what he desired most in the world, young images of himself who would follow him to secure his vanity? These children would remember him in their lives. With flesh like his, a nuclear weapon would chime into the world that he had extorted. Who are we if we don't leave a future behind?

'What's going on? What are they going to do to me?'

Finding no compassion, Ruth screamed. This wasn't what she was promised. It didn't make sense to tell her she would be fine when her pain told her otherwise. Wasn't she the one he loved the most? And yet, he pathetically continued to tell her she would be okay because his mother had seven children, and all were natural births. That might be the way his mother had them, but it wasn't for her. She was not a peasant.

'This is my body.'

No one could stop her screaming. Her insides were being pulled out. The things inside were growing bigger by the minute, and they were thriving, kicking, and grabbing. These things had razors in their hands. They were slashing about with anger and with fun. This is not how kings are born, by tearing at her delicate flesh from within.

'Give me an epidural,' Ruth screamed like a shrieking Valkyrie and then an opiate. Ruth didn't want to suffer any pain; it was her body. Kill the babies if you must. Just please don't let me be hurt.

Her slenderness now was against her, especially around her hips. It wasn't possible to have a normal birth. Get rid of these monsters, and she will have more, but the next time it would be different.

'You'll be fine,' the beast pacified her while ignoring the blood pouring out from between her legs. Rivers of blood for his fabled children.

Time after time, Ruth screamed for mercy. It was awful. Cecelia wanted to put her hands to her ears to block out her screams, but the wrench of compassion was pulling her apart, and now the red congealing liquid was pouring from the table on to everything.

Yet, utterly immune to Ruth's pain, Dr. Deer's interest diverted to see if the straps around Ruth's ankles were still secure. A final surging scream was met with the hand of benevolence. Ruth passed out. It came as another metal instrument was handed to Dr. Deer to exercise the passage of birth of the newborn.

The first son was pulled out, crinkled and fighting and feeling the sting of the cold air about him. Eyes, ears, legs, head, and arms were pulled out, still intact and ready for the world. It was just as well that Ruth wasn't conscious when the second son entered the world, marbled with its mother's blood.

Two tiny boys, one larger than the other, had begun their lives, tempted by the dry world about them to take their first breaths before crying. It was a wonder to his father to see his firstborn's little fists curled and punching the air. Mr. Blaine laughed with pleasure. This was his son. He had done this. This was his creation. This child was telling the world that their father, the emperor, was here.

So, this was what it was all about. Two more males taking their places amongst the living, two more voices, two more sets of human rights had made it. Cecelia had released Ruth's hand to step back and survey the scene. The father had taken his first son, wrapped in a blanket as the still bloody child cried, bleating like a young lamb while trying to escape his father's hands. Did he want to go back to where it was safe and warm?

'You will be a rich man,' Mr. Blaine said to his son, holding the child high in front of him. 'And people will bow at your feet, just like they do to your father.'

Still, the child cried, unimpressed by its father.

'We need to do the medical checks on your sons.' Dr. Deer's expressionless face was waiting to receive the first son. The second son had already been taken off quickly.

'What do you mean?' Mr. Blaine didn't want to be parted from his possession.

'It's procedure. We must check his heart and see how his limbs are. We need to know if he's healthy.'

'All my children are healthy. They don't dare be ill.'

'If you refuse them their health checks, then let it be understood that you take the responsibilities.' Dr. Deer was indifferent to this man's claim to fame.

Stark eyes against indifferent eyes, the child was given to a nurse and taken away to be first weighed and then checked out and cleaned. The first indignities of the miracle of life.

So, this was life. Cecelia walked out of the delivery room to get washed up. Two of the fertilized eggs were allowed to live, while the others had been macerated and flushed away.

Exhaustion filled Cecelia's head and body as if it had been her who had given birth to the unidentical twins.

14

———————

One hell of a Saturday, and it was still not over. In the tumult, Cecelia had forgotten about Peter and how he was, and their pending life together. New lives alter everything.

What would she do about Angelina's story? Somehow, after the birth of these two young and real boys, it didn't seem to matter what happened about the third child any longer since some good had come out of his supposed death. For death is death, and it was a finality. Their removal from her womb gave the remaining two a greater chance in life. It's the way life is. Sometimes it's necessary to remove something to make room for others to grow.

Tomorrow, Cecelia promised she would talk to Ruth to find out how she was. But for now, Ruth's body was a mess. A lot of stitching was required to repair the raw ends of her womb. These two babies' entry into the world had cost their mother dearly, and they didn't even know it.

Unusual for Peter not to come to dinner, Cecelia waited for him in the dining room. For now, the children were born. She could start thinking seriously about her new life with him. How was she going to ask about seeing him at Angelina's funeral? If she told him she had seen him there, it would mean she owed him an explanation as well. Lying to Peter was harmful to their relationship. Even if it was a strange relationship, she still owed some allegiance.

Angelina was dead and laid to rest, and nothing could harm her or the fetuses anymore. So what did it matter? Sometimes you have to say goodbye to sadness from the path where others got off, and soon, your time would come when you must make your exit. It would be better for her if she thought this way. It would be safer. Mr. Blaine had the sons he wanted, and Ruth, the product of greed, had paid for it in pain.

Time goes by quickly after a disaster; she thought while watching dinner being brought to the first table. Soon the landlord would bring Peter's and her dinner of gammon and pineapple. Peter would miss it unless she explained to the proprietor that he had been to pay his respects at the church this afternoon. But first, perhaps she had better go to his room to see if he was there, just to check. How different she felt today after witnessing two new births. A time to understand your own worth and the journey everyone takes to get here.

Dashing up the stairs to his room, rapping on his door and waiting told her that Peter hadn't returned. It was now her responsibility to save his dinner. Yes, this is what a wife does for her husband when he wasn't there. What sort of pretty wedding band would she wear on her finger?

So, with an apology and a brief explanation that Peter had been held up, she asked if Peter's dinner could be kept —then an angry-looking Peter arrived with a rabid face almost foaming at the mouth.

'Leave my dinner there,' Peter ordered the landlord.

Speaking to him as if he was a servant. 'I'll be back in a few minutes.'

His friendliness to Cecelia was also thwarted. A brief glance at her before turning away as if he didn't know her or, if he did, he despised her.

What had happened? Did she or anyone deserve to be treated like that?

His lousy temper bewildered Cecelia. A changeling had taken his place. A man she thought she knew had become an ogre. She didn't like him like this.

While watching his dinner cooling, this became a time for examination. If he could change this quickly, and for no apparent reason. Then he was dangerous. He reminded Cecelia of her mother.

Tersely and with exact manners, Peter arrived to take his seat. She couldn't help watching to see the nature of his mood now. Purposely silent, upright, sitting opposite her, Peter was waiting for her to say something. Her refusal was adamant. He had scared her, and she wasn't going to instigate a conversation with him. But his leaden stare was penetrating through the shell of her skull.

She looked up. 'Is there anything the matter?' a lame and nervous question, yet by his behavior, it was the only one to ask. How this reminded Cecelia of her father towards her mother.

'Do you remember when I told you I found that woman?'

A humble, 'yes.'

'Well, she wasn't the one. I found out today that I was given the wrong name.'

'Oh dear, I'm sorry.'

'What are you sorry about?'

'Well, for you and the trouble it's causing you.'

'Don't worry about me, it just means our future is delayed for a while, but I'll find her. I always do.'

'Is this really your problem? You can resign. You said you were going to. So, why not quit now and leave the problem for someone else?'

'It's a matter of honor.'

'Well then, stay and work on it, but please stop your temper towards me. I haven't done anything wrong.'

'You're right. I mustn't be like this towards you,' he smiled. 'I shouldn't show you my bad side.'

Mentally, Cecelia sat up. Never had she expected that Peter could have a bad side. Those awful years of her mother taunting her father with her vicious temper came flooding back. She could hear her now. On and on, she would spit wicked abuses, telling him he was stupid, worthless, and worse, impotent. Why didn't he answer her back? Why did he cower when she emptied her foul mouth?

'I don't know what I ever saw in you. Everyone told me you were useless. I thought they were wrong, but it turned out you're worse than useless.'

Dad stood there taking it. He always looked so sad.

Only once had Tina tried it on her, and never again. An almost forgotten memory buried deep within the dust of shock, but now had found life again by recollection. Her mother raised her hand to her once when she was drying the dishes. There wasn't any reason for it. But it was enough. She had seen episode after episode of her father's despair, and this would not happen to her. Picking up the carving knife still lying on the draining board, Cecelia stood her ground and threatened to use it on her mother. And she meant it. Cecelia's frantic self-protection had been driven by fear.

Never had her mother looked so surprised. In some

ways, she seemed as if she was strangely proud of her daughter?

'What is this?' smiled Tina, surprised. 'The baby tiger can bite?'

'Go on, try it and find out for yourself if your blood is red,' urged Cecelia's brilliant eyes, pointing the knife and stabbing into the air.

'You are most definitely not your father; you take after me,' Tina nodded and smiled before wandering off. Never did Tina try this again. So why hadn't her father been able to do that to save his pride and her respect for him?

'I am never like you,' she screamed after her mother. 'Never—'

She looked up to find that she was now back here in the safety of the present with Peter, in the reliable and worn-out present which was always renewing itself.

'It means we will just have to wait longer,' Peter looked at his dinner while gathering his thoughts before deciding to eat. He took up his fork and poked the pineapple about the plate before it joined the sweet corn.

'Wait longer?' she puzzled.

'Yes. We will get married a couple of weeks later. You know,' Peter looked up from cutting his gammon. 'The more I think about getting married, the more I like the idea. I will have a wife,' he nodded cheerfully. 'A wife who will look after me, who I can confide in, and I will look after her,' he chuckled to himself.

Who was he? watched Cecelia analytically, for now she was unsure. The man who had left to clean up minutes ago was not the man now sitting opposite her. She had seen a glimpse of someone else, a man of intolerance, bad manners, and arrogance. A man who she could not possibly like and certainly not one to be married to, either. What did she know about him? Nothing. But there was one question itching for an answer, which was why he was at Angelina's funeral?

'How did your day go at the funeral—I mean, the church?'

'Funeral?' he looked at her face with enigmatic surprise.

'Sorry, I got my words mixed up, although, to me, they both mean the same.' She was sliding on ice.

At first, he was surprised and then amused. Still holding his knife and fork, he smiled and regarded her as if she had taken a wrong turn and collided into his mind. 'Strange you should say that. I ended up going to a funeral. I found myself caught up in this crowd of mourners, and because I had completed what I had gone to do there today, I thought I would go along with the funeral-goers and see who it was.'

'Who was it?' Cecelia's eyes were trapped on his face, waiting to hear what she was now fearing what he would say.

'A lovely looking young woman who was in the wrong place at the wrong time. Very sad, but this sort of thing happens.'

Coincidence. The crime of coincidence.

His gammon lay on his plate, looking like the meat of death. Raw, now that the pineapple had been disposed of. Stab marks had hacked it to pieces. Yet, when she blinked, the piece of cooked pink flesh was still intact. Cecelia twisted her eyes, feeling she could be sick.

Should she own up to being there at the funeral herself? No, she wouldn't. She wasn't prepared for this in-depth discussion.

'And how is your uncle?' Peter looked at her mouth and then her eyes.

'I don't think it will be too long now. He's getting frail.'

A discernible smile rested on Peter's lips. He couldn't wait until she told him that her uncle was dead. Under the cloak of his eyes, he was already attending another funeral.

While her meal waited to be enjoyed, her appetite had left. Uncomfortable thoughts were now troubling her.

'How did you get into your line of work?' Cecelia asked while trying to place a piece of gammon and pineapple together.

'You want to know about my history from when I was young?' He rubbed his chin as if he was checking to make sure he had done a good job of shaving today.

Is it a good or a bad thing to delve too deeply into someone else's life? Peter was in his early forties; he would have had a past as she had. No one goes through years of life without ugly problems and passions arising.

There was something exotic and mysterious about him. He could have been a Heathcliff from *Wuthering Heights*, a man unknowable to anyone and who always arrived with a fortune. This gypsy, a bohemian who is answerable to no one. Who ruled his own world and dealt out his own sentences? And isn't that the romance of someone like him which makes you believe he had a contract with the devil? If he didn't, you would want to know why.

Was she in danger of making him into something he wasn't?

'I suppose it was after my brother's death—'

'How did he die?' Cecelia's curiosity had turned morbid.

'An accident; the police confirmed it was an accident.'

Tight with interest and a little fear, Cecelia waited for him to continue. His eyes were already regaining his steps back to the past to clarify and develop that picture which still held court in his mind.

'Sad and tragic, and yet my parents blamed me for what

happened. Of course, it was never me. Call it their grief. There was only one year between James and me, you see. I was eighteen, and he was seventeen.'

His cutlery had settled back on his plate as he took hold of his glass of water. A sip to wet his palate, and then his eyes moved elsewhere in time.

'Presumably, my parents thought it was my responsibility to be my brother's keeper, and to a certain extent, James was obedient to me. But though he was taller than me, by an inch. I was the stronger and the more athletic of us both; he knew this; he was always challenging me.' Peter smiled. 'And I always won.'

Could water be turned into wine? Whimsically, Peter looked at his glass and put it down. Some things happen in life, which goes against the logic of nature.

'As I was the eldest, it was natural that I would be stronger and cleverer and wiser than him, but it wasn't enough for James. He always wanted to beat me. But there can only be one winner in a family, particularly amongst brothers.'

Should she tell him to stop now? Telling his story must upset him and yet he was smiling.

'It's a shame he wanted to prove himself against me, as he would never win—'

Staring into space and watching the gowns of mists pull their veils away to give him a clear view before shrouding his eyes again. He was back there once more.

'They found him hanging by his neck in a shrubbery. He believed me when I told him I had been able to do that, and do so while still avoiding being hung, that is. I never thought he would try it. And so, my parents blamed me. Accidental death—'

'Oh, you poor thing,' cried Cecelia, for the images which

Peter had conjured up were now accessing her mind with a vivid array. She could see what he saw, or at least, she could imagine it.

He barred his hands to Cecelia, anticipating a hug of emotions. And this was his story and his past. He didn't want her entering.

'That was twenty-five years ago. People die,' Peter laughed, now embarrassed. 'My brother has passed through the biggest mystery in life, as I will do, but now. I'm hoping it will be later rather than sooner. You have given me a reason to live. And we shall live and live grandly. I would never have thought I would do or say this. I just hope that I haven't tampered too much with fate's grand plans, and if I have, I hope I will be forgiven. What do you think?'

Cecelia didn't know what to think. Here sat this handsome man, Peter. A man who was very cultured, intelligent, and yet, who was also guarded, and sometimes a monster. What landscape did he travel to and inhabit? Would it be so different from hers? Possibly.

'I think we should eat our dinner before it gets too cold.'

Obediently, Cecelia picked up her knife and fork, and with a quick stolen look towards Peter, she began to eat. She had never experienced what it was like to have a brother or sister, a relationship to cherish, or one to curse for the rest of her life.

Forgotten was that other man who walked in with destruction.

Sunday morning came, which should have been a time for a lie-in. But as Cecelia snuggled under the covers and listening warmly inside to the noise bustling outside her door, her cell phone buzzed. She didn't need to think too hard about who it was. Her guess was correct. Ruth was ringing.

Ruth demanded that Cecelia visit her. What? On a Sunday.

Cecelia could have refused because this was one of her days off, but her mind counseled that if she wanted this story, she had better play sweet. And another thing, she now had an enormous debt to pay off. She had to get serious with her life.

Better get up and dressed and on with life, as you never know where this opportune visit would take you. Perhaps Ruth, now that they had suddenly shared something extraordinarily special, would offer her a job as her PA or something. But who was she fooling? This woman used people, took what they had to offer for her own self. Just like her husband, this couple were users of humanity's generosity.

Eight on a Sunday morning, and breakfast was being served, brings in a host of wonderful expectations. Cecelia could smell toast and crispy bacon and hear the bubbling coffee percolating. Of course, she was tempted to stop for a few minutes and eat her fill, but Mrs. Blaine was waiting, and every second counted and totaled against Cecelia. A quick look into the dining room assured her that Peter wasn't in there either. He was probably lying in bed and enjoying his long Sunday morning sleep. One day, she romanticized he would be lying beside him. And yet, he had never kissed her.

'I'M IN AGONY,' said Ruth when she saw Cecelia coming through her suites. 'And they won't give me anything. Do you know what they did to me? They split me up the middle so they could get the brats out. They've ripped me apart. Slit my clitoris and circumcised me. I'll never be able to feel anything again—and Hadleigh was the one who gave his permission to do this to me. I shall never forgive him —never.'

'I'm so sorry,' Cecelia came closer; the drip and beeping machinery held her back. For the first time, she felt sympathy for Ruth.

She who had slept her way to the top had been robbed of any future sexual pleasure. It was a high price to pay for her love of power and money.

'I'll never be good enough for anyone else. No one as damaged as me will be wanted by anyone.' Ruth's eyes squinted to fine slits, searching about her room for revenge from the mutilation which had been done to her. 'I'll get my own back on him,' she murmured to herself. 'No one does this to me and gets away with it—oh, my god. I can't even go for a pee. They've got me hooked up to a catheter—look.'

There was blood in Ruth's urine; she wasn't faking what she was saying.

'You've got to help me. You've got to get me something to take. He doesn't want me to take anything because of the babies. He says I must breastfeed them, but I'm refusing until he gives me something to help with the pain. I've married a monster.'

'What do you want me to do?' Cecelia looked horrified. How could that man do something like that to this woman?

Savage.

'Get me some medication—I need something to help me. It's driving me nuts.'

'I don't have any paracetamol on me.'

'Fuck paracetamol. I want morphine, it's the only drug which will stop this. And I know where to find it. They will have morphine in this place—for god's sake, it's a fucking clinic, isn't it?'

'Yes, but I'm not allowed to deal out any drugs. I don't have a license.'

'You don't need a fucking license. You're such a stupid bitch. Don't you realize the pain is driving me insane? If I had known what he was going to fucking put me through, I would never have agreed to it or married him. I hate him.'

'I'm sorry.'

Ruth's eyes, doused in evil were flashed at Cecelia.

'If you want to help me, I will tell you what to do—I don't have anyone else who could do this for me—so I'm relying on you.'

'What do you want me to do?' Cecelia was nervous.

'It's in his office. Go to Deer's office, and on the back of the wall when you walk in, there's a painting. Look behind the painting, and you'll find a safe. Open the safe, and you'll find Deer's own private stash of morphine. Yes, you may look shocked; but Deer is an addict. I want one of those vials.'

'Even if I could do that for you, I don't know the safe's combination.'

'In my purse over there on that chair, open it, and inside you will see a frog engraved on the inside. Pull the frog, and you will find a piece of paper with the safe's number.'

How did Ruth get the combination of Dr. Deer's safe? Nothing was going to be banned from Ruth.

Cautiously, not liking what Ruth was asking her to do, Cecelia picked up the purse to look inside. A bright green silk frog with green cubic zirconia was sparkling at her and daring her to touch its embroidered body.

'Before this all started, Hadleigh and I had an interview in Deer's office.' Ruth watched her from her bed. 'My husband signed a contract which Deer put into his safe. I watched him very carefully when he opened it, and I remembered the numbers. I'm not stupid, you know.'

'I don't know if this is a good idea.'

'You know what this life is all about?' Ruth's question wasn't waiting for an answer. 'It's about taking chances. You'll get nowhere if you don't gamble.'

Staring at Ruth, Cecelia could see the price of her chances. To her, it seemed she had robbed more than she had stolen.

'For god's sake, you've got to do this for me. I've no one else I can ask. I'm being tortured. My vagina has been split up the middle, and all my goddam entrails have been ripped out. What have I done to deserve to be punished like this?'

'Okay, I'll do it,' yet she was thinking, what will you do for me? The frog's glittering eyes were provocative. It was daring her to touch him. Pulling at its twisted green face. A pocket came away to reveal a piece of paper inside. There were numbers written on it—The numbers to Deer's safe.

'You will find he has half a dozen syringes in his safe,' Ruth continued from her bed, her eyes anxious and needy and believing that soon her pain and discomfort would cease. 'Bring me one.'

'I don't know how to inject,' panicked Cecelia.

'You don't need to. I can do that for myself.'

'And another thing; what if Dr. Deer's office is locked?'

Garnished with pain, yet Ruth could still smile. 'You see, unlike you, I plan for everything. That's why I'm here, and you're there. That's the difference between us. I always get what I want because I make certain of it. Inside my makeup pouch, you will find a key. Take it. This will open the door for you.'

Hesitating again, Cecelia found the green-colored makeup container which held the key. In a way, Cecelia wished she hadn't found it, as this was taking her on to the second step.

How on earth did Ruth get that key to Dr. Deer's office?

'I won't be long,' Cecelia said, biting her lip. Adrenalin was pumping freely through her veins, making everything she did brighter, sharper, and more painful.

Since the Thomas episode, Cecelia always veered for the safest course in life, but after that interview with Angelina, a change came stamping through into her life, wrecking her safe and sane rut. There was no turning back now.

Resenting what she was asked to do by a woman who made sure she only feathered her own nest, Cecelia took the walk to Dr. Deer's office while reminding herself how she should be and look. Not to bring attention to herself, she held her back straight, stood tall, and walked with purpose as if she had every right to be there. It worked; passing three people, they gave her nothing except a quick glance.

In the depth of her hot and sweating hand was the key. In her palm was the key's imprint. Trying not to fumble, she pushed the key into the lock and turned. But in that fractured second came that question. Will this key open the door? The soft click rewarded her with an entrance as the door sprung open. Just like in Alibaba, opium gold was waiting to be collected.

Impeded by the knowledge that this was Dr. Deer's territory, Cecelia walked on knives to cross the room to the painting. Nothing special. The picture was an artistic projection of an ideal countryside. Inanimate eyes wouldn't tell on her; she was safe, even though she knew what she was doing was wrong. But did her wrong outstrip Dr. Deer's and his slaughter? It didn't matter if you had good lawyers.

Feeling her fingers over the gold leaf on the edge of the

painting, a little tug, and it pulled away with a click. Behind the image was Dr. Deer's private safe.

She had better be quick. Holding on to her feelings was becoming costly. Taking the piece of paper now screwed up from her hand, she read the numbers and turned the dial. Seven forwards, twenty-eight back. Numbers seemingly picked out at random, but a memory and an identity belonging to this safe and owner. Was this somebody's birthday? With every click of the lock, the tension in Cecelia's body tightened.

The porthole opened to reveal a cave of fantastic acquisitions. Stacks of money, letters of worth, and a stash of what Ruth had desired. Collecting a vial and one of the syringes, Cecelia closed the door and then pushed back the painting. Her deed had been completed, and it was time to hurry back to Ruth to give her that fix. Yet Cecelia stopped to look about her to see if she had left anything of herself. Nothing.

Out of the office, she rushed back, just in time to see a nurse coming from Ruth's room. All the medical checks completed, blood pressure, heart rate, and the catheter had been made afresh. Then Ruth, eager-eyed, told her to leave her room.

'You have no idea how grateful I am to you,' said Ruth, holding out her empty hands, anticipating they would be filled with what she desired. Peeling off the cellophane, all the while her slender fingers were trembling, she couldn't wait to put this opioid into her vein.

'You mustn't take too much,' cautioned Cecelia.

'Don't worry; I know how to handle myself.' Ruth pushed the syringe into the bottle top. 'In that drawer there, you will find a stocking. Get it for me.'

Passing the stocking, Ruth wrapped it around her arm and pulled it tight. Now tapping her arm after filling up the syringe, Cecelia watched with alarm as Ruth pushed the needle into her vein.

In seconds, relief flooded Ruth's face, and the lips which had pulled so cruelly down now relaxed into a smile.

'Thank you,' she whispered calmly. 'Put these things into my purse now and give me my purse. I need them close by me.'

'What about breastfeeding?'

Ruth sighed. 'Then they will have their first fix of morphine.'

15

Not regretting what she had done for Ruth, Cecelia left her room, thinking about what she had just achieved. It was now Sunday. The day Dr. Deer was most likely to take off, which would be a good time to do what she knew she had to do. Here was her chance. While she had been in the room, her quick glance around had revealed that Dr. Deer had his own refrigerator with a freezer.

What was stored in it? Possibly the usual things one would find in a hospital. Vaccines, medications, and things that needed to be cooled or kept in frozen storage to preserve their life. So, apart from his own stash, which he kept in the safe, what else was in this frozen tank? The only way she would find out was to look.

It was just an idea, but one which fascinated and tempted her thoughts to suggest this needed investigation. And as it was a Sunday, this was the day to check out her hunches and find out why that container had any business being in Dr. Deer's office.

A fertility clinic is a place where dreams are made which

nature can no longer disappoint, for everyone should be allowed to have children. And once the genie has been released from its bottle, the barren become fertile.

Back along the corridors to Dr. Deer's office, Cecelia wondered how many children had been created here. How much laughter has echoed because of this human intervention, and then how many had been destroyed? All the sons and daughters never to be known or suffer the pains of living are lying somewhere ingrained in the earth. She could not help wondering about her own life and creation. Where do we begin, and where do we end? Was it always by accident or is it all at the point of a whim? How can you plan for any child when the rush of the sperm to win is the first part of the race? And then the requirement to be fit and prepared for the world when you're born.

It was her opinion that all the answers to her questions would sit waiting in Dr. Deer's refrigerator.

With the key, Cecelia gained entrance again to his office. The seconds were ticking away. This time, it was the cooler which was her goal. No hesitation now. Her quick breaths were timed with her every action. Cecelia had rehearsed this type of scenario before. Everything action was calculated.

The drone of the fridge was running, humming a secret language recorded by the ancients.

In this sarcophagus, Cecelia's faith was placed on what was stored in it. If she had any insight into Dr. Deer's mind, such things as evidence would never be disposed of, for that time might come when he would need it. And he would be stupid or vain enough to store the proof, depending on how you looked at it.

Her terrified heart was bouncing around her chest, as if eager to get out. Oh, if only inanimate things could talk, what would they say to us?

She nearly crossed herself standing in front of the tomb.

This cooling system was like any other domestic cooling system which you keep in your house, but this one contained ghoulish secrets. And the seconds were passing by.

Breaking open the door to the freezer, came with a hiss as the seal released the frozen air. Or was it her imagination? Balanced on a white wired shelf was a plastic container. Once upon a time, it could have held sandwiches, or leftovers from a previous meal. Her heart kicked again as she held the icy container in her hands.

What a simple little device to contain such knowledge. It came with a push on lid which easily clicked open under some pressure.

Already she knew what she would find. Trapped in time, a small frozen body the size of an unborn child waited. A child who lay in eternal sleep, its broken body torn asunder, had now been pushed back together again. The littlest Humpty Dumpty who could never be put back together again was here. Jagged flesh of his tiny leg had once thrashed, kicking life with promises that one day, he might be an athlete had now been put to rest. He was sleeping, never to be awoken again. You were a sacrifice; you weren't needed. One day, you might have been needed for an army.

How cold it was to touch. She had to touch him, didn't she? Because it was so perfect. Sleeping now, never to arise.

His unwavering blue-eyed focus stared out at her with eyes that had receded a little into the skull. He was still waiting for that life, haunted by the promise.

When this child was placed in the frozen casket, was it still alive? This was the next question which planned to haunt her.

Taking her cell phone from her pocket, Cecelia took

several photographs of the child. He was not so dissimilar to his new born brothers. She took another picture of the name tag clipped onto his tiny wrist before closing the lid on its sad, staring eyes. But she wondered at the reason for a name tag?

If she were religious, she would have said prayers for this little child and had given it a proper name so that heaven could call him. But now she had to forget about it or suffer a fate like Angelina had suffered, the regret and remorse, and life's injustice. A heart of ice is the only possession to get through living, for the time had come when she must think of herself.

Closing the door behind her quietly, with the beating of her heart riding in her ears, she started walking. She had what she needed, and now it was getaway time. Mr. Blaine had turned the corner and was now walking towards her, a frown curling his eyebrow.

By not looking at him, it was as if she had never seen him, denying him the opportunity to speak. He had no power over her except if she gave it.

Was it possible that she was turning her life around? Had she taken that step to shut that door to her past? It felt like she had climbed out of a repetitious circle. Such a feeling was refreshing. To have control of her life without regret or pain was something that had always been out of reach. It made her feel fabulous. With desire, she wanted to shout with happiness. There was nothing to fear anymore except fear itself.

Cecelia left the clinic, hailing reception with a wave of her hand. No, she wouldn't hide anymore. She had the run of the clinic and no one knew how to stop her. The knowledge was recorded in her camera, and her camera was in her purse.

How the hours disappear when one is happy; it was not yet three-thirty in the afternoon, and the forever sunshine city laid a gray finger on its folks. Cecelia did not feel cold as she usually did this time of year, but the sun was draining away fast. Perhaps it was time to go back to her lodgings. She grinned as if to remind herself of what was now contained within her cell phone's memory. There lay the evidence.

THIS WAS a new day in her life. She would walk so far before taking the Metro to air her thoughts on what she should do next and how she should write her piece for her newspaper.

Life was simple if you knew how to work it.

'Have you got something to say to me?' Peter was waiting when she entered the bed-and-breakfast.

It was a stunning accusation which stopped Cecelia right in her tracks.

'I don't understand what you mean,' Cecelia frowned worriedly.

'I want to know how you feel about me. I got the impression you are cooling towards me. Is it because I was angry last night?'

'Oh, that.' The relief was so tremendous, she wanted to laugh. The coil of stress had kept her tight.

'Do you find me a joke?'

'No, no, it's not anything like that.' This underhanded, secret life was proving difficult. 'It's been complicated with my uncle. He seems to be going rapidly.' And then she thought of Angelina as her face misted. Her disadvantaged corporeality came between Peter and herself. 'I heard last week that one of my friends had died suddenly.'

Peter frowned.

'You might have seen the report in the newspapers.'

No, he didn't know. He was waiting for her to carry on. His eyes focused on her face, waiting.

'I spoke to her a couple of days before she died—' Why was she telling him this? 'She looked well and happy then. I feel it was my fault what happened to her.'

'Death is natural.' His face looked relieved. 'I understand. There must have been a great deal going on in your mind, your uncle, and now your friend. I wish you had told me before. And there was me making demands on you all the time. Oh Clara, you are such a wonderful person. I know we will be very happy together.'

Now it was her turn to watch him, to look at his face and listen to his words and form that necessary opinion about him in the calm, objective light of her mind. Hadn't she realized from her first big mistake with Thomas that it's fatal to judge only by appearances? Good men are dressed from the inside and not from their exterior.

While she liked to look at Peter, she didn't know if she wanted to be with him or not. He often made her feel uncomfortable, and really, what did she know of him? Except that he probably had money, and he didn't need to work. Yet, there was something else, something which she couldn't explain or put her finger on, but he wasn't normal, was he? He never tried to touch or even kiss her. Now that wasn't normal, was it? While Thomas could not take his hands off her.

Supposing they were married and on their wedding night, supposing he was frigid. Oh no, she couldn't put up with that. Not to kiss or touch; not to legalize the forbidden fruit and then for her to find out he didn't like them. What a horror this would be.

If she had imagined herself to be in love with him, then this dream she had nurtured had to be stopped.

'Peter,' Cecelia pulled her lips in, already regretting what she was going to say. 'I'm sorry, but I don't know if what we have between us is enough to sustain a special relationship to last us a lifetime. I think maybe we should end it here.'

'And when did you decide that?'

'Just now, although it has been running through my mind for a few days. We don't know each other well enough to make a lasting commitment like marriage. A few days spent in the same boarding place are not enough.' She smiled from the embarrassment; it was one of the hardest things she had ever done in her life. An unplayed hand will never tell you how this decision will pan out in the future. He might turn out to be the most wonderful guy in the world, but for now, the voice in her head was telling her no, it's not safe. Having jumped that first hurdle, Cecelia was strangely relieved. 'Just because you and I are lonely, this is no reason to start a life together.'

'There is someone else, isn't there?' he was frowning. He was upset and unable to comprehend what she meant, and now he was becoming angry. The veins at the side of his brow were beginning to appear, raised by temper. How dare she decide for them both?

'No, there isn't anyone else.'

'You didn't go to see your uncle today, did you?' he spat out.

'Why?' she was curious now. 'Where do you think I went?'

'I saw you from my window. You went out early, and this time, you didn't take the route you usually take.'

She lowered her head; she was guilty. At last, he had found her out. But why was he checking on her?

'You're right. I didn't go to see my uncle. I told you a lie,' she shrugged. 'But it was necessary. I don't have an uncle. My friend was in distress…'

'Is this another of your lies?'

'Which is why we wouldn't be good for each other.'

'Because of the lies? That's your opinion.' He was staring fiercely at her, like a man who was suddenly reduced to a little boy. 'Why did you lie to me? What was the purpose of that—I trusted you?'

'I know, I'm sorry, but there are reasons for it which I can't tell you about.' She shrugged. 'I'm sorry.'

'No,' he grabbed hold of her shoulders. 'You can't do this to me. I've made plans for us both.'

Pulling herself from out of his grasp, Cecelia, now shaken, took a step back from him. 'It's better you know now rather than later. I'm sorry, Peter, I shouldn't have played with you.' He frightened her. This time, she had become Thomas to him, the breaker of hearts.

'When did you decide you didn't want anything to do with me? I know you were attracted to me in the beginning. I could have put my life on it.'

Yes, when had she decided? Did it start when she saw him at Angelina's funeral? Perhaps that's when the doubts crept in. And yet, he had already explained himself to her and why he was there? But now, he was waiting for her condemning answer. But he was losing her; she was already slipping through his fingers.

'I know you care about me—I know it. What did I do to make you change your mind? If you want all my fortune, you can have it. The only thing I want now is you.' he was extraordinarily hurt and petulant.

'Oh, Peter, I'm so sorry.'

'Please, please give me another chance, and I will be

better for you.' Frantically, he stopped to search his world, and there wasn't anything he could find to give her. He couldn't understand that he wasn't enough. 'I know what it is. You're angry at me for hoping your uncle died sooner.'

'No, Peter, I told you I haven't any uncle who's dying.'

'It's because I got angry last night. That's it, isn't it? I lost my temper.'

'No, Peter, stop this. It's all over between us, whatever there was. But it doesn't mean that we still can't be friends.'

He was staring into her eyes, trying to understand the thoughts which were going on in her head. With such a distressed face, he looked for help. But there was nothing. He was suffering the worst emotions of rejection.

'I can't believe that you don't love me anymore.' And then he turned on his heel and walked away to take the stairs to his room.

This had been so difficult for her, but she could see more clearly than he could, and yet, she still felt sorry for him. It was just a silly little daydream, and Peter must understand this. As time went by, he would find faults in her. It was inevitable. Staying in a place like this only showed the best of oneself. He will get over it once a few days had passed, and then he will realize that this was for the best.

But he was so sad that it surprised her.

16

There was no reason for Cecelia to go to work tomorrow. She had everything she needed on her cell phone's camera. Nor was there any further need to stay at the bed-and-breakfast place. Her work was done. Now she had to write the story about the death of a baby, the third child.

With her plans now changed, she couldn't tell Peter she was leaving, especially after yesterday evening when he didn't come to dinner. His vanity had been bruised enough. Instead, she would write him a note and leave it in the reception before she left. No forwarding address or other contact details. Their relationship, however fleeting it was, had to be snipped off now and permanently.

Of course, it was mean of her, especially as she had lied to him. She should have realized then when she needed to lie that there was something wrong with her side of the relationship. But nothing much had happened between them to call this a true union of hearts. Honestly, what was she thinking if she thought she could find love in a bed-and-breakfast hotel? To everyone else, this would have been seen as nothing more than a casual friendship. And the funny thing was, she was relieved that it was over. Perhaps she was not meant to marry and do that thing of settling down; what a load off her shoulders.

Life now had given her a fresh start. She couldn't afford to feel guilty, not one bit. Every strength she had, she needed for herself. In one way, it could be said that she was as bad as Ruth for the way she used people. She grinned at the analogy. You could say that, but perhaps in her case, it was different. With a story like this to tell, she needed to be free to report it to the world.

Another responsibility to face and a decision to make, she should telephone and give in her notice to the clinic. There would be people relying on her. But perhaps she wasn't as responsible as she thought she was, or maybe this was the greedy development of her new self. It was so wonderful to be free.

Passing through one resolution to another came fast. Her mind had been cleared of all the ifs, buts, and doubts. A clear path now lay in front of her, with all the decisions made about what she should do. She was now striving forward to make this world her home by putting her mark on it.

The ideas she had about Ruth taking her on as her personal assistant didn't matter anymore. She didn't need to rely on anyone's help because now she was better positioned to help herself. This was a more satisfying feeling, knowing she could care for herself without depending on others as she always had. If she was honest, Peter had only been there to be that last prop if she didn't make it.

Going down to the dining room with the knowledge this was going to be her last meal here was exciting—as it was scary. In less than two weeks, she had completed her mission, and it had all been strangely easy. She had everything she wanted and in such a short time. Yes, luck had been on her side, but don't forget there was also her own ingenuity. In one way, it felt strange to be leaving this hotel, but this time, she was leaving it as a success.

So much had happened to her since that day, not even a month ago, when Angelina had approached her. And she had chosen Cecelia to speak her mind to. It didn't seem credible that Angelina would not hear it on the news media. But Cecelia would honor it and tell her story to the world. So much trust there. With this story, Cecelia would do her best to make sure that no one could terminate a life when it was formed and viable.

Poor Angelina, what must it have been like to feel the still living and warm baby in her arms, which should have been in someone else's? This experience must have altered her mind, especially when he opened his eyes to her. Easy now to understand why Angelina couldn't cope with its death. When that insignificant life sought her for help, it was too late. Buried in her mind was that she had abandoned him. And for that, she could never forgive herself. She took her own life by falling in front of a bus. It must have been one of those insane decisions made on the impulse and never to be regretted because it was always too late. Die now, and you won't have to face that image again. Poor Angelina.

Dr. Deer took opiates to cope with it, while perhaps for others, their choice was simply to go mad. Everyone has their own strange place to go to when the mind becomes distorted and diseased. Often it is to that parallel world called paranoia. How easy it is to sort out everyone else's problem when you yourself are free from them.

Cecelia could smile at this now. She had fought her way

through it and survived. This world did not differ from what it always had been, dull and moving along slowly, yet how different it looked to her now.

Monday morning and Peter wasn't at breakfast, which was a relief. And yet, in the strangeness of perversity, she was thinking about going to his room to see if he was okay. Not a good idea, she warned herself.

The biggest surprise came with clarity of thought that he wasn't her knight in shining armor who was racing to save her. He was just a sweet and good-looking man who was also gentle and well-mannered. Just your everyday gentleman who sometimes lost his temper. Poor Peter.

She scratched her head. What was it that was different about him compared to everyone else? Because there was something different about him which she couldn't quite connect with. It was there, staring at her straight in the face. Inside, he was empty. Empty of heart and love, poor man. But she wasn't going to sacrifice her life for him; no, she wasn't going to play that game anymore even though she felt sorry for him.

She wished him well and hoped he would find the girl of his dreams, but sometimes, he made her feel uncomfortable for no reason at all. Perhaps this was more than enough. She smiled indulgently at his face, which she had conjured up, thankful that he had found her attractive to want to spend his life with her. It was a compliment.

How does anyone start a letter to say goodbye? No one gives you a lesson on this. The only words she found herself writing was to tell him she was sorry. But for some reason, this made her feel extraordinarily guilty. She could see him with sadness now, a lonely stranger.

She was back on the road, trying to make the world right for herself.

But didn't he realize that throwing all his money at her, someone he hardly knew, wouldn't make her care about him or love him? Money only buys companionship; it doesn't buy love. It was just like her to contemplate a relationship when trying to change her life around by writing this incredible story.

In Peter's own way, he was innocent about life as well, perhaps more than she? But this letter had to be written. As cruel as it may seem had to be done. And with black inked letters on the white virgin paper, it felt like death was being served.

When you want to break away from the person you once were, you sometimes need to jump, which is what Cecelia felt herself trying to do. Make that leap into the unknown and take the next new identity which comes around.

'Take care of yourself,' Cecelia added to the note. 'I know you will find the person you are looking for. I'm just sorry that it wasn't me.' Or rather, she didn't pen this into the letter. She was glad now that it wasn't her.

Sitting at breakfast, Cecelia ate all she was entitled to. Usually, it was either a slice of toast or, alternately, a bowl of cereal. Today, though, her decision ran on the course, that it would be better to fill her stomach substantially with a cooked breakfast. The future wavered with uncertainty. And a full stomach would help. Except for some dry food in her little apartment, there was nothing much else to eat.

With every person entering the dining room, Cecelia looked up, hoping for Peter to come in and join her. But no, he was still sulking. It was better this way.

Bringing down her two large, heavy suitcases and one small piece of hand luggage stuffed full of the extra new clothes. She was glad to put them down at the reception to pay her bill. Her fingers were already stinging from the weight. This part would be the nightmare seeing how much she owed, but it wasn't as expensive as she expected, which was a pleasant surprise.

Only now, just as she was leaving, did she find out what the proprietor's name was, Mr. Carter. Now she wouldn't have supposed him to be called that. But then, she hadn't supposed anything interesting about him at all. But he was kind, asking her if he should call her a cab and if there was anything she wanted to leave for him to store so she could collect it later. Funny how things turn out. She didn't think he liked or even approved of her.

'It was good having you stay with us, Miss Tinder,' he didn't need to look at the registrar. He already knew her name, which was very flattering. 'We've all been worried about you.'

'Worried about me? Who's been worried about me?' she frowned; why would anyone be worried about her?

'It's the man you were spending your time with here.'

'Peter Thornton?' Cecelia's frown came from puzzlement. What was wrong with him? Was it because of one time when he was obnoxious? But things like that often happen after a bad day.

'Yes, he threatened one of the other guests.'

No, she couldn't believe that. Peter was a gentleman, true he sometimes could be a little moody, but that was usually when he didn't get his own way, like a little boy.

'One of the female guests suggested you should come and join their table. They liked you; they wanted to advise you about him.'

'Advise me of what?' how ridiculous this was. Here she was, a woman in her mid-thirties, and she didn't need anyone to look after her? It was insulting. Although if they were concerned about her, there must have been a reason. It was nice of them she supposed to care about her.

'It happened a few evenings ago when he came to your usual table and saw that it had only been set for one. When he was calling me, one of the female guests explained you were dining with them. That's when he exploded. If I hadn't come out when I did, I believe he would have assaulted the woman.'

'No, never. Surely not.' She couldn't believe this, not Peter. It was impossible, especially when she had caught him smiling at the other guests. It was they who behaved poorly. When she had mentioned their attitude to him and how strange they were acting, he told her that people often got like that towards him and guessed that it must be because he was here on his own.

'Being a man and traveling on my own is not so romantic as it may seem. Especially when you have to say no to some people, particularly women when they set their cap at you.'

How rude some people could be.

'We have all been concerned about you, Miss Tinder.'

There was an expression of concern and kindness on Mr. Carter's face. He could see she didn't believe him.

'Does Mr. Thornton know you are going?' Mr. Carter asked politely.

'I'm leaving him a message. Would you mind giving this to him when you see him next?'

'No, I don't mind at all,' Mr. Carter smiled, taking the sealed envelope from her; he ran his eyes briefly over it before putting it into one of the pigeonholes. 'Have you told him where you are going?'

This was rude because it was private. 'If you mean, do I intend keeping in contact with him? No, I don't.'

'Good,' he replied. 'You've got to be aware of handsome

young men traveling on their own; it's not natural,' and then he squinted his eyes, conscious that she didn't believe him. He decided he should explain himself further.

'Ah, I see. I need to explain myself further.'

Cecelia looked up at Mr. Carter for he was about to embark on a story, perhaps one of his making or perhaps one which had happened.

'I came downstairs one night, seven days ago. It was three-thirty in the morning; I needed to check something. And wasn't I surprised when I caught him letting himself into the house through the emergency door? I stepped back into the shadows, thinking he was a thief and believing that I should get to the telephone and ring the police when I saw it was him.'

Cecelia couldn't believe that this man. Why was Mr. Carter talking about Peter this way? It had to be another person he meant and not Peter. For Peter always went to bed early; he needed his sleep. Which was something she hadn't approved of because it suggested to her he could be boring by going to bed just when things were happening.

'We are not against any guest staying out as long as they want. The way they live their lives has nothing to do with us. As long as they respect this boarding house and are decent to others, and pay their way—we all have to get along with each other, don't we? What I couldn't understand is why he didn't ring the doorbell; I might have complained a little about the hour in the morning, but nothing worse than that.'

Was Mr. Carter so sure that they were talking about the same man? Peter had confessed many times that he enjoyed a good night's sleep and that there weren't enough hours in the night to achieve this.

No, the attention Peter attracted must be out of jealousy.

They had probably found out that he was wealthy. It had to be this. Reviewing all her options, Cecelia kept mute on the matter of Peter.

'I won't tell him what time you left and where you went,' said Mr. Carter conspiratorially when Cecelia finalized her bill.

She smiled and politely said thank you, yet it had spooked her what Mr. Carter had to say about Peter, the man she had seriously thought of living with. Mr. Carter was very kind, but she could form her own opinions about the people she mixed with. Of course, Mr. Carter meant well, but it's how people treat each other, which is the difference.

Now she was leaving to go back to her flat and start her life afresh. And Mrs. Rudge loomed clear on her menu of thoughts. It was she who spooked her in the first place, telling her that someone was looking for her. And now, why hadn't she thought of this before jumping to conclusions? It could have been Thomas, but it probably wasn't for that was too long ago. But you never know. One day, he would leave his oversized wife.

And as for Mrs. Rudge, she was at that age when facts were not as clear as they used to be. She was always prone to be a bit of a gossip, helping nature a bit by providing extra flourishes and trimmings to her story to make it more interesting. Going home now was making her nervous.

Stop running away from life, Cecelia commanded. It's no good always being fearful and imagining things. This was no way to live. People are all stories unto themselves, and everyone's perspective on life differs from each other. Certainly, older people get frightened of life when there is no need for it. They tend to be afraid of the future with all the changes coming with it. Well, she was not going to be like that. She would never be old or frightened. She was going to be one of those people who changes other people's lives. One who affects life and is not affected by it.

It had been on her mind to go by train, but with her luggage being so heavy now, the chances were that she would drop her bags at every step. Besides, these cases had become far too heavy to carry any distance. It would be much better if for this last time she went by cab.

Coming back up the stairs, Mr. Carter was still by the window, watching her.

'I've changed my mind,' she said when he opened the door to her. 'Would you call a cab for me, please?'

Five minutes later, the cab arrived at the lodging house, and Mr. Carter came out to help the driver put her cases in the cab.

Once inside the cab, Cecelia gave her instructions for the driver to take her home. So, this would be the final farewell. Looking out of the window, she waved to Mr. Carter as the cab started its journey back to Cecelia's studio apartment. Such a great deal had happened since she had left there. It was as sad as it was happy; life was a big adventure.

Money was there to help you get out of a problem, but only when you can afford it, and really, she couldn't. Because of the debt she had accrued since leaving her apartment, she regretted her reckless decision. This, she realized, had been made on impulse and her fear brought on by the death of Angelina.

Good and bad sensations came with the journey home. It was like going back through her life once again, to find the missing ends of herself. The parts she didn't like, which were now waiting to be exorcized. She needed to stand up to the old part of her life and exile it to another place.

The kaleidoscope of life was now falling back into place. The promises she had made that she would not return here again were replaced by the fact that she was going home.

Yet, it was the smell of her apartment that needed standing up to first. Stale as if life had stopped living, the place required serious airing, and serious living in.

'Hello old key,' she took out her key from her purse. So much had happened in the short time she was away. So much had happened to her. She had been to the college green around the edges of life, and now she had returned a graduate. Although, what she had graduated in was not a certainty, perhaps how to outwit people.

She had come home. And what she had remembered when she left, dashing out of her apartment like a bat out of hell, was that it was an absolute mess.

'My goodness,' Cecelia said when the door swung open.

And it was a surprise because her flat was tidy. This was not how she remembered it. Her bed was made, and the drawers on her dresser were shut closed, which was strange but gladdening. She renewed her ownership with it by touching its smooth, shiny surface. There wasn't any dust, but of course, there shouldn't be. She hadn't been away long enough for that. And yet, the smile on her face was cautionary because her fancy suggested she needed to give the place a good cleaning on her return. Strange, because she didn't remember any of this; her drawers were shut, and even the bed was made. But she must have done, as there was nobody else to do this except herself.

It was now nine o'clock in the morning, and the clinic would wonder where she was. They were now probably realizing she wasn't going to turn up for work this morning. They might even suspect she was dead. Why not? Since death seems to be the latest fashion.

Impossible to go to work. By now, Dr. Deer would find his safe had been tampered with and that someone had taken some of his stuff. He would find that one of his syringes missing, and after counting the vials of morphine, he would see that one of them had gone as well. He wouldn't be happy, and he might even succumb to his daily paranoia.

Perhaps he would look around with an open mouth and wonder at himself. Could it be he that used it? Had he done this coming out of his trip with a loss of memory? He had never once lost his memory; he knew himself and his habit. Which meant that someone else had entered with a key.

The worst problem was that if someone had a key to his door and managed to open the combination of his safe, what else had they found? Now Dr. Deer would be talking to security to find out if any unwanted visitors were recorded on his office security cameras. This was what she would do and think if she were Dr. Deer.

Security cameras! She had forgotten about the security cameras. A stupid mistake. Once they knew who it was and seen her on the footage helping herself to his stash, he would get in touch with the police and tell them that his office had been burglarized—or would he? If the law came into his office, they would fingerprint everything, which might mean even the cooler. And what was in that cooler? Cecelia grinned. Evidence.

Forensic investigation would be too complicated. Too many secrets. It wasn't safe. Unless he took the baby out of the freezer for disposal. But if he rid himself of this little body, his insurance would be gone, for Cecelia judged this must be his insurance over Blaine. People like Mr. Blaine were dangerous, which is why Dr. Deer needed his guarantee. But the price of keeping a little dead child would also be as incriminating for him as well.

Like Dr. Deer, she wouldn't trust Mr. Blaine if anything should happen to his children. An unlikeable man, who wasn't to be relied upon, the dealer in the deaths of millions. So why would one more matter?

For the second time, Cecelia felt sorry for Ruth. A stupid woman whose life's aim was to secure herself a rich husband, so she would never be in want again. One only had to look at them to see there was no love between them. And now she was lying in her room, her used-up body attached to a syringe of agony.

Should she give Ruth just one last call to see how she was? Or wasn't it more to the truth that she wanted to know what happened after they had found out Ruth had been given morphine? Because that was something which could not be concealed. What was the harm in phoning to find out? After all, it was Ruth's own private cell phone.

Quickly making herself some coffee, Cecelia switched on her cell phone and saw that someone had been trying to get through to her for over forty times. It could only be Ruth.

'Hello Ruth, it's me, Cecelia.'

'Who?' asked Ruth; she hadn't recognized her voice.

In a panic, Cecelia knew what she had gone wrong. She had given her real name instead of the other. She snapped off the call instantly. For two or three minutes, Cecelia sat on her sofa, thinking about her mistake. What did it matter now if Ruth knew that Cecelia was her real name? Did it matter? No, probably not.

'Ruth,' Cecelia had relented and rang again. 'I'm just calling you now to see how you are. It's me, Clara. How are you?'

'Clara,' she sighed. 'Is that your real name?' poor Ruth sounded tired and worn out.

'For you, it is.'

'You're not coming to work here anymore, are you?'

'No, I'm sorry.'

Cecelia could hear her breathing heavily and guessed that she was stoned out of her head.

'I thought we two could be friends.'

Cecelia put a hand to her mouth. She had the idea there could never be any friendship between them. They were so very different, but life changes on the spin of a wheel or the flip of a card.

'Everything's gone bad, Clara; Hadleigh is blaming me for it all. The oldest twin is blind, and it looks like the youngest one will not survive.'

'Oh, I'm so sorry,' gasped Cecelia.

'Yeah, well, I'm not. I think we were owed this. We have done something very wrong, but Hadleigh won't admit it. I didn't want any children—not at all. I'm not a mother, but a social climber.' And then she giggled. It was so strange to hear her laugh.

Cecelia didn't know what to say to this strange and unhappy woman.

'I can't even get a divorce from him; he is convinced I can have more children for him and his empire. Unfortunately, when Deer scrapped out that third child, he ruptured my womb, which is why he was tearing me open to get to that last child. This kid never cried because he was already dead or almost. I don't care anyhow. I'm not a good advertisement for motherhood, am I?'

'How are you now?' this was all Cecelia could say.

'High as a kite, and I don't care. But I won't be like this forever. Once I am strong, I'm getting out of here, and I'm not going back to Blaine. He has ruined me, but not everyone wants children, at least, I hope not.' She was falling asleep because she yawned.

'Did they find out about the heist from Dr. Deer's safe?'

'Yes, of course, and now they are looking for you. I suggest you leave the country or something. There again, wherever you go, Hadleigh will find you. He always does. He's got someone on you already, looking for you. Don't try to go to the police; they won't help you. Anyway, thanks for what you've done. I'll try to put in a good word for you.'

Someone was looking for her. Someone who now had a picture of her would one day soon find her and—. By switching off her cell phone completely, there was no way they could track her. Someone was hunting her. But what would he do to her if, and when, he found her? Turn the question around for an answer. What would she do to a person who knew her darkest secrets? That is easy. For Cecelia, these people wouldn't be safe until they were dead.

17

———————

Everyone has a voice they can use, and after the first spate of panic on where she would run and hide, Cecelia recognized her only salvation was to write the story. Under this story, she would find her mercy because she had something that was dangerous to them. A live baby has been pulled out of its mother's womb in a gruesome way. No one should do this when there was a good chance for life. It's only a woman's body and her rights for so long, but it belongs to the child when life kicks in and is viable.

She wouldn't go out of this apartment until she had written her story.

'I've got a story for you,' Cecelia was on the mainline phone to her editor.

'You've got a story for me. I've got a story for you,' snapped Don, the newspaper editor. 'Don't come back. You're fired.'

'I'm sorry I left without telling you about what was going on—'

'Your position is filled. There are a lot of hopefuls just

waiting outside to step into someone else's shoes, and you have obliged.'

Oh dear, this was going all wrong. And now he was about to hang up on her.

'You're right, and I don't blame you for doing it. I would do the same if I were you.'

'Too right, well, what did you expect?'

'I've got a big story for you—'

She caught his interest. 'A big story?'

'Yes, that's why I had to go undercover.'

'Cecelia, you've never written a big story in your life.'

'Yes, I know. I want you to trust me. I think I've put my life in danger.'

'Then go to the police.'

'I can't; these people have connections with the police.'

He was now listening, and by the deadly silence at the other end, he was also thinking. 'When can you get it to me —and what's it about?'

'Abortion.'

'Oh, abortion. Yeah, I know. The pro-life group has been on the march again—it was in all the papers, including ours, and on the television. There's nothing you can say about it that's new.'

'When a fetus reaches over eight months, is that called an abortion as well?'

'What are you saying?'

'I'm saying that at a certain clinic, there are fetuses or rather children that when they reach a certain age, they can be delivered and will survive, but because of people's image and vanity, the unborn are terminated. Are you getting this?'

'Yeah. Is this for real?'

'It's as real as it can ever be. They are pulled out from the mother bit by bit. Sometimes these children are still alive.

They can open their eyes to take that first and last look at the world.'

'You've got to be kidding me.'

'No, unfortunately not.'

'And you have evidence of this? I mean, you have proof?'

'Yes, I have the story; I can give you names and photographs.'

'Oh my god, not photographs. You mean, this sort of thing really happens?'

'Yes, Don, it does. And the way they can get around it is by pulling the infant to pieces—bit by bit, in what is classified as an abortion. If the fetus is taken out by cesarean and cries, then it becomes a real baby. Do you hear what I am saying?'

'This is sick.'

'Yes, but it is being performed.'

'Okay, get the story to me as soon as you can. Where are you now?'

'I can't tell you until I get this story down and off to you.'

'Well, you take care of yourself, kid. I don't know how dangerous it is, but I'll take your word for it.'

18

Never had life been so exciting as it was now. Her world from the past was flying by her with the screams of an angry banshee. She was alive and living; she was that free radical in a body full of healthy tissue. This baby was dangerous. Cecelia spelled the word out to herself. Yes, it was her that was dangerous. And honey, she loved it. Move over, Mickey Spillane. There was a broad in town now. And now, because she was alive, there was someone after her. For the very first time, Cecelia wanted to live.

Three exhilarating days passed, and for almost all this time, Cecelia sat at her desk typing and editing her piece. Whenever there was a sudden noise on the block, she knew that someone had come for her. To live on the sharp edge of life made every moment of the day special. And Cecelia was grateful for every passing second.

Plenty of baked beans in the flat and cans of tomatoes. This was what she was living on, that and the coffee she was rationing. Once it ran out, she would drink hot water. She could exist like this for a while, everyone could who was determined to reach their goal.

It was on the fourth day after another one of those nights of sleeping in fear when a knock hit her door. Mrs. Rudge often got lonely, and knowing that Cecelia was at home all day would give her a knock just for a quick chat. Sometimes Cecelia would let her in and make her a cup of tea. Pleasant enough to have this break, but often it wasn't. Usually, Cecelia looked to the window as if she hadn't heard or pretended that she was having a bath.

The knock said that it was Mrs. Rudge again, but this time it was okay because Cecelia was coming to the end of her edited story.

'Hello, Mrs. Rudge,' she said as she pulled open the door.

But it wasn't Mrs. Rudge. Peter was standing there.

'Hello Clara, it took me a long time to find where you were,' he was looking for her to let him in.

'Peter, what are you doing here? Didn't you get my letter?' nothing could have prepared her for this.

He had gone out of her life; she had left him to be added to her memories. It was like someone had left the graveyard and turned up to stake their claim on her life. And to be honest, she had not given him a thought. There was too much going on in her life to worry about a past love.

'Aren't you going to invite me in?'

He was smiling at her, sweetly like he used to, and this was how best she remembered him. She stepped aside, feeling that somehow she owed this to him. Should she say that she was pleased to see him when it was pretty obvious she wasn't. How on earth did he get her address? Surely the hotel wouldn't have given it out to him.

'So, this is where you live?' he stood in the middle of the room surveying her home with interest and wonder. 'And this is where you have escaped to? It's homely; I'll give you that. But what confuses me is that you could have had so much with me.'

'I'm sorry, Peter—' Oh no, we were going to have an analysis of what could have been.

'No, don't be sorry. You've made my life very interesting.'

What did he mean?

'You have surprised me, Clara, more than you will ever know.'

'I'm sorry, Peter. I don't know how many times I can tell you I'm sorry. We were never meant to be together. And given time, you will see this too. I know I've hurt you.'

'Perhaps at first, you did. I didn't know what I had done to upset you. You know, you really are an enigma.'

He wasn't frowning now; it was as if everything which perplexed him had become more clear.

Should she ask him to sit down? He was making her feel so guilty.

'Would you like to sit?'

'You don't know how rich I am. I own three Picasso—originals I'll have you know. Not just one, but three, and even a small Van Gogh. Although personally, I don't know what they see in him. However, if a part of his life makes me prosperous, then I'm all for it.'

But he either didn't hear her or was ignoring her. This was such bad timing. She thought, though surprise she might have been pleased to see him, but she wasn't. Her nerves were in shreds. There was something menacing about him. He didn't like being stood up. And he was not satisfied with her apology, either.

'What do you want from me, Peter? Why are you here?'

He grinned; he was pleased with himself.

'A proposition. I am going to make you a proposition you can't refuse.'

Oh dear, not again.

'Don't you understand, Peter? I don't care how much money you have or how handsome you are; because you are, Peter, you are very handsome. You could have anyone in your life. You have so much to offer other females, so you would never be lonely, ever again.'

He always listening politely to what she said before answering her; good manners goes a long way.

'But Clara, dear, it's not them I want. It's you.'

She sighed; he was not going to give up. She could tell this because he was smiling.

'Peter, I am sorry, but we don't have anything in common. I am a journalist, and potentially I might now be a highflyer. I don't want a safe life going from country to country, looking at paintings, and being polite to everyone, then going to bed at ten. I want an exciting life, and I have it. You would do better to find someone sweet and gentle, and this is not me, not anymore. So, it is goodbye Peter. This is the end of whatever it was you think we had.'

'Perhaps you should listen to my proposition first.'

Another exasperated sigh. He was not going to give up.

'I like you, Peter, but I can tell you now that I'm never going to fall in love with you.' It was a big mistake to open the door, but he would have come back again, so it might as well be now rather than later.

His expression dropped a little, but he was determined.

'Perhaps,' and then he smiled to himself before looking up. 'I know all about you—'

'No, you don't. You only think you do. I lied to you all the time. I don't have a large family. Yeah, I have some cousins somewhere, Canada and New Zealand, I think. And as for my mother, I don't care if she is in hell.'

'Well, that sorts the family out,' he grinned, pleased with himself again. 'My father and mother want nothing to do with me either, but that's fine by me. They always favored my younger brother.'

Restless, Cecelia turned away, again wishing he was gone.

'I don't care about families—yours or mine. I just care about you.'

She had to be firm. 'Peter, listen. You don't know me, and you would be shocked if you did. I am a bit of a wild child. I've done things that I am ashamed of. Yes, I have, Peter,' she nodded quickly. 'But as it is my life, and I can do as I want. I'm getting on with my life now. It may be a bit late, but it's better to start now than never.'

'I know what you're doing. I now know everything about you, thanks to a very wealthy friend of mine.' he waited a few seconds to deliver something explosive. 'Did you know there is someone after you, Cecelia? Someone who is dangerous?'

He caught her with a crack of thunder, a lightning strike which had electrocuted her with a shocking surprise.

'You're in great danger, Cecelia. Someone has sent someone to take care of you.'

Cecelia gasped. It was true—All her thoughts collided into one big bang. But how did he know that, and how did he know her real name?

'I am here to offer my services to help you, Cecelia. I will take you away and protect you. Believe me. I know how to protect a person.'

'You are telling me that someone is trying to kill me?'

He nodded. That was enough.

'I thought—but I was not sure,' she stopped, and took her eyes to his face. 'But, if they are out to kill me then, how could you protect me?'

'Because I am the one they sent.'

19

I t was bizarre because she had fainted. The world had run off with her consciousness, and upon giving it back brought her back to this life on her small sofa.

'It's excellent, Cecelia,' Peter's voice came from her table. 'But I don't think you should publish your story. People won't like it. I am afraid it is too gory. And another thing, people won't believe it.'

'What are you talking about?' Cecelia pulled herself up to sit on her sofa. She saw Peter had her hard, labored story in his hands. How dare he read it? She swung her legs over, holding her hands out to him for her edited piece. All her hard work was in his hands. Don't say he was going to tear it up.

'I was sent to kill you.' He turned to look at her. 'Isn't that strange? What are the odds that we should meet like this, at the same lodgings and even at the same table? That we should gravitate towards each other must suggest we were meant to be?'

He was her killer in her own home, and she had known him all along.

'I don't believe you.'

'No, I didn't think you would, and in your place, I wouldn't believe me either, but that's how it goes.' He smiled and looked at her sofa. 'May I?'

Quickly, she moved from the sofa and went to sit in the highchair. Peter noted this and grinned. He liked this about her; she always surprised him.

'Mr. Blaine, Hadleigh Blaine, have you heard of him?' he didn't expect her to answer. 'He's been one of my customers for a very long time now. I've earned a large proportion of my wealth by removing the people he doesn't like or who have got in his way. He has been very generous with his money for my services.'

Her hand had gone straight to her mouth, hearing this. This wasn't a dream or a fantasy. This was real. Here was Peter, the handsome man with whom she shared so many meals, and he was now telling her he was a cleaner.

'But you led me on a merry dance. I had to kill young ladies to get to you although, thinking about it, when Miss Angelina Joseph broke her contract by telling you; she had to die. We can't have people being disloyal to the clinic. And poor Miss Mantle; you told Ruth Blaine that you were her. And it all would have gone well if only you hadn't peeped in the freezer.'

'So, Samantha's death wasn't suicide?'

'She threatened me with a knife. That was a surprise, but I told her that her time was up. I must admit she made a fight for it. Shame, though. She had me running after her because she nearly got away. She certainly had spirit.'

'You are a monster,' Cecelia cried, visualizing the last moments of her friend's death.

'So, I have been told. Oh, and by the way, what did you think of the apartment when you returned?'

She did not know what he was talking about. What did he mean?

'I could see you left your apartment in a bit of a rush. What was it you were running away from?'

Staring at him again because he was talking in riddles, and then it clicked.

'It was me,' he laughed. 'I was the one who came back to tidy up for you, although I had didn't realize who I was tidying up for. I think I did a good job, don't you? Although if I had known it was you, I would have done an even better job. I believe one should always clear out the inside of the cupboards at least once a month—'

He cocked his head to the side as if he was considering another aspect of her.

'Didn't you notice that someone had been here? The good little fairy had come to tidy up for you.'

He grinned at her puzzlement.

'That's one thing about me. I am well organized although there wasn't much in your tinned goods cupboard. Bake beans, Cecelia, and tin tomatoes; we should eat better. I was very disappointed to see the variety and level of your stock; I had very little to work with, which was why I had left it. You should see my color coding, Cecelia. With that you would never lose anything again.'

He was playing with her now, taunting her.

'I have just one thing to ask before you kill me.' her life was going to be snuffed out before she was ready. And was she afraid? No, she wasn't. Well, fancy that. Her time had come, and she wasn't even scared of it.

'And I've got something to ask you first,' he was grinning. The mischief had lit up his beautiful, sparkling blue eyes.

Whatever he was, a contract killer, a rich man, there was

no denying he was a handsome man, whose only probable flaw was that he was a psychopath.

'Do you want to hear my offer?'

Offer? She didn't know whether or not she wanted to.

'Okay, you hear my offer first, and then you can kill me, but you must make certain that my story goes to my newspaper.'

'Oh dear, now that's going to be a problem. It's the story which I've got to quench, and then you, of course, you are almost as important as the story. I can kill you easily, but are you prepared to die? Do you really want to die just when the fun has started?'

'Yes, I am prepared.'

'Are you sure? Don't you want to listen to my proposal first?'

A deep sigh, 'Very well, go on, tell me your proposal.'

'I don't have to kill you, you know,' he smiled.

'So, why are you here if you don't want to kill me?'

'If you had been someone else, I wouldn't be having this conversation with you.'

He scratched just above his right eyebrow.

'I can tell you that when I looked at the security footage, I couldn't believe it was you. Not my sweet and lovely Clara, as that was what you were calling yourself. And there you were, Cecelia, going to the safe and helping yourself to a syringe and morphine. You; a drug addict. I couldn't believe it. I've looked at your hands and arms for any proof of this. Although you could have been injecting it in the veins on your legs.'

'I'm not a drug addict.' Cecelia was insulted.

'No, I thought not, and I am glad about it. Disgusting habit. Never touch drugs, my motto. Was it you who gave the morphine to Mrs. Blaine? Of course it was. I see that now; how very charitable you are. Now that wouldn't have been me doing it for her. Taking a chance like that for someone, which to my mind isn't worth the life she has. Why did you do it?'

'Because she was in pain and suffering. So, what was your offer to me?'

He grinned broadly, pleased now they had got to talk about his plan to her.

'If you marry me, I promise you will always be safe. No one will ever come after you, but only if you marry me.'

'You still want to marry me?'

'Oh yes, that has not changed.'

He must be mad.

'But you can't ask me to make a promise like that.'

'If you don't marry me,' he sighed, 'I have no choice but to kill you. I gave my word to them that when I found whoever it was who discovered their secret, I would end their life. We can't have people threatening to tell other people's secrets, can we?'

'Do you know what their secret was about?' suddenly, she was angry. 'I saw you at Angelina's funeral. What I am trying to reveal was her secret. She was the one who told it to me. It was her mission to let everyone know how murderous these people were.'

'Ah, the blond-haired beauty, fortunately, she went quick. She didn't even know I was following her.'

'And you killed her just because they wanted her dead?'

He shrugged.

'Hadleigh Blaine certainly got his money's worth out of me. Three if I kill you, and all for the price of one. If only you had said something to me beforehand about Samantha

Mantle. But, never mind, she's gone now. But if you like, I can turn over a new leaf and stop by not killing you. Just marry me, and you will be safe.'

Marry the man who was sent to kill her. Should she consider his proposal and marry him and be his prisoner wife forever? Yes, the alternative was frightening. But wouldn't marrying him be a life sentence worse than death? How bizarre her life had become?

It was not long ago she would have said yes and eagerly married him. He was everything that a woman wanted. Good looks, excellent manners, and he was also wealthy. But things had changed; Cecelia had found her own self-worth, and realized she didn't need a powerful man in her life anymore. She could do this life on her own.

There were other things about him that were necessary to consider. He was controlling and possessive. She could just imagine the interrogations that he would put her through. Better to get this over and done with now. Being dead was better than being married to Peter.

'I don't love you, and I'm afraid I will never come to love you. So, you might as well get it over with now. Just do it quickly, I don't want to suffer. Please.'

The astonishment on Peter's face was incredible.

'But you don't have to love me. I am okay about that. It is not a requirement.'

'No, no. Don't you understand I would sooner die, rather than be married to you.' Cecelia nodded eagerly.

'You mean you would prefer to die instead of marrying me? You would have half my money, I promise.'

'I don't love you, Peter. I'm sorry. I don't want to be married to you.'

He stared at her hard. It was a look that promised her certain death.

From underneath his overcoat, he took his gun from its holster.

'Do it now—' Cecelia yelled, startled that her death was now imminent.

He nodded, now holding the gun in two hands. The countdown was in his eyes. Was this really happening? Pulling back the hammer, he aimed the pistol at her.

Oh dear, I am really going to die; Cecelia couldn't believe this was going to happen; it was not how she had seen her death. But neither was she going to look. Squeezing her eyes together, this was her end, and she would not run away. There was not even time for a prayer. It was happening now.

The noise that sealed her death was quick, although they say you never hear the shot that kills you, but she had. Opening her eyes, Peter still had the gun in his hands.

'I can't do it,' he said, putting her cushion down. He had used her pretty cushion to silence the shot.

She was alive. And as she looked at him, the feathers were falling.

'You are the first person I have never been able to kill.'

Peter was bemused and even puzzled and neither was he angry. He wasn't anything except perhaps resigned. Putting his gun away, he came over to her and placed his hand gently on the back of her neck. Swiftly, he pulled her towards him to kiss her on the forehead.

'Look after yourself, Cecelia, for me. I'll do the best I can for you.'

'And is that it?' she held her shaking hands together. She was still alive.

'This must be true love?' he grinned at her. 'I never thought that was possible. I suggest you find yourself somewhere else to live. You are too exposed here.'

'Okay,' she whispered, her voice still hoarse.

Baffled, she watched as he let himself out of her flat. She had lived and died and lived again in the space of a minute.

20

Over the next few days, there was a spate of deaths in LA. It was thought to have been committed by a single hitman. Dr. Deer was one of them, and so was Mr. Blaine. Shock ran all around the world. But this was short-lived as the world fell silent when what had been discovered in Dr. Deer's freezer was revealed. One fully formed child, broken in pieces, had gained his revenge. His mother, though, Mrs. Ruth Blaine, had disappeared into the heavy morning LA smog.

Once in a while, a card or a letter would arrive, no name but a message to remind Cecelia to take care of herself. After a while, these messages stopped.

REVIEW

I would appreciate it if you reviewed my book as this would make my day.

Thank You...

www.ingramcontent.com/pod-product-compliance
Lightning Source LLC
Chambersburg PA
CBHW020751190726
48285CB00006B/1984